———— ★ ————

While Coffin sat thinking of his own problems, the fire burned in the rough ground beyond the old Atlas factory.

When did it start? It must have started in the early afternoon, because such fires burn slowly. The fire burned the mound of wood and leaves that a sex-less figure had put together, which he or she had lit and upon which, so a watcher said later, he or she had climbed. Hard to believe, and the wit-ness did not have good eyesight. Not climbing, perhaps, but dragged?

First smoke, then flames.

The body burned, the hair smoldered, the body fats caught and melted, the skin crisped.

———— ★ ————

GWENDOLINE BUTLER

THE COFFIN TREE

WORLDWIDE.

TORONTO • NEW YORK • LONDON
AMSTERDAM • PARIS • SYDNEY • HAMBURG
STOCKHOLM • ATHENS • TOKYO • MILAN
MADRID • WARSAW • BUDAPEST • AUCKLAND

THE COFFIN TREE

A Worldwide Mystery/September 1997

First published by St. Martin's Press, Incorporated.

ISBN 0-373-26250-7

Printed in U.S.A.

AUTHOR'S NOTE

One evening in April, 1988, I sat in the Toynbee Hall in the East End of London, near to Docklands, listening to Dr. David Owen (now Lord Owen) give that year's Barnett Memorial Lecture. In it, he suggested the creation of a Second City of London, to be spun off from the first, to aid the economic and social regeneration of the Docklands.

The idea fascinated me and I made use of it to create a new world for my detective, John Coffin, to whom I gave the task of keeping the Queen's Peace there.

I have to acknowledge with gratitude the technical advice given to me by Frank Domingo, the forensic artist, formerly of the New York Police Department, and Detective Lieutenant William L. Harrigan of New York Housing Police.

Thanks, too, to Colin Wilson and John Kennedy Melling.

The Coffin Tree grew in London's Second City. The upper branches had been struck by lightning several years ago, a blow that would have killed some trees, but this one struggled on, putting its strength into its lower branches.

There were three great, thick, heavy branches, each one that could be cut down and made into planks.

No one owned the tree....

ONE

THAT HOT SUMMER when the old Docklands of London sweltered in the great heat and drought was talked of and people made jokes about the saint who sat on the gridiron, this was the summer when John Coffin walked his Second City of London and felt that life was unravelling about him.

He was seriously worried about the death of two young men, two detectives. The deaths were said to be accidental, but two accidents were two too many.

He walked and observed and distrusted far too many people; this was his burden at the moment, he was lonely and perturbed. Something had to be done and it was for him to do it.

WHEN A NEW, smart and very expensive shop called Minimal opened in Calcutta Street which was the busiest street in Spinnergate, the locals didn't know what to make of it.

Phoebe, who had inspected the area a week or so ago when she considered moving to London from Birmingham, had noticed the shop at once. It was in her nature to look over a district before she moved there (and she was almost certain that she would be doing so) and the Minimal shop caught her eye.

She was now moodily running over a rack of high priced shifts, watched by the manageress who wasn't sure what she had in Phoebe. Rich lady incognito or shoplifter? That was Phoebe's dark outfit with a large shoulder bag because she planned to stay the night.

Minimal certainly did not apply to the prices of the clothes sold there, she considered, wondering how many sales were made. It might describe the decor which was white and empty.

'Not even a chair to sit on,' as one of the girls from the chorus in the musical currently running at the Stella Pinero Theatre complained. 'Not even a curtain to draw when you try on. Just that little bamboo screen which hides nothing... I don't want everyone seeing me in my bra and pants for free... Let them pay and buy a ticket.' The musical was not playing to full houses.

'There is a curtain of sorts behind, Philly,' said her friend, Eleanor. Eleanor Farmer was older than Phyllis Archer by a few months but they resembled each other in their long fair hair, blue eyes and neat footwork; not strictly pretty, they were good dancers. They were known as Ellie and Philly and regarded as almost twins; they always worked together if it was possible.

'Net, net and full of holes.'

The holes were embroidered and pretty but you were certainly visible through them.

In spite of these drawbacks, both Ellie and Philly tried on several garments each with little intention of buying, although Ellie was tempted by a short tunic and flared trousers with a distinguished label, and Philly would certainly have bought the off-white Donna Karan body and skirt if she had not overused her credit card and been overdrawn at the bank.

But each of them bought a white cotton shirt, so they went out carrying the black on white Minimal carrier bag in triumph. The bags looked good slung over the shoulder.

It was a hot summer's day and as they stepped outside, they sniffed the air. It didn't smell so good, but little Londoners both, they were used to the strange city smells.

Still, this was richer and sharper than most.

'Something's burning, Philly.'

'Something not nice.'

'Nice when it was alive, maybe, but I think it was dead.'

'Put your hanky to your nose, Philly, and run for that cab.' Cabs were few and far between in this part of Spinnergate so you grabbed one when you could.

They barely noticed Phoebe but Phoebe noticed the two girls because it was both her habit and training to notice people.

'They're girls from the show at the Stella Pinero Theatre.' The manager spoke somewhat nervously; she was a jumpy young woman, stylish but on the alert. 'I recognized their names from the programme: Phyllis and Eleanor, they kept calling each other Ellie and Philly. I was at the show— I didn't recognize their faces, of course, but you could tell they were dancers. Stella Pinero lives near here. Do you know her?'

'Of her,' said Phoebe. 'I do indeed.'

'I had Miss Pinero in here the other day.'

'Did she buy anything?'

'A silk shift.' She nodded towards a display of three shifts, one blue, one yellow and one black; they looked good, you had to admire the professionalism and skill of the establishment. Which made it all the more surprising in Spinnergate which was not a rich, upmarket area.

Here in the Second City of London where John Coffin was chief commander of the police force, responsible for the keeping of the Queen's Peace in the turbulent boroughs of Spinnergate, Leathergate, Swinehouse and East Hythe, the rich inhabitants (and there were such in the new expensive residences lining the old Docklands) drove to Bond Street and Knightsbridge to shop and the poor sped towards charity shops and the large department store in Swinehouse which held regular mark down sales.

'That one over there, but in cream. She has wonderful taste.'

I bet, thought Phoebe. But I'd better not buy a cream shift. Not that she was going to.

'The black would suit you.'

Phoebe fingered the thick, lustrous silk, taking in the price with some amusement: Stella might afford it, she wouldn't. (Although she had heard that the Stella Pinero Theatre was not doing too well financially just now. But Stella herself had a TV series going and had been filming abroad. Money there, no doubt.)

'I'm trying to cheer myself up before an important interview,' she confided. 'I thought if I found something really good, I could call it a happy omen.'

The manager studied Phoebe. 'Would you wear it to the interview? Do call me Eden, it's more friendly.'

'No, I wouldn't wear it, just a cheer up thing really.' Phoebe studied her face in a long wall mirror; she didn't look as good as she would like. She rubbed her cheek thoughtfully. 'That your name? Unusual, isn't it?'

'It's a family name. The other one is Brown, so you can see my mother thought I needed something livelier.' Eden was a small, neat blonde with tiny hands and feet and big brown eyes, her olive skin suggested that the blonde hair was dyed.

Well done, though, Phoebe decided, and no roots showing. Phoebe was tall and slender but she had good muscles and was limber and athletic.

'No, I wouldn't wear it,' she said, turning away from her image. 'This is my interview gear.'

'What about this dress?' Eden came from behind a white screen with a plain linen dress. 'This is anthracite grey.' Her customer seemed to go for dark colours. She did not understand about the interview. What was she being interviewed for, for heaven's sake? A funeral parlour? Surely something cheerful and strong was the best bet? 'Very nearly black...I have it in tangerine, too.' She pointed to a flame-coloured dress.

'I like it,' said Phoebe, ignoring the grey linen and going towards the flame-coloured one. She studied the label and assessed the price from that particular Milan designer.

'Try it on.' Eden knew that once a customer had tried on a garment you were that much closer to a sale.

Phoebe held it up against her. 'No, I won't do that... Tell you what—keep it for me.'

'Well...'

'I'll put down a deposit, and if I get the job, then I'll come back and buy it.' Then she had another thought. 'No, I'm going to take both. And I'm going to take them with me.'

She had no doubt she would get the job, for which she was highly qualified, and John Coffin was head of the force in which she would be working. He would be on the interviewing committee. They had once been close, very close, but that might mean he would feel obliged to be neutral. But there were other factors...

Still, she was tense.

'And if you don't get it?'

'Oh, to hell with it!'

'It's unusual,' Eden said doubtfully, thinking of her deposit. Who was this woman?

'I'm an unusual woman.'

You can say that again, said Eden to herself.

'No, I think I'll get it,' said Phoebe absently. She stared at herself in the looking glass again and moved her finger down her cheek. 'Do you know, I think it's swollen...I've got bad faceache.' It might be more than toothache and that was why she was taking two dresses. She had to opt for life.

'It's tension.' Eden was sympathetic. 'I get red blotches all over my face when I'm tense.' But she was still worried about the bill.

More tension than you know, Phoebe admitted inside her head as she held the dress against her. More than I'm going to admit to. Her mind made pictures; this tension comes in packets, personal packets named Phoebe Astley and a more formal packet labelled Job Description.

Inside both packets was the name of John Coffin because he came into both bundles.

In the past they had known each other well, too well, he might now think since his marriage. They had met recently in Birmingham where she had been working, heading her own small unit. The case he had been engaged upon then had been both personal and painful, she had helped him, he would be the first to admit, but they had walked carefully around their past relationship.

She didn't know what truths and lies he had told but she had let him have more than her average number of lies. He was going to find out now; the matter would not come up at the interview session, of course, although she could imagine the amused, informed stare from his blue eyes as the matter of her married status came up. Nothing much would be said, he had probably long since checked that particular untruth anyway, but later, ah, yes, later…she would be asked questions.

The truth will out, she said to herself, although as a serving police officer she knew that it did not always do so.

The maddening thing was that he would understand, and might not laugh. He had a kind heart beneath the steel.

Stella Pinero was lucky and Phoebe hoped she knew it. She had heard that Stella had tantrums, but then she was a beauty and a celebrated actress, and was entitled to her tantrums; they came with the job. And for all Phoebe knew, Coffin enjoyed the tantrums, she could see he might.

He would certainly know how to control them; the man she remembered had known well how to give as good as he got. Except that love did hobble you and the word had reached her that he loved Stella extremely.

She was going up for this interview for a position which she truly wanted and which offered interest and great responsibility as well as some danger, and it wasn't going to help that she had once been in love with John Coffin.

Once or still? Be quiet, she told herself.

She had her own reasons for leaving Birmingham upon which she would certainly be questioned at the interview but she had already settled on the half-lie. Later, to John Coffin, she would have to be more truthful.

Phoebe dug into her shoulder bag. 'I'll give you a cheque, all right?'

'Sure.' Eden added cautiously. 'Make it a third, please.'

'No, I'll pay for the two. How's the shop doing?' Phoebe was writing her cheque; she was calculating, a substantial sum by her standards.

'Fine,' said Eden. She was of the opinion that this was entirely too personal a remark. 'We're opening a branch in East Hythe next month.'

'Is that so?' Phoebe handed the cheque over and waited for her receipt. 'How many does that make?'

'Three. One other in Swinehouse. Horrible name, isn't it?'

'You don't live locally?' You couldn't if you hate the name that much; full of history that name is, even Phoebe knew that. Pre-Norman, pre-Saxon and probably pre-Roman.

'No, I drive through the tunnel. Still Docklands, though.'

The new Thames tunnel joining London north of the river and the Second City was a great link; Phoebe had driven through it herself this morning, fighting traffic all the way and had thought it a great death trap with poor lane discipline, but that was Londoners for you. A lawless lot. Still, no one dead by the roadside that she had seen.

'I'll be looking for a place if I get the post. What's it like round here?'

'Can be expensive. Depends. Spinnergate's your best bet. I'll be looking there myself soon. I'll be looking for a lodger too; we might suit.'

'I'll remember what you say.' I'll remember everything. I usually do, it's my job.

She rubbed her cheek. The pain in her cheek was not

really bad but it contained just the hint that it could get to be nasty and that worried her. She knew she had cause for worry. There was pain and pain, and this could be a bad one.

Outside, a church clock sounded the hour. Forty minutes to her appointment. Just time to drive and park the car and take three deep breaths. She had reconnoitred the route earlier and knew where to go.

She smiled at Eden as she pushed the heavy glass door. 'See you again.'

'The dresses suit you. You'll enjoy wearing them, I promise.'

Phoebe paused at the door. 'Can you smell burning?'

Eden sniffed. 'It's some way off. Sort of strong, though. There's an old chap round here has a lot of bonfires. And he's not the only one.'

Albert Waters had had one fire already today, possibly that was what they could smell?

'If I didn't know better,' began Phoebe, then stopped. 'What does he burn?'

'What?'

'Nothing.' If I didn't know better, then I would say it was flesh burning.

Phoebe walked to her car, parked just around the corner, this spot too had been prospected earlier; she sat still for a few minutes recalling the scene behind her, remembering Eden, the shop with its contents, and the outside in that busy street. On one side there was a grocery store and on the other a chemist's shop: both old stores but with a certain prosperity. Further down the street was a bank, and a pet shop where a small white puppy slept in the window. He had a basket, a cushion, a bowl of water and a few hard biscuits. Phoebe had hoped that someone would buy him soon; it was no life for a dog in a hot window.

She fixed Eden in her memory: the pretty blonde with the small hands and feet, and the big ego. She felt sure about the ego. Once inside Phoebe, all these details would be there for ever, and would pop out whenever required without effort on her part. Press the button, the right button, and out it came. It was the way her memory worked.

Having fixed it all, Phoebe started the car and drove away. The car window was open so that the smell of burning came into the car and drove away with her. The smell bothered her.

Mortuaries burnt odds and ends of human remains, so did hospitals, but she had studied her map and there was no hospital near here.

It had been a quiet, ordinary shopping day; both women if questioned would have so described it, but there is always a subtext.

Eden took the opportunity of an empty shop to make a local telephone call. She dialled the number and hung on for some time waiting for an answer.

'Oh, come on, Agnes. Where are you? Two days I've been ringing you and you know we need to talk.' She went away to make herself a cup of coffee. 'You do flutter around, Agnes, just when you ought to stay put.' The two women were business acquaintances rather than close friends; they worked for the same organization, but Eden liked Agnes Page. 'Probably popped over to Paris without telling me to look for clothes.' Or New York or Milan or Hong Kong. This was fantasy as all the clothes were purchased by the buyer, a hirsute woman with blue hair and long red nails who had been in the rag trade for decades and Agnes was on the accounts side, but it was a game they played between them, that one day, they would open a shop and buy from all the best houses. You needed a fair bit of capital for such a venture. 'Money, money, money,' hummed Eden as she drank her coffee.

On her way to her crucial interview, Phoebe wound up the car window to keep out the smoke.

The fire was burning and the smoke was blowing John Coffin's way.

HE FELT THE FIRE too. There had been a fire in his life for a few weeks now, and on the day of Phoebe Astley's interview for a job in his force, he began talking about it openly to a group meeting in his room.

They were the interviewing board being entertained for drinks and coffee, all carefully selected men and women.

They would be interviewing the shortlist of three candidates.

He poured out drinks, letting his eyes wander out the window, wide open because it was so hot.

The Second City of London shimmered in the heat. In the distance was the river, but all he could see was the roofs of Spinnergate with—far away—the tower blocks of Swinehouse, and beyond, the factory tops of East Hythe.

For some years now, John Coffin had been chief commander of the Second City's police force, responsible for maintaining law and order in this most difficult and rowdy of cities with a millennium-long tradition of being obstructive to authority. The Romans had suffered from its citizens as her legions had landed at the dock now being excavated by the archaeologists from the New Docklands University, digging up camp sites where the soldiers had been gulled and robbed by the locals. The English folk who settled when the Romans went picked up the same tricks and became as bad, worse really, because, being English, they kept a straight face and made a virtue of it. Norman, Plantagenet, Tudor: this part of London was not controllable, it kept its own laws. They withdrew behind the walls of London and its tower and left the villages and hamlets along the river to get on with it. And, with the river for their thoroughfare, so they did.

With every generation, the population grew, so that by

the time Victorian notions of morality arrived, there was a dense population obstinately reluctant to be evangelized.

The hot air came heavy with the smells of the living and the long dead that came floating in through the window and hit Coffin in the face. He hoped he wasn't going down with one of the odd viruses which were on the move in the Second City this summer. He couldn't afford to be ill with Stella in the state she was in over her theatre (or was it his sister Letty's theatre? It had been Letty who had helped put together the St Luke's Theatre complex, now renamed the Stella Pinero Theatre).

He handed round the drinks: whisky with ginger—he ought to shudder and his Edinburgh half-brother—lawyer William—would certainly do so, but it seemed to be what Alfred Rome wanted.

'Sir Alfred.'

'Ferdie, please.'

Sir Alfred, Ferdie to his friends, he must remember that, was the warden—he preferred the title to vice chancellor or president—to the very new university tucked away in the east of the Second City, in the Bad Lands, not hitherto considered educable, but no doubt Ferdie Rome would change that. He was of the new breed, educated at Ruskin College, Oxford, then at Birkbeck College in the University of London, then a short period in the Cabinet office. The unusually rapid promotion suggested to Coffin that this was a political appointment, which made Sir Alfred all the more formidable. Tough, square-shouldered and completely bald in his late thirties, he looked fit for anything. Coffin now had two universities in his area and had to protect both from the rebels and the lawless.

Coffin carried two glasses across the room to where two of the women, Jane Frobisher, banker, and Professor Edna Halliday, economist, stood talking. Edna's stocky figure was in skirt and shirt but Jane, usually impeccable, was wearing a long-sleeved silk dress—she looked hot.

'Jane, gin and tonic; Professor, white wine.'

Three other members of the group were senior policemen, two from this force: Chief Inspector Teddy Timpson, CID, and Superintendent William Fraser, from the uniformed wing, and the third, Chief Inspector Clare Taylour, from the Thames Valley. The extra figure, there to keep the balance, was a figure from the outside world, a journalist and barrister: Geraldine Ducking. When you said outside world, that was with reservations because Geraldine came from a family deep rooted in the old Docklands. It was for this reason Coffin had called her in. Geraldine was the tallest and largest woman there, but she dressed well, so that her size was unnoticed, and she had small, neat hands and feet.

Clare Taylour had refused wine and spirits and was drinking mineral water; she was a calm, forceful woman who intimidated most people, but not John Coffin, who had known her for years. Today she had a bandage wrapped round her ankle and was limping. 'We're all walking wounded today, look at Geraldine and Jane—she says she's been sunburnt.'

Coffin carried whisky round to all the others, including Geraldine whose favourite tipple it was, she was a self-proclaimed deep drinker, but managed to stay remarkably sober. She was also one of the cleverest people Coffin had ever met. She held out her hand, on her arm was a dressing. 'Wasp bite,' she said.

Among this group of people were some of his closest friends and colleagues; outside of Stella and his sister Letty, these were the people he liked and trusted.

And there had been Felix, the happy man, aptly named. Twenty-eight years old, ambitious but friendly, and now dead.

Dead for a month. One young friend gone by violence.

He looked round at them: Sir Alfred he knew less well but he was beginning to enjoy the sight of that sturdy figure always wearing what looked like, but surely couldn't be, the same suit and the same grey suede boots. He had small feet and delicate hands. Jane Frobisher, talking away with her usual animation, but she did not seem as happy as usual in her lovely clothes that Coffin, under the tutelage of Stella, could recognize as couture. Of course, bankers earned that sort of money, even in these days of recession. Professor Edna Halliday, by contrast, looked as if she had got out of bed and put on whatever was to hand. Skirt and striped shirt were clean but creased, her hair pinned back with a casual hand so that bits of it were escaping. But it would be wrong, he thought, to describe her as unattractive. On the contrary, she was full of life and humour and he knew for a fact that she had a string of lovers, usually two at a time. He had never been invited to be one himself (the list was by invitation only), she liked them younger, much younger. This did not seem to be held against her by other women and she got on with everyone. Clever lady.

You never noticed what Clare Taylour was wearing and that was probably part of her own skills and why she was such a success as a detective.

The two policemen had the right anonymous clothes as well, although Teddy Timpson was young enough to wear a sharp tie. Fraser was in uniform and putting on weight.

Coffin felt sympathy there; his hand strayed to his own waistband. Marriage seemed to be fattening; accordingly, Stella had put him on a starvation diet. He didn't get enough exercise, that was the trouble.

Coffin was on the committee but would not be chairing it; that task fell to Teddy Timpson. He would also withdraw when one of the candidates whom he knew appeared.

'Important looking lot, aren't we?' said Sir Ferdie jovially. For such a tiddly little job—he did not say this aloud but Coffin could read his thoughts.

'I've been lucky to get you all,' he said. 'But it's an important job, more important than it looks.'

An innovation of his own. The officer appointed would have the rank of chief inspector or superintendent, according to age and experience, and would liaise with all the important institutions in his bailiwick.

There was too much what Coffin called 'loose crime' floating around.

The unit would be small but hand-picked.

As had the committee been; it had been carefully put together whether the members knew it or not. At least one of them was beginning to suspect and to wonder if acceptance had been wise.

'You ought to look after us, though,' said Sir Alfred, 'important we may be, healthy we are not. Now there's me, on tablets for my blood pressure, there's Geraldine who's had collagen injections—'

'Oh, surely not.' Geraldine was not famous for her beauty but she had kept what looks she had and glowed with health. Coffin hoped she could not hear what was being said. Geraldine was younger than the other women there, in her early forties, whereas they were in their fifties. She had the careless charm of someone who always got her own way. She was generous, cheerful and interested in men. She had made one careful advance to the chief commander, more as an experiment than anything else, but she had not been annoyed when he did not respond. She was younger than the others but a little bit older than she admitted.

Coffin knew all the ages. Among other things. 'Oh yes, I recognize the shine. And one of us has just had an operation for cancer and we're probably all on tranquillizers. Not you, of course.'

'How do you know all this?'

'By keeping my eyes and ears open. You ought to do the same.' Perhaps I do, Coffin thought, perhaps I do. I don't know everything, but I always know something—that's my job.

Years as a detective had made him observant of friends and foes alike. It was automatic with him. For instance, he had seen Sir Alfred travelling to London from Oxford (where they had both been attending the same conference) on a second class ticket in a first class coach. Naughty or just absent-minded? He had seen Geraldine entering the block of buildings in East Hythe which housed a doctor, a solicitor and on the top floor, an inquiry agent.

Josh Armer, the solicitor, was not the most respectable lawyer in the business and was friend to more criminals than Coffin cared to think about. Professional friend, of course, Josh always sent in a bill. The phrase 'there is no such thing as a free lunch' might have been invented for him. A plump, gently spoken man, Josh was a classical music fan and supposed to be an expert on Rachmaninov.

Arabella Hammer, the female inquiry agent upstairs, was his equal and they were reported to be lovers.

Then he had remembered that Josh Armer belonged in this district, one of the families that had lived here for decades in a vast kindred. There weren't so many of them left now, but they popped up occasionally. Geraldine's family was such another.

You had to remember that some of these dockland areas were like villages where kids married to live near mum, just as mum and dad had in their generation. There was a lot of intermarrying and probably a bit of incest as well. Such a way of life was dying out of course, but pockets still remained. Kindred loyalty went back to the Anglo-Saxons and earlier, when an eye for an eye meant just that.

'What's the name of this new unit?' asked Sir Alfred, examining his papers. 'Seems to have escaped me.'

Coffin let his eyes flicker round the room before he answered. Teddy Timpson had married a local girl and that meant he was sometimes biased. The trouble with being a detective was that you automatically suspected everyone of having secrets.

Especially when you had one or two yourself.

Coffin said, 'The provisional name is Unit AN, but it hasn't got a settled name yet,' he went on. 'Perhaps the committee can think of one.'

'Leave that to Geraldine, shall we?' said Ferdie. 'She's the word girl.'

'Long time since I was a girl,' called Geraldine over the top of her whisky, 'but thank you for the name.' She took a swig of her drink, but actually, as Coffin observed, drank very little. 'When are you going to let me have a look at your mother's memoirs? I could make a lovely TV series out of them.'

He laughed. 'That's what worries me.'

'What a lady!'

A lady, in the genteel, white gloves and carrying-a-handbag style, his mother had never been, thought Coffin. A wanderer, an adventurer, and several-times-married lady, probably several times a bigamist and probably a liar into the bargain, leaving behind three abandoned siblings who only discovered each other late in life. There was John Coffin himself, his beautiful sister Letty and industrious William in Edinburgh and goodness knew who had sired him.

'I think Stella wants to get her hands on it.'

'I bet she does... Where is she now?'

Coffin hesitated. 'In New York at the moment...'

'I thought it was Spain.' He saw the glitter in her eyes which was not drink nor sympathy. 'It *was* Spain.' Damn you, Geraldine, for being so well informed. 'But she flew straight on to New York.'

He let them linger with their drinks for one more minute, then he caught Teddy Timpson's eye and nodded. Time to begin.

Round the table, they shuffled the papers in front of them. Why did a committee always fidget? But they always did, some worse than others; this lot were moving the papers as if they were about to play a hand of cards with them... In a way they were—poker—but they didn't know it.

'We have three candidates, whom we will see in alphabetical order,' began Chief Inspector Timpson. 'Two men and one woman.'

He had their names in front of him: Simon Daly, from the Met, a very strong record and destined to go high; James Wood, who was from his own force, ambitious, pushing, a difficult character but able.

And Phoebe Astley.

'The woman is good,' he had said to Timpson. 'She was doing a very fine job where she was. I was surprised when she put in. She deserves serious consideration. You'll know when you see her.'

And that is where I will go out, Coffin nodded to himself, partly because I know Phoebe—she is a friend and for a time was more than that so I don't want to seem prejudiced—and partly because I am absolutely determined she is chosen.

And also because I have fixed it that you will, Phoebe.

I want you here, Phoebe, and I want you now.

He looked across at Teddy Timpson who stared back. Both of them were skilled at communicating without words. They were both remembering a conversation that they had had earlier in the month, and behind that conversation was a train of events which explained why he wanted Phoebe on his team.

HE HAD SPOKEN to Teddy Timpson two weeks ago. Not a man with whom he felt wholly at ease or wholly safe. He had a lot to tell him; information that Timpson had to be told, but all the same, Coffin had edited it carefully. Placed as he was, at the top of an uneasy pyramid, he kept a lot quiet inside him. Some topics were hotter than others.

Security, for instance, where he was in communication

with various government agencies. Sometimes he was obliged to pass on all he learned to the responsible units in his force; at other times, he kept details to himself.

For a few months now he had had meetings in the old City of London with a committee made up of men from the Treasury, the Bank of England, the City of London, the Inland Revenue and the hard boys from Customs and VAT, a man from Scotland Yard and Coffin; the major clearing banks were represented also.

The committee was called the Resources (Police: London) Committee—RPC for short—and a man from the Treasury kept the minutes, in his head presumably, since no one ever saw them again. Too secret. Coffin made his own notes of what went on. There was never an agenda, the Chair, Althea Adams from the Bank of England conducted the meeting in her own terrifying way.

The resources of the three London Forces, the Met, the City of London, and his own, it did not discuss. Money, it did.

They were a group of men of influence and power who were really looking into what one member called 'dirty money'.

Coffin found these meetings, which took place at irregular intervals and in different rooms, both stimulating and alarming. He enjoyed meeting all the trained, tough-minded professionals.

Earlier in his career, he would have found them intimidating, products as they were of schools and universities he had never entered; the Treasury man, Winchester and New College (of course); the two men from the clearing banks, Eton and Trinity, Cambridge (again, of course) and Althea, Cheltenham Ladies College, Girton and Harvard (this time, not of course, but predictable). Now he took them as he found them: clever and hard-working.

Besides, he had done his homework: he knew that Althea had a sick child whose care preoccupied her, that the Treasury mandarin was about to divorce his wife, and one of the men from the clearing banks had just come through a gruelling treatment for cancer.

He hadn't been able to get much about the Inland Revenue and Customs chaps, which he regretted because he suspected them of being the prime agents behind this committee.

What the committee made of him, he did not examine, but he kept quiet and took it all in. He was not surprised at his own self-confidence, but he did remember the thin youth with the dark hair who would once have been ill at ease in such company. Anyway, what could they have said of him? There's John Coffin who's having a bad time with his missus?

It was with all this in his mind (and when he already knew that Phoebe would be up for the new job), that two weeks ago he had suggested that Teddy Timpson meet him for a drink in the pub near Spinnergate tube station, a comfortable establishment too far away from police headquarters to be used by the local coppers. He sat waiting in the Black Dog where they had no air conditioning on this hot day so that the ice in his glass was melting fast. It was not like DCI Timpson to be late, he was a brisk and cheerful man.

But he found himself glad of the quiet time. It wasn't the best of days. He was alone in his home in the tower of the old St Luke's church, now converted into the three flats with the theatre complex adjacent. Stella was away, filming in Spain, leaving him in charge of the cat and the dog. The dog, Bob, who answered to any name and the cat, Tiddles, who never answered at all unless it suited, were his sole companions.

His sister Letty was in Scotland visiting brother William, probably with a view to extracting some money from him for her reeling property empire. She'd be in for a disappointment there, he thought, as William was a tight man

with money. Still, it would be an interesting meeting—
Greek joining battle with Greek. On the whole, he backed
Letty but you could never be sure.

Then, like someone probing a sore tooth, his mind went
back to Stella. She had telephoned from the airport in Madrid to announce she would not be home just yet, love, but
was flying into New York, stop-over in Paris.

Not even Heathrow, London, he had noted glumly, as if
she couldn't bear to be on the same island. And to be called
'love'—that was bad, very bad. No one really close to
Stella was ever called love in that way; it was what she
called a fellow actor for whom she had small regard, or a
bad director.

What had he done? Or not done? They had parted on
warm, even passionate terms; he remembered it well, that
night before she left, now it had all gone cold.

He would find out in the end; Stella never kept anything
to herself when she was angry which he had to suppose
she was, but he wasn't sure he wanted to know. He didn't
enjoy these ups and downs with Stella. He had thought all
that sort of thing was in the past, when, God knew, they
had enough of them. They had met when young, too young
probably, loved and parted, met again briefly before moving away from each other, and then coming together when
his sister Letty had created her St Luke's Theatre complex.

Happy ever after, he'd thought. He watched Teddy
Timpson come through the door.

'Sorry, sir. Got held up.' The man looked flustered and
hot.

'Have a drink before you say another word.'

'Thanks...lager, please.'

Teddy didn't drink a lot, unlike some of his colleagues,
but he probably had other vices. 'I got held up. A double
stabbing in Cock Street, in the Little Cockatoo pub.' He
drank thirstily. 'It's always been a bad place...it's the land-
lord.'

'Stabbed?'

'No, he did it. His wife and the barman, they were having it off and he found out. Well, he always knew, I reckon, but only took off today. I blame the weather.'

'At least you've got it tied up.'

'Not on your life: he denies it, says some man walked through the door and knifed them both.'

'Where was he?'

'Hiding in the cellar.'

'What about the knife?'

'We can't find it. And no witnesses, the pub was empty.'

'Is that likely?'

'It is round there,' said Timpson gloomily. 'They know when to run. Anyway, he had a bright idea, he set the place alight.' He lifted his sleeve to his nose. 'I still stink of smoke.'

'Did the whole place go up?'

'No, no, he didn't make a good job of it.' He grinned. 'Mind you, it wasn't a bad idea. Fire does destroy.'

'I've said a bit already as regards what I want to talk to you about. I won't procrastinate any more.'

'Yes,' said Timpson cautiously. 'You've said a bit. Not a lot.' Procrastinate… He's an intellectual, my guvnor; he doesn't know it, but he is. Timpson thought about an earlier chief who might have said: This is the business, boys. Or, in a jokey mood: Up boys and at 'em.

'It's about the new unit.'

'Yes, the one that's going to be liaising with all City institutions and all police units as well.' The word was that there wasn't much money and it was going to have to work hard. 'A political invention to keep critics happy,' was what someone had said. 'It's going to be smallish, isn't it?'

'Money,' said Coffin, then sat thinking about how he should put it to Timpson, whom he had used before as a go-between because Timpson's negotiating skills were well known. 'Money's short.' He had every reason to be think-

ing about money. At the back of his mind, not to be dis-
cussed now with Chief Inspector Timpson, was a big
money problem. He would be seeing Archie Young, now
CID supremo, later.

Timpson waited. Money came in everywhere. Who knew
better than he did?

Coffin looked at Timpson, wondering what the gossip
was and how much he knew. 'There's quite a lot going on
at the moment.'

Timpson kept a careful opaque look on his face.

'You guessed?'

'Word has got around.'

Coffin nodded. Thought as much.

Timpson was cautious enough to say nothing more: if he
hadn't been told, he wasn't to know. He knew how to be
blind, deaf and dumb when he had to be.

'This unit needs the right top man. Or woman. I think it
ought to be a woman, I've worked with her before and I
think she has the right qualities. You are chairing the committee and I will withdraw when she is interviewed, seems
fairer.'

What's fairer got to do with it, thought Timpson. 'Sure,'
he said aloud. 'Of course, we have to consider all three
candidates.'

'Of course we do.'

They seemed to be understanding one another and Coffin
was satisfied. 'Have another drink?'

'My round.' It gave Teddy Timpson an obscure pleasure
to buy a drink for the chief commander whom he both liked
and found alarming. He cast around for something to say
that would end the meeting on the right note. 'Saw Miss
Pinero on the telly last night,' he came up with. 'She's
brilliant.'

'Brilliant,' agreed Coffin with a tight smile. He knew he
had got what he wanted. He stood up. 'I must go. Another
appointment.'

'THEY'VE DONE excellent work,' he said to Superintendent Archie Young just an hour later on this same day, two weeks before the crucial committee for Phoebe. They were in his own home in St Luke's Mansions; in his flat, not Stella's, which was on the ground floor. They still kept the two going which was perhaps one of their mistakes. Didn't happily married people live under one roof? Or did you only meet the survivors? From Coffin's tower he could see over all his turbulent territory, make out the roof of his headquarters where a new floor had been planted on top of the building, not adding to its beauty but certainly providing much needed space. And if he tried hard enough, he could see the top of one of his new universities and one of the hospitals—the big new Second City General Hospital. When he looked out, he tried to admire the charm of what he saw and not think about the terrible responsibility that they represented.

'You have to hand it to the blokes who trail through financial records and know what's going on.'

'More so when equally clever minds are doing their best to hide it.'

Archie had climbed the career ladder quickly: the next promotion, already in line, would make him chief superintendent. He was clever, and sensible enough not to be *too* clever; a steady, reliable man.

'It's their job,' said Coffin, without much admiration; they had landed a mess on his lap.

They had talked about this several times before, but always in this unofficial way. At the moment, since Stella was in New York (or so he believed), and Archie Young's clever, high-flying wife was absent on a course in Cambridge, they were eating together. A modest meal sent in from the local fish and chip shop which did a splendid order and deliver service.

Coffin handed out the chips and fish which they were eating in his kitchen. In his youth, in that far away and long ago London, he would have eaten out of the newspaper but he graduated long since to the white porcelain which had been chosen, and not by Stella, and to pouring out some red wine which was about the only thing that stood up to fried cod. (Once it would have been a pot of strong tea, and still was for many and why not?)

'I had a session with Teddy Timpson today. He was agreeable.'

'He usually is.'

'Yes, no trouble there. I think we'll get the right head for this little unit.' Even to Archie Young who knew so much about him by now, he was careful about naming Phoebe. People could tell a lot about the way you spoke of a person.

And there is always a hidden agenda, the subtext.

'By the way, your own promotion has gone through. You're up, Archie, but keep quiet for the moment.'

Archie Young allowed himself a flush of pure pleasure and wished he could smoke, but the Coffin establishment was a No Smoking house. Coffin did not go back to the main subject of their meeting until they had almost finished.

John Coffin commanded a police force small by the standards of his big brother the Metropolitan police force which towered over him; small by the standards of some of the big north country forces; he knew that the Met joked about the Toy Town City force but he could afford to ignore that now because he was feeling his own powers.

Rivals and even friends had expected him to fail, but he had built up a very good set of teams from the mixture of local units he had inherited. He had created his own promotion panel which he watched over while allowing its independence. But he had seen to it that the weaker officers were weeded out and clever, hard-working men like Archie Young got fast promotion. He had men and women around him now that he both trusted and liked. 'I've kept you up to date: it seems that drug profits and other illegal monies

are being fed into British banks. The powers that be...'
even to Young he did not name them. That might come
later, but he was still bound by an oath of secrecy, '...are
worried that it could damage the whole banking system.'

'Money's money,' said the pragmatic Young.

'Apparently not. Might seem so to you and me but the
City says not...' The City in this context meant the bankers
and financiers of the First City of London, the money establishment. 'We seem to have been given a special part.
It looks as though a group of banks here in the Second City
have been targeted. I suppose they thought we'd be grateful. They had us down for a collection of innocents.'

Young accepted this silently for a moment, then said: 'I
bet I could name the banks.'

'I bet you could.'

They had three banks whose origin was far flung and
international, but which gave a good rate of interest on
savings and so were much used by the small depositors of
the Second City.

'Not only us, of course. The cash is being spread around
widely, and as I've let you know, action is being taken.'

'Sure.'

'But it's up to us to clear out our own little pigsty... A
lot of the money is being laundered here.'

Archie Young chewed a bit of cod which was unexpectedly solid; he could see the cat eyeing him hopefully.
'Acting on your instructions...'

'And your own wits,' said Coffin quickly.

'And my own wits,' went on Archie, 'I've had a couple
of men out there working on it.'

He put his fork into his food and began to stir it round
as if he didn't see it at all but something quite different.

'It's been a tough game to play, John.'

The use of his name, so rarely used even between the
two friends, was significant.

'Yes, it hasn't brought them luck.'

Two men, two deaths.

Felix Henbit who had died of an overdose of sedatives and drink. Suicide? Or accident? No one could believe in the suicide.

Mark Pittsy who had died in a car crash.

Apparent accidents, both of them.

'Rotten luck,' said Archie, 'some cases are buggers.' He shook his head. 'You get a run of accidents like that sometimes and I hate it.'

'We have a problem, Archie,' thought Coffin, but he did not say it aloud. Instead: 'I'm not happy.'

'Who could be?'

'Felix Henbit had a wife.' He made it a statement; he had liked Felix but kept his distance.

'Yes, likewise Pittsy; not long married. Also a sister in Cleveland who seemed a bit remote.'

'I'd like to meet Mrs Henbit.'

'I think you should. She'd appreciate it, a nice girl who's bearing up well. All the usual support groups have been in touch to see how she was getting on.' Mary Henbit had been bleeding inside but hadn't let it show too much.

'I'll get round there.' He might take Stella if she ever came home again which he sometimes doubted. She was good on such occasions, other women liked her.

Coffin looked down at his plate of chips. Not my mother, vanishing lady, my mother, you'd be home alone. She'd be long dead now. Or was she? His mother seemed just the sort to read you could live to be a hundred and sixteen and decide to do it. He pushed his plate away; the chips didn't appeal so much.

The two men talked for a while longer, then Archie Young went off—still flushed with the news of his promotion, and wishing his wife was at home so that he could tell her—soon after the meal was finished. Promotion had come very quickly; he knew he owed a lot to the chief commander, but he also knew he was a good officer.

He didn't have the older man's imagination, and sometimes he thought the Big Man let the parameters of his imagination spread a mite too far. He was thinking that now.

Coffin had not told Archie Young all his thoughts even though he trusted him. He never did tell anyone everything. He had seeded the corn and must now await events.

LATER, ON THE DAY of her interview, while Phoebe prepared herself for it and then went through it and got a hint of her success; and while Coffin sat thinking of his own problem—all this while the fire burned in the rough ground beyond the old Atlas factory.

When did it start? It must have started in the early afternoon because such fires burn slowly. The fire burned the mound of wood and leaves which a sexless figure put together, which he or she had lit and upon which, so a watcher said later, he or she had climbed. Hard to believe and the witness did not have good eyesight. Not climbing, perhaps, but dragged?

First smoke, then flames.

The body burned, the hair smouldered, the body fats caught and melted, the skin crisped.

PHOEBE, WHO KNEW she had interviewed well, who was sure she had got the job, waited for Coffin to telephone her, and when he did not, tried to telephone him at home. He was not there so she left a message on his answering machine.

Phoebe came back into the picture and Stella returned to the fold on the same day, which was a complication. Both of them left a message on his answerphone.

Flying back today, fondest love, Stella. Get out the champagne. That meant she was in a good mood. Not necessarily forgiving (what was there to forgive, he asked himself), but certainly loving.

Phoebe Astley made her plea. *Can you give me a bell? I am staying with a mate who has a place near the Tower. We could meet for a drink. I mean we'd better, hadn't we? We've got to talk.*

Coffin smiled wryly as he put down Tiddles's food and pushed the dog's nose out of the way. Phoebe always had rotten timing, that was one thing he now recalled about her. Stella, on the other hand, had the impeccable timing of a top actress.

Well, he would ring Phoebe, but in his own time; Phoebe had to learn about timing, and now it was Tiddles and the dog who came first.

He fed them both, washed his hands, because cat food (they both ate cat food, fortunately the dog could not read) smelt.

'The thing is, Tiddles,' he said. 'To be quiet but not furtive.' He considered the problem while he fed the dog.

'I know: we'll go to the Half a Mo.' He was pleased with Phoebe and his own plans. As he left the interview room—without speaking to her—he had seen her talking to his assistant. She had a carrier bag from Minimal at her feet. Good girl, he had thought. Instinct, that's what she's got. Without knowing it, she has started work for me.

THE PUB, CALLED Half a Mo by its regulars was placed on the junction by Halfpenny Lane and Motion Street, outside Coffin's bailiwick and into the City of London.

Small and dark, it had always been popular with those seeking privacy. Coffin had arrested more than one villain there in the old days. Its real name, shown on the board swinging above the door, was the King's Head, and there was a bearded head wearing a crown and clutching a glass to be seen, although wind and rain had weathered it. Only strangers to the district called it by that name.

The Half a Mo had changed since Coffin's last visit. It had been brightened up, more lights, more paint, more noise. It had never been noisy, as he remembered it; people had muttered quietly over their drinks. Usually because they were up to no good. Now music blasted from several sources, but, as he reflected, this too was a good protection against conversations being heard.

In fact, he could hardly hear what Phoebe was saying; she had kept him waiting, which just confirmed what he thought about her timing.

She was sitting opposite him, looking bright-eyed and alert, and a good deal thinner than when he had seen her last year in Birmingham, where she had helped him through a difficult patch. She looked thinner, but that might be due to a smart-looking silk dress she was wearing.

'How are things now?' She lifted up the gin and tonic which had always been her tipple.

It was a routine question to which no answer need be given.

'Fine,' he said. Which was half true and half not true. He had survived a board of inquiry, some hostile media criticism, and been told that he could be sure of a KBE in the next Honours list. Also, he still had a wife, at least he thought so; he would know more about that when he met Stella off the plane tomorrow morning. 'And what about you?' Their past relationship meant that there was real feeling in the question.

'Oh well, as you say, fine...' She sipped her gin and looked away.

'I was surprised when you put in for the job.'

'I heard about it on the grapevine and thought it was one for me... Of course, I didn't know much about it then, it was just a whisper.' Now she did know. Or as much as he had told her and as much as she had guessed.

'What about your husband and the children and the dog—do they like the idea of your working in the Second City?'

Phoebe looked away. 'Do you like my dress? It's new,

I bought it to celebrate getting the job. I know I *have* got
it; I was tipped the wink.'

'Come on, Phoebe.'

'They don't exist; there is no husband, no children, not
even a dog. I made them up. But I expect you know that.'

'I did check.' He looked at her without a smile. 'Why,
Phoebe, why?'

She shrugged. 'Well…I didn't think I'd ever see you
again after you swung into my office that day in Sparkhill,
you hadn't answered my party invitation. You just came in
because you wanted help. And you looked so married.'

'I didn't know that. I didn't know being married changed
the looks.'

'Well, it's changed yours. And for the better, I may add.'

Coffin just stopped himself looking at his reflection in
the wall mirror. 'But you were doing very well in the West
Midland force.'

'You checked that too?'

He was silent.

'Of course you did, you're a thorough man, John, always
were…I suppose I will have to call you Chief Commander
and Sir now.'

'You needn't call me anything.'

'I have called you some names in my time.'

'Sorry, Phoebe. I expect I deserved them.'

'I'll tell you one day how much you deserved them.'

Coffin felt his spirits sinking. 'I hope we are going to be
able to work together.'

Phoebe moved sharply. 'Will we be? I'll be heading my
own little unit and you are the big boss.'

'I'll explain.'

'Perhaps you had better… When you telephoned in
Sparkhill after I applied for the position, I knew you wanted
me. I don't say you fixed getting me the job, although you
could have done, but you didn't do it for love of me, so
what else is there?'

First of everyone, she had caught on to the hidden agenda.

'I knew you were the right person.' He got up. 'What about something to eat? The food used to be reasonable here, and I'm hungry.'

When he came back with a plate of sandwiches, Phoebe said: 'I was surprised when I got a packet of photocopied advertisements from *Second City News*... A couple of dress shops, a fast food chain, not one I knew, two hairdressers...I didn't think shops were touting for my custom, and then I remembered a copper who had sent me an advertisement for a new restaurant with the date and time and question mark scribbled on it and I thought, well, I know someone who does that sort of thing. Perhaps when he doesn't want to commit himself too much.'

Coffin offered her the sandwiches. 'Cheese or ham?'

'Cheese. And then I thought: But, the John Coffin I knew was never anonymous about work.'

'I'll take the ham then. Pickle? I remember you liked it.'

'Not onions though. You have to know someone very well to breathe onion over them. Of course, I do know you well, or I did. I thought: whoever sent those papers to me was nervous. And the John Coffin I knew was never nervous without cause.'

'I always valued your powers of observation and deduction. You are the right person for what I want.'

'Yes, but what is it? I am to run a small unit which will communicate with all principal institutions in the Second City. I shall have the rank of chief inspector, which I am glad about, by the way, but not much money to spend.'

Coffin looked about the bar which was crowded, but no one was taking any interest in them in their seat by the window where they could not be overheard.

'Yes, you will be all that, and the unit and your position were not invented for you, but as soon as your name appeared as an applicant, I decided to make use of you.'

'Oh, thanks.'

He ignored her sharpness—it was part of Phoebe. 'Let me explain: large sums of dirty money, money from drugs, and crime, are being put through the City of London banks. We are getting our share. This is seen as threatening and damaging.'

Phoebe, listening, absently popped a pickled onion into her mouth. 'But I'm not a financial—' she began.

'Stop and listen, the financial side is being handled by the Met and the City of London squad working with the Second City fraud experts… We're only small but I've recruited some good brains.'

Phoebe choked on the onion and Coffin stood up to hit her on the back.

'Oh, come on, Phoebe, listen. You will have two juniors working with you. Your ostensible job will be to liaise with all the institutions in the Second City, you know that, that was your remit.

'But I am going to use you in another way.' He moved the dish of onions away so that she could not get at them. 'Some money is being laundered, here in the Second City. Where, we can guess; from that we can move to guessing by whom, but they are getting help from someone close to us.

'Two of my young men who were working on it are dead. Felix Henbit and Mark Pittsy. Felix was a clever and resourceful officer; Pittsy was brilliant—he would have gone right to the top. Both of them died in what were supposed to be accidents. The papers that I sent you came to me anonymously. I don't know if they have a connection, or who sent them but I sent them on to you. Not exactly anonymous; I thought you'd guess they were from me, but I didn't want to make any comment; I wanted you to take them cold and react.'

Phoebe looked down at her new dress. 'They took me into Minimal.'

'That may have been exactly the right thing to do.'

Phoebe remembered some of the other names: Dresses à la Mode, KiddiTogs, Feathers and Fur. 'You may have to give me a dress allowance if I'm to shop at all of them.' But probably they were not all as expensive as Minimal; the names suggested different markets, and Feathers and Fur might be quite specialized.

Coffin ignored this; life with Stella had taught him caution when discussing money spent on or for clothes. 'What we have here is a classic murder puzzle: someone is picking off my men. I don't think that Felix Henbit or Mark Pittsy died because they had drunk too much; coppers do drink, but those two were careful men. Somehow they were killed.

'I'm not sure of what the motive is: whether it was because they were close to me, or because they had enemies I know nothing about, but I feel the motive must lie in the financial investigations they were both working on. I want you to investigate their deaths.'

'Don't you trust your own men?'

Coffin was silent. 'I have built a good structure up here. I took over a rambling set of CID and uniformed units and I've built up a force with its own identity. But I've had to do it on the quick. Of course I trust them but this is murder in my own backyard. I want you to investigate it for me.'

'I see.'

'You will have yourself and you will have me.

'My own feeling is that someone is protecting the machine that is feeding the illegal money into this area. We have a Minder, and I want him or her caught. I want you to identify the Minder.'

Phoebe considered, she knew now what she was taking on. 'I shall want back up. Leg work, help with interviews...'

'You'll get it.'

'Forensics...'

'You'll get it. Once we identify the Minder, then we will get the proof.'

Phoebe's mouth went dry. 'I never thought I'd hear you put it that way round.' For the first time, she saw the metal in John Coffin. 'I think you'd better get me another drink because I see what I am; a kind of stalking horse. If I succeed at all you want, I stand a good chance of getting killed myself.'

When he came back with her drink, she noticed he had got one for himself too and it looked strong. Good, at least he cared something for her. 'I almost wish I hadn't put in for the job.' She looked down at her new black dress, the colour of which now seemed uncomfortably appropriate.

'Phoebe, why did you apply? The truth now. I want you for this job, confirmation has to go through channels, but I'd like you here now. Only I need to know why you wanted to come.'

The drink lessened the dryness in her mouth. 'Oh well, you might as well know: I put away a rough type with a long record who threatened to get me personally, if you know what I mean... He comes out about now. Could be out already. I thought I'd be better off down here in the Smoke where he wouldn't have the contacts.'

Coffin considered. 'Doesn't sound like you, Phoebe.'

She looked out of the window. 'Well, there was a sort of an affair.'

'Ah, yes, that would complicate matters. So it got personal... He still wants you?'

There was a long pause. 'It wasn't quite like that. You see the affair, such as it was, was not with him but his wife.'

'Now I *am* surprised.'

'It was something that just seemed to happen... I wasn't too happy, neither was she, poor girl, but for me, it was a mistake.'

'Only not for her?'

Phoebe nodded. She was thinking about Rose with sadness and liking, but not love, not physical love. 'No. I'm afraid I treated her badly. You might be surprised to learn that treating their lovers badly is not the prerogative of men.'

Stella herself could not have delivered a shrewder blow. 'So you've run away?'

'I've run away. Don't we all?'

As THEY TALKED, the fire had been quenched and the blackened shrivelled body found; from one hand an unburnt finger stuck up as if in accusation.

The inhabitants of this particular area were few—a small terrace backed on to the open ground—moreover, they had among them the eccentric figure of Albert Waters who had built a small replica of Stonehenge in his back garden and who was now erecting the Tower of Babel in the front. They took it for granted that this fire was something to do with him.

He was into suttee now.

TWO

A QUIET BUZZ sounded in Coffin's pocket. 'Damn! I've been summoned.'

'Still attached to your bleeper?' said Phoebe.

'As ever.' He also had a portable telephone but he preferred a call such as this and then to go to his car phone. More protected.

Phoebe raised an eyebrow, a sceptical gesture she should have denied herself when she knew how much she was going to depend on him. 'I thought with your new eminence you would have given that up.' He wasn't a man who minded being laughed at, not as much as most men, but you couldn't go too far. In the past she often had.

He stood up. 'I must go to the car. How did you get here?'

'I walked.' I was on the verge of going too far, she thought, I must remember, I must remember.

'I'll give you a lift back.' To where you are staying, he meant, wherever that was.

She would have known his car from any other man's as soon as she looked at it. Nothing flamboyant: a good dark-coloured Rover, you could tell he had some money; he hadn't had once, but always bought the best he could afford whether it was a car or a coat. No litter in the car, but a neatly folded raincoat on the back seat with a pile of road maps. He liked to know where he was going. She had used to wonder why he didn't carry a compass as well. Not a joke to make now. He was quieter and more controlled than he had been once, gentler perhaps, but in a grim mood. He was angry.

In the car he listened to Archie's voice. 'I don't know if

you want to come, but you need to know. A body on a bonfire, looks deliberate.'

Phoebe watched and listened as Archie poured out his words. There was a faint scent on the air: Stella, she thought, her scent, and was horrified to feel a stab of jealousy. She was wearing Giorgio herself: strong, assertive and sexy and she had better give it up because if you want to be anonymous, and professionally this might be wise at the moment, then this was not the scent to wear. People remembered it. What Stella's scent was, she could not recognize.

'Is it still burning? Under control? But the body? Yes, I get it.'

Whatever Superintendent Young had to say did not please the chief commander because Phoebe saw him frown.

'Right, I'm coming. I want to take a look for myself.' He turned to Phoebe. 'You'd better come along too. There is a fire and a body and it doesn't look like an accident. And an old man I know seems to have something to do with it.'

He looked at Phoebe's smart dress. 'Will you risk that? You can never tell when you go to an incident.'

'I'll risk it... Did you notice—no, I don't suppose you did—that the large woman on the committee was wearing another version of this dress in red?'

'That was Geraldine, she always wears red when she's on the warpath.'

Phoebe blinked. 'And was she?'

'She must have been. Powerful lady, Geraldine. Keep on her right side if she comes your way.'

'And will she?'

'Can't tell. She knows the district pretty well. I think she may even know old Waters, the man who seems to have something to do with this new body.'

'It doesn't connect with that other business?' She would

always refer to the problem in this elliptical way from now on. 'Only connect,' E. M. Forster had said; he ought to have been a detective, she thought.

'I hope not, or the whole thing will be even crazier than it is now, but who knows, he's a strange man, but no, I don't see a connection... Superintendent Young is there and he is one of the people you've got to know.'

And to get on with, Phoebe interpreted this as meaning. 'I know something about him already. I know he worked with you before you came here, that he's got a good record, that he's done two courses at Saxon Police College, and always come out among the first half dozen, but that he always says his wife is the clever one.'

Coffin started the car. 'You have done your homework.' But he had expected no more of her and would have done the same himself in her place. She had perhaps demonstrated to him the range of her contacts, which interested him, and made him wonder who was using whom in this new appointment.

'I've met his wife, by the way.'

'How was that?'

'Oh, just by chance, at a meeting in Birmingham University: she was the guest speaker.'

'Interesting, was it?' He was guiding the car through the traffic which was unexpectedly heavy on this hot evening where the going down of the sun had not lowered the temperature much. He glanced at Phoebe's dress, there wasn't much of it, so she was luckier in the heat than he was.

He didn't believe for one minute that she had met Alison Young by chance; she had gone to the meeting on purpose, part of her pre-planning.

'Yes, it was interesting.'

Archie Young was not himself an interesting speaker although it was well worth listening to what he had to say. He got his facts right.

He turned left at the traffic lights, leaving the busy main

road through the Docklands behind him and driving into a
side street lined with small houses with neat front gardens:
Palgrave Drive. Beyond Palgrave Drive was Frances Street
which was less neat, and from Frances Street he drove
down the poetically named Golden Alley. Golden Alley
was not neat at all since several old cars and various abandoned shopping trolleys had been left there to rust, next to
a gas cooker of antique appearance.

'We are in Swinehouse now and you'd better get to know
it.' He was driving slowly. 'When can you start?'

'I've already asked for a transfer. I have some leave.
Straight away, if you want.'

'It'll have to be unofficial, but that suits me; I want you
here, working for me, quietly.'

'OK. Suits me too.'

'Where will you live?' The car was bumping over cob-
bles. The only good thing about Golden Alley was that it
was short, it led into Brides Street. Every time Coffin came
this way, he thought that if a modern Ripper got going (and
praise be, it would not be in his time and his bailiwick) it
would be in Brides Street. Brides Street was narrow, lined
with houses in which people lurked rather than lived.

'I'll look around. Rent something till I sell my place in
Edgbaston.' She looked out of the window with interest.
There seemed to be property for sale and to let around here.
And she had not forgotten Eden Brown's invitation: she
liked Eden and it would be interesting to start off with her.
She did not anticipate staying, she'd need her own place in
the long run. But Eden was clearly quite a girl.

You could smell the fire now.

Brides Street wound its way into Fashion Street where,
by contrast, the houses were pretty and well painted. Coffin
came this way at irregular intervals to visit an interesting
old inhabitant called Waters who had built Stonehenge in
his garden. The neighbours had complained, so he removed
his Henge, stone by stone, and built a pyramid in the back

instead with an attempt at the Tower of Babel. His pyramid had a little door and Mr Waters lived in it himself when he felt like it, as did several itinerant cats and an old urban fox.

Behind Fashion Street was a stretch of rough ground in which Albert Waters sometimes operated and where he had once built a mini earthwork that he called Waters's Way. Beyond the now weed-overgrown earthwork, lay the Swinehouse football ground.

In the rough ground, was the fire.

A fire engine, an ambulance and several police cars blocked their way. A small crowd was penned behind a police barrier.

'I smelt a fire burning when I was shopping,' said Phoebe.

'Yes, Calcutta Street, where you were, is parallel with Fashion Street but nearer the river. The wind must have been blowing your way. It's a funny district, I've smelt some weird smells there myself, almost as if the past had caught alight and was burning.'

He was recognized as he walked towards Archie Young and a shout came through the air. He had no difficulty in recognizing Albert's voice. 'Come over this way, sir, and I'll tell you all about it. I am an innocent man.'

'Be quiet, Bert, I'll speak to you later.'

'What's he on about?' he said to Archie Young as the superintendent came up.

'Oh, some of the neighbours thought the fire was his fault; he's always up to something, and he's been talking about the Great Fire of London for weeks now.'

Albert was still calling out and Phoebe heard him shouting about 'Your lady wife,' and to her horror realized he meant her.

'Shut up, Bert,' said Coffin, he looked annoyed. 'Archie, this is Phoebe Astley who might be joining us as head of our Liaison Unit.'

Archie held out a hand, he knew how to read this, she would be joining them. 'Glad to see you here. We've got something interesting for you.'

'Let's take a look then.'

Young led the way through a gate into the patch of ground. 'Was a row of allotments once, you can still see the outlines of the beds, and Waters uses that old shed over there.'

'Oh, does he?'

'For purposes of his own, which are God knows what. Anyway, that's how he comes into it. He's always over here so whatever goes on, the neighbours just assume it's him. And he admits himself he had started to build something here.'

He was walking ahead of them. 'This is it.'

A circle of blackened grass which was sodden where the fire hoses had played ran round a large pile of what had been wood and straw and wooden boxes. On the top lay a blackened hard object. Over everything was the sour, nose-pricking smell of burnt flesh.

'The police surgeon couldn't get too close—the heat; the fire chief said to leave it to cool down, but he had enough of a look to say it was human. Once.'

'Badly charred,' said Coffin.

'Yeah...the wood and hay and stuff were smouldering for some time and no one took any notice; they thought it was old Waters burning something. It seems there were two fires: Albert started one in the morning.'

Coffin walked right and then the other way, widershins.

'What does Albert have to say about it?'

'He'll tell you himself, only too anxious to talk. Says he had an early morning bonfire... He admits he started to build something, not sure what, but invention gave out so he was waiting for the gods to give him a clue. But he denies putting a body there.'

As he would do.

Something in Archie Young's voice made Coffin look at him. 'So? So what?'

'One neighbour said she saw a person she thought was Albert, climbing on to the pyre. Albert says no.'

'Well, he didn't get burned to death which bears that out. And he's not a liar; inventive, yes; mad, yes, and often a nuisance, but not a liar.'

Phoebe in her turn had walked round the bonfire site. The ground all round was muddy and trampled down. But she spotted something lying further away on the grass.

'There's a shoe here.'

Coffin nodded. 'I know, I saw.'

Young said. 'It's left there till we've photographed everything. That's about to be done; just waiting for us to clear away.'

'It's a woman's shoe. Neat, high heeled. Looks expensive.'

'Doesn't mean the body is that of a woman,' said Archie Young carefully. 'The witness we've got said she saw a man. Or she thought so, wearing trousers.'

'Women wear trousers.'

Young didn't bother to answer that. His wife wore trousers, Stella Pinero wore trousers, half the women he worked with wore trousers. 'When the body is examined we shall know the sex.'

'I wonder what sort of trousers they were,' said Phoebe. 'The sort of trousers can tell you a lot about a woman. I mean, tight jeans, flares, jodhpurs, Turkish trousers, caught at the ankle.'

'She just said trousers, I think that was all she could see. Ask her if you like, she lives next door to Albert Waters—she made a statement.'

Phoebe looked at Coffin. 'Go ahead,' he said. 'I'll have that word I promised Albert.'

'Right.' She could read his face: Be my eyes, he was saying, be my ears, then report back. I want to know.

'Number six, Fashion Street,' said Young. 'I think you'll find her there, I saw her looking out of the window. She'll probably enjoy a visit, I think she's hoping to be on the evening TV news.'

Phoebe walked away while Coffin turned towards Albert Waters who was leaning against the fence and smoking a pipe.

'I haven't smoked a pipe for years, but I needed it today and one of your chaps let me go and get some pipe tobacco... It isn't what it used to be, I think the tobacco leaf has changed. You hardly ever smell a decent pipe smoke now.'

'Not many people smoke them these days.'

'Not in public, in private maybe.'

Coffin leaned against the fence beside the old man whose hands were trembling. 'You're talking too much, Albert,' he said kindly.

'I always do when I'm nervous; you should have known me in the war, Hitler's war, even I'm not old enough for the Kaiser. Talked a blue streak, I did then.'

'What did you do in the war?'

'Gunner. Not in the air, thank God, that was the killer, I did have a tank all round me.'

'So what's making you nervous now?'

'What do you think? I did light a fire there, this morning. I thought I'd get rid of some rubbish. It smouldered all day but I didn't take any notice; it couldn't harm anyone, I thought.'

'Didn't the smell worry you?'

'I had some old mattresses on them filled with horse hair, I thought it was that.' Albert looked tearful. 'You don't think of bodies...then I saw the flames, and I thought: Here you are, better have a look at that... Then I saw what was burning up there. It was me called the police. Police first, fire brigade next.'

'You knew it was a body?'

Albert chewed at his pipe. 'Smelt it. I knew that smell. Told you I was in a tank, didn't I? Smelt a jerry like that. One of ours too, mate of mine.'

'All right, I understand. The smell reminded you of too much.'

Albert kept quiet for a moment. 'I could do with a drink.'

'Later, Albert. I'll stand you one myself.'

Albert grinned—he had a pleasant grin, and Coffin could see the cheerful young cockney who had gone to war. What ever happened to him in that tank in that desert?

'You built the bonfire?'

That roused him. 'No, I did and I didn't. My bonfire wasn't the size of what this one was. I had a few planks of wood out there. I was going to build the Ark but I couldn't seem to get going. The invention drained away. Does sometimes. So I left it there, what I'd done, and waited for inspiration.'

'How long?'

Albert considered. 'Week or two. Might have been. Inspiration's been a bit slow lately. You can't call it up to order, you know. Wish you could. The Greeks had a special god they used to call up when they needed help. I wish we had one, I could do with one like that.'

So could I, thought Coffin. I wonder what the right god for detection would be? Bacchus, Thor? Wrong pantheon, of course, but Norse or Greek, he didn't expect an answer.

'Anyway, this morning I thought I'd have a burn up, bits of this and that, like I said. It raises the spirits.'

Coffin wondered who or what spirits he was hoping to raise. 'If you didn't build the fire up, then did you see who did?'

'No, not to notice.'

'Your neighbour says she saw a man—you, she thought—piling it up and then someone—a man, perhaps you—climbing up on it.'

'Think I'd burn myself?'

Coffin shook his head. 'No.'

'She can't see anyway, not Mrs Thorn, can't rely on her.'

'And you saw nothing? Sure of that?'

Albert said: 'These last days, I've been working on my construction in the front.'

'Oh yes, I heard about that, the Tower of Babel, isn't it?'

'Mini,' said Albert with dignity. 'Mini Tower of Babel. You have to keep yourself within your own limits.'

Coffin looked towards the remains of the bonfire which was now being photographed. The full police operation was in action; two big vans had arrived, one of which would be the incident room and the other, if he knew his friends, would be the canteen.

'Come and have a drink,' he said to Albert, 'there'll only be tea or coffee in the van, but I keep a flask of whisky in the car in case.'

'I'm a case,' said Albert happily, ambling forward. 'I'm definitely a case.'

Coffin looked towards the house into which Phoebe had disappeared. He trusted her, he had to trust her. He trusted himself, he trusted Archie, he had to trust Phoebe, and outside of that, he trusted no one.

There was Stella, of course, mustn't forget Stella, whom he had to collect quite soon at Heathrow.

PHOEBE COULD SEE the two men walking towards the police coach from where she sat in Mrs Brenda Thorn's bow window. She had a cup of tea in front of her and a chocolate biscuit. Mrs Thorn was explaining that she had certainly thought it was Albert Waters who was building up the bonfire because everything that went on over there always *was* Albert, but her eyesight wasn't too good as she was willing to admit, so she might have been mistaken.

'Right,' said Phoebe, wiping melted chocolate off her

fingers and hoping it wouldn't get on to her new dress. 'So why did you think it was a man?'

'I could see between the legs, dear,' said Mrs Thorn. 'Another cup?'

Phoebe thought about a short skirt, shorts, even tight jeans. 'No, thank you.'

'Besides, he looked like a man. Big. Men are big.'

'Usually. Mr Waters isn't big though.'

'Big enough, bigger than me,' said Mrs Thorn who was built like a square-shouldered eight-year-old with heavy bones and short legs. Her top half and her bottom half did not match.

'So when was this?'

'Morning, late on.' She could see this was not precise enough. 'Before the one o'clock news. Before *Neighbours*.'

That made it about twelvish, Phoebe thought, before my two-fifteen interview. 'Is there anything else?'

The teapot came into operation again as Mrs Thorn filled up her cup. 'I don't take sugar, dear, I daresay you noticed, I have to watch my weight... No, nothing else, I wish there was. Who did you say it was that got burned to death?'

'I didn't, we don't know yet.' And whoever it was might be dead when put on the bonfire. I sincerely hope so. 'We have to establish identity. Any suggestions?'

'No...'

That's it then, thought Phoebe; she stood up, not much to report to the chief commander. What would she have done if she was still in Sparkhill? To begin with, she would have known much more about the street, probably have walked down it once or twice in the recent past—she liked to know her neighbourhood. She would have been able to talk to the community policeman who, if he was doing his job, would know Mrs Thorn.

Mrs Thorn lifted the teapot, then put it down. 'Empty... I usually drain it. Grew up during the war, you see, rationing, no waste…' The teapot seemed to improve her memory. 'There is something.'

'Go on.'

'I think there was someone else there, another person on the other side of the bonfire. It was only just lighted then and smoking.'

'What did you see?'

'Nothing else. I went to my washing to stop it getting kippered and then I didn't look again…I was watching TV.'

'Well, thanks. Thanks for helping.'

'It wasn't the first fire he'd had, you know. He liked a bonfire, but don't we all, I'm fond of one myself. We had a beauty down here for the coronation.'

Phoebe made her way to the door. 'Did Albert live here then?'

'Always lived here, never lived anywhere else. His mother before that, and her mother. There used to be a lot of them. "Wherever you go, there's a Waters", Mother used to say. Not true now. Only Albert left.'

COFFIN AND ALBERT WATERS had been joined by Superintendent Young who intended to keep a friendly but watchful presence on the scene. Around them in the long coach, the mobile incident room was busy setting itself up. Phones were already ringing on two desks (no one was answering them, Coffin noticed), while a young policewoman sat staring at a laptop computer. The screen woke up and started to spell out a message to her, she did not react.

Albert Waters did though. 'I know her, she used to walk round here when she was training.'

The WPC turned her head and gave him a smile.

'You've got a lot of friends,' said Coffin.

'Wouldn't call Brenda Thorn a friend, she doesn't like me. But then I don't go a lot for her. She says I built the bonfire, well I didn't. If she'd looked she'd have seen me at work in the garden at the back. I saw her, getting her washing in.'

'SO THIS CONFIRMS his story and hers,' said Coffin, as he and Phoebe exchanged information. 'He saw her doing what she says she did do.'

'But she didn't see him. I did ask, as I left, I said: "Did you see Mr Waters when you got the washing in?" and she said that no, she hadn't seen a thing, but Albert could be invisible when he liked. And she didn't mean it kindly, not really friends, those two.'

'So he says.'

'I think the really important thing that comes out is that she thought there were two people... One who climbed up on the fire and who was wearing trousers and was big, and one the other side.'

'But invisible?'

'That's right,' said Phoebe. 'I think she was hinting at Albert.'

'A hint isn't evidence. Do you think she saw anything or anyone?'

'Yes,' said Phoebe, 'I think she did.'

'Can't say who or won't say? In your opinion?'

Phoebe shrugged. 'I think she's gone as far as she can.'. To herself, she added: Give her a hot, full teapot and who knows what might come out?

Coffin said: 'I'm going to walk the ground again. See what I can see. Come with me.'

Lighting was being set up as night came on. The body was being moved under the careful eye of the police surgeon and a pathologist; they were moving it carefully because burnt bodies are fragile.

Coffin watched for a moment, then eyes down, paced the grass. 'It rained yesterday,' he said to Phoebe, 'so the ground is soft... Do you see what I see?'

'Yes, tracks, wheel marks.'

'Paired wheel marks, as if a trolley or some such was used. The wheels dug in, so the trolley was heavy.'

The marks, which had already been taped off by the police team, were patchy, sometimes you could see them, sometimes not.

The two of them walked back to the road where the body was about to be put in an ambulance. Archie Young was there talking to another officer.

'Has Waters got anything to pull or push with two wheels?'

'The tracks, you mean? I saw those. No, he says not. He says he has a wheelbarrow and a supermarket trolley that he nicked, and nothing else. Those marks were not from a wheelbarrow or a trolley, though. I know what you are thinking: a body could have been moved out to the fire on wheels.'

Coffin drew back the covering: a curled up, blackened form, head down, arms extended. It was impossible to guess the sex or age. But Coffin knew what he was looking at: 'This person was not dead when burnt, but died while burning.'

He turned back to the road. 'Let's go.'

Phoebe walked beside him, just for a moment she thought she got a flash of a face she might know—or could have known if she'd concentrated—in the little crowd of onlookers, then Coffin touched her arm and she looked away.

'Can I drive you anywhere?'

'No, I saw a tube station not too far away. I want to walk, get some air.' The corpse had made her feel sick. 'And get to know the district a bit.'

'Right.' He hesitated. Was a warning justified or even wise? Phoebe had her prickles. 'Look after yourself.'

'Oh, I will, don't worry. I know how to watch my back. And nobody knows me.'

Phoebe had her own reasons for not wanting to be driven home by the chief commander. She needed to think.

That night as Phoebe got into bed, not in the flat of a mate as she had told Coffin (God, the lies she had told that man), but in the rented room in a small guest house which was all she could afford, she thought about the day.

She had the position she wanted, she was back in London, but she was broke till she sold her house, sensationally unhappy and now she was anxious.

Frankly, after today, she wondered what she was getting into.

She rolled over in the narrow bed and considered. Now I must do something highly sensible. And also a good career move.

For a start, she would call on Eden Brown and see if she could join up as a lodger. I don't think she'd want me if she knew what I was working at. Bad for trade.

Don't tell her, said another voice inside her.

Had it been Eden watching the bonfire? No, probably one of those mistakes.

She touched her cheek which was tender, the pain was still there. Was it worse? She reached out for the bottle of painkillers.

Some pains you could exorcize, but others not.

As soon as Coffin got back to his home in the tower of the old St Luke's church, the telephone rang. He considered ignoring it but it might be Stella with a change of plans.

'Hello.' He kept his voice cautious.

'Geraldine here.'

'Ah.'

'You made a good appointment today.'

'The committee did.'

She laughed. 'Your choice, though.'

'I was open minded. Didn't want to influence things one way or another.'

'Not what I thought. She was the best person for the job, you thought so and I thought so. I'd like to meet her. What about coming round for a drink?'

'She's still based in Birmingham; she's got to find a place to live.'

'Oh, no trouble there, plenty of empty flats and houses; one benefit of the recession if you aren't a property owner.'

There was a note in her voice that made Coffin wonder if she had his sister Letty in mind; Letty had invested in a lot of local property and was now suffering some pain. He said nothing, Letty could look after herself in his opinion and would certainly break back.

'I'm entertaining on Sunday morning from midday onwards...my At Home. My little salon.'

Geraldine's salon was famous. She lived in a large, early nineteenth-century house where top Customs officials had held sway while the Docks were still alive.

'When's Stella back?'

He looked at the clock, past midnight. 'Today,' he said, 'today.'

HE WAS THERE EARLY, having been woken by a telephone call he would rather never have had, but Stella's flight was early too, a wind behind them, and as he walked in, Stella walked towards him.

She was wearing a full pale yellow skirt and a white shirt and she looked more beautiful than he had ever seen her.

She ran towards him, cheerful and full of energy, not at all as if she'd just been travelling all night. She threw her arms round him. 'Lovely to be back, heaven, heaven.' She kissed his cheek. 'I've brought you a present. Well, several... Oh, you smell of smoke...it's in your hair.' She drew back and looked at him. 'You look peaky... What's wrong? Bad time?'

'I'll tell you in the car.'

He did tell, an edited version; he could trust her, but for her own sake it was better not to say too much.

'Those poor young men... I remember Felix.'

'I thought you would. I was going to ask you to visit his wife with me.'

'Of course, you know I would... But that's not all, is it?'

The traffic was building up as they crossed the river; it was still early but commuters were driving into work.

He told her about the body on the funeral pyre.

'Burnt. Totally burnt, how terrible. Who was it?'

'I've heard now: it was a young woman.'

'She was dead?'

Alive or dead, that was the question.

'She was alive when she set the fire and she meant to do it. Suicide. She left a note.'

Stella looked at his face.

'It was Felix's wife.'

Alive or dead.

Suttee.

THREE

THE MOMENT STELLA came back, the theatre came to life: a new play opened in the big theatre in the old church (now called the Stella Pinero Theatre), an innovative piece was rehearsing in the theatre workshop, and the drama school had a new intake. It was Stella who had waved the magic wand, and life began again.

He realized how much he had missed her.

She had returned with all her usual enthusiasm and cheerfulness to breathe energy into the schemes at the theatre that she had left behind.

Coffin relished this side of it; the glitter and sparkle that Stella brought with her made a counterweight to the tragedies that hung over him. Felix, Mark Pittsy and now Felix's wife.

Suicide, of a particularly terrible kind. How could she do it?

'I don't know, darling,' said Stella as she unpacked her presents for him. 'But if she was in great pain in her mind, I suppose physical pain might not matter so much.' She contemplated a day in which she herself could do such a thing and could not find it there. No, she would always battle on. 'I couldn't do it.

'No, I'm such a coward... I'm surprised any woman could, but they do, in India. There, it's part of the culture, or it was, but this was her own private hell, poor love.'

Coffin sat on the bed and watched her unpack. 'Here's a bottle of your favourite Jack Daniels. I know you don't drink as much as you did, but it's nice to have it by you.'

'I drink enough,' said Coffin gloomily. Especially when

she was away—he'd had plenty this time, but life had been tough.

'But not as much as once,' she said, her voice firm. 'And if you stick to the best whisky and champagne, you won't go wrong.'

It was the sort of remark he loved her for, redolent as it was of her own zest for the superior.

'Geraldine has asked us to one of her mornings.'

'Oh, we'll go, she always has the best people there. And with this new play coming on, I could do with nobbling a few critics.' Stella held up before him her latest purchase from Bergdorf Goodman. 'Look at this, isn't it lovely?' It was a plain, short little shift of black. 'You'd never believe how much it cost.'

'I expect I would.' Coffin was beginning to be an experienced husband. 'Especially when I see it on.'

'Oh, you are a love. And quite right. A cheap dress.' (Cheap by Stella's standards did not necessarily mean a small price.) 'A cheap dress often looks good when on display and a couture dress nothing, but when you wear them...ah, that's when cut and fit show.'

She seemed prepared to elaborate on this but Coffin said: 'She wants us to bring Phoebe Astley.'

'Ah.' She was perhaps not best pleased to find Phoebe Astley so ensconced in his life. 'Well, of course. I like Phoebe. Of course, I've never really got to know her,' she added carefully.

'I need her in this job, Stella. I couldn't see anyone else doing it. I wanted her here.'

'I know. And I've decided to be big about it.'

'And she's clever and ambitious; she'll move on.'

'Think so?'

He nodded. He felt like opening the bottle of whisky already; Stella, when she started to probe, could get close to the bone, very close. He had told her some of the reasons for wanting Phoebe to head the Unit, but not all the secret investigation as well. It was really better not. Safer.

Because he might be the ultimate victim, and he didn't want Stella involved. She was not for burning.

'Well, I won't ask why you really wanted her,' said Stella, letting him know she could read his mind more than a little, 'but why did she come?'

'I'm not sure,' said Coffin slowly. 'I know what she said, but I'm not sure if it's the truth.'

'And I'm not to ask?'

'Oh, just a love affair that went wrong.'

'Just,' said Stella with a little nod. 'Just.' She continued with her unpacking, while her husband watched her, leaning across the pillows. 'You look lovely in bed, darling. At your age.'

'Thank you.'

'You're really unhappy and worried. I could feel it while you were making love to me, not really there.'

'Not true.' Perhaps it was though, horrible thoughts had intruded.

'You're getting to be megalomaniac, you know, dear. I hate to say, but I've seen it growing on you.'

'You mean paranoid.' He rested back against the pillows. 'You could be right.'

'But I love you, and you have a lovely, smooth...'

'Say any more and you'll make me blush.'

'Temper,' finished Stella sitting on the edge of the bed and giggling. She threw across to him a soft, silk dressing gown. 'Here, in thanks for your lovely smooth, rounded temper.'

'There's terror about,' he said gripping her wrist. 'It's an infection. Like the Plague. It's got me; I don't want it to get hold of you.'

'It won't,' and added with her elegant, brutal honesty, 'although I am often afraid of almost anything: of the dark, of spiders, of being ill in a strange place.'

She removed her wrist. 'You've got quite a grip, you know; you'd have made a good actor, I think.'

'Why do you say that?' One or two of his colleagues would have called him one already.

'You get the action to fit the words; you grabbed my wrist at just the right moment. It would have looked good on stage.' She got on with her unpacking. No more presents for him appeared, but a small collection of carefully wrapped parcels were placed on her dressing table. Stella always brought gifts back for her friends. Those who were closest to her at the time (and they varied, usually being people she had last worked with or would be working with next), could count on a bottle of scent or a little piece of jewellery or a special silk scarf. Stella prided herself on her presents.

'Well, you won't want me to go and see the poor woman now. She's dead, poor love.'

'No.' Coffin was up and finishing a cup of coffee. Tiddles appeared at the window and was let in. 'He must have good take-off, that cat,' he said as he opened the window. 'I never know how he does that jump from roof to windowsill.'

'He's eaten enough birds,' said Stella, 'he's probably got little wings developing under that fur.'

Since a veterinary surgeon's intervention had rendered Tiddles neutral, he was he or she as it suited them. Even before the operation, the vet had said that Tiddles was a natural neuter; there were a few around even in the cat world. Unlike their dog who was defiantly male with wide and catholic sexual interests.

'I'd like to see the house myself, though,' he went on. 'Her death worries me; from what I'd been told she wasn't suicidal. And if she was, it's a terrible way to go.'

'What would the house tell you?'

'I don't know...how disturbed she was, perhaps. A woman's eye might be a help?' He looked at Stella.

She shook her head. 'Take your Phoebe.'

He did not rise to the hidden barb in that invitation. 'You'd do it better.'

'Where's she living?'

'Hasn't got anywhere yet as far as I know. She has to sell a place in Birmingham then she will buy, I suppose.'

'So she's here for ever?'

'Nothing's for ever, Stella.'

'Right. Well, she could have my flat and I could move in up here...silly having two homes, anyway.'

With some pleasure, Coffin realized that Stella was protecting her property: him.

'I'll put it to her.'

'I've been thinking so for some time,' said Stella.

THE CHIEF COMMANDER was usually tied to the pattern of events in his diary, but in between two meetings, he telephoned Phoebe; she had scribbled a number on a piece of paper before going off last night.

It was not, as he had been led to believe, the house of a friend, but what sounded like a small hotel. He knew some of those small hotels in Docklands, not cosy.

Phoebe was not there, so he left a message asking her to telephone and returned to his routine of work. He was reading a government report (to which he had made a contribution) on child abuse, when she returned his call.

'Where are you?' He could hear voices and the clatter of china.

'I'm in Max's Delicatessen, round the corner from the St Luke's complex. I needed a cup of coffee.' And some aspirin, her tooth was throbbing.

'Oh, you've found that out, have you?'

'I was just scouting round.'

With your usual sharpness. Of course, she knew exactly where to go, knew he lived close by, knew how often he went there with Stella and without her, and probably wondered if she would see Stella Pinero there. For all he knew, Stella might be there now.

'It's a nice place to eat,' he said, 'is Stella there, by any chance?'

'I don't think so.'

Ah, so you have checked. 'I want you to come with me to the Henbit house.'

'Yes…I've heard about the wife… It was her on the fire?'

'Who told you?'

'I asked Teddy. He seemed to think it was all right to tell me.' Her tone was dry. 'I think he was in shock himself… I am too, if you want to know. Utterly shocked. She left a note, I understand?'

'Yes, that was what put them on to it. No one would have thought of it being Mary Henbit otherwise… Why there? The identification is only provisional at the moment and not for public consumption, but there seems no doubt it's her.'

'I suppose there's a PM?'

'Yes, I've asked for it to be hurried along.' She always asked the sharp question. 'Stay where you are, and I'll pick you up in my car. I'll be driving, nothing official.'

'I'm very comfortable here. On my second cup of coffee.' He could still hear voices and laughter behind her.

But she was watching for him when he drove up and got into the car without drawing attention to herself. He could see Max's back through the plate glass window as he served a customer. A tall man carrying a big bunch of flowers was just going in whose face he recognized as that of a famous stage designer. There was a bright yellow poster advertising the new show at the Stella Pinero.

Phoebe settled herself into the seat by his side. 'Been doing some work. The crime rates have gone up in the Second City. Three per cent.'

He knew that, but had not expected her to know. Nor was he totally pleased.

'How did you get that?' He tried to keep the irritation out of his voice; he wanted to be able to work with Phoebe, he needed her, and this inquisitiveness of hers was valuable if directed in the way he chose. But Phoebe had never been controllable, as he was now remembering. Nor did she always tell the truth; he was remembering that too.

'Oh, I always get what I want...I found an old mate working in Records...'

'The one you aren't staying with?' he asked drily. He was beginning to feel that he was like the man in the story who let the djinn out of the bottle and then couldn't get the djinn back in again.

Phoebe was unblushing. 'Oh, you found that out? The telephone, I suppose. I had to have somewhere to stay so I found this cheap hotel. Just for the night.'

'Stella says you can have her flat if you like.'

'Might drop in to Minimal and see if Eden Brown still has a vacancy.'

He slowed down at the traffic lights while he considered this. Eden Brown was the woman who managed Minimal, one of the small chain of dress shops whose advertisements figured in the newspaper cuttings he had sent her.

He had meant her to take an interest and she had done so. But was it wise to get too close to Eden Brown who might be innocent of all ill doing in connection with the dirty money, but who might know exactly what was going on?

'Remember you are working for me and with me,' he reminded her.

'You mean: keep my nose out of what doesn't concern me?'

'Yes.'

They drove on in silence, each of them assessing the position of the other. Phoebe did not mean to be hindered

by the chief commander: if she did well in this private
investigation, then her position at the head of the unit to
which she had as yet to be officially appointed would be
very strong.

Nor did she mean to stay in it overlong. Her ambition
went beyond it.

There is always a hidden agenda.

'I am beginning to get some things clear in my mind:
you want a woman helping in this investigation, and I can
understand that because the involvement of the dress shops
and possibly other similar places. Easier for a woman. You
wanted a woman not connected with your own force and
new to the district. That suggests to me that you don't trust
your own force.' She stopped. 'Did I say that aloud? It's
quite brave of me, I expect you are angry... Oh, I quite
understand that I am in the same dangers that the two men
were.'

'I *am* using you,' admitted Coffin as the lights changed
and he drove away. 'But you are using me too.'

'As long as we both know where we stand,' said Phoebe.
Then she said, as he accelerated: 'But I have never known
for sure with you and I don't know now. But I'm not going
to ask questions. You've got Stella.'

Once again there was a pause: 'Let's leave it there,' said
Coffin.

'Conversation closed,' said Phoebe brightly.

THE HOUSE in which Felix and Mary Henbit had lived was
in a neat crescent of semi-detached houses recently built
and sitting uneasily on the site of the old biscuit factory,
as if they felt its ghost.

It was going to be generations, Coffin thought, as he
stopped the car at the kerb, before his Second City in the
old Docklands really settled its identity.

'Is the house open?' asked Phoebe.

'I've asked for someone to be there to let us in.' He

nodded towards the door where a uniformed WPC was trying to look as unobtrusive as possible while being aware of the neighbours looking out of the windows up and down the street. 'A friend of Mary Henbit had a key and went in to see how she was, one of the Wives Support Group, and that was how she came to find the note.' He was as aware of the silent watchers as was the WPC. 'Let's get inside quickly.'

The house was quiet and still, a small pile of bills and unopened letters on a table in the hall. A vase of flowers, long dead, with the leaves and petals spattering the floor.

'The house has been looked over but I want to see for myself.'

'What worries you?'

'It was such a terrible way to go, I ought to have done more,' he said. 'And don't say it's not my business, it's all my business.'

Felix Henbit had been his business, Mark Pittsy had been his business. Phoebe, if she got into trouble, would be his business.

Phoebe stood in the middle of the hall and looked up the stairs. Ahead of her were three doors, each open so she could see into the bedrooms and the bathroom. On the ground floor was one large sitting room with a dining alcove at one end. Straight ahead was the kitchen.

'What do you want me to do?'

'Look around. Use your eyes. See what the place says to you.'

'What the place says now,' Phoebe said, 'is that they were a happy young couple, recently married with new furniture which they looked after. They may have had debts and quarrels but that isn't written in the furnishings.'

'Look at her clothes, go through the pockets; look in her handbags, see if there is a diary, or anything to explain why she did what she did the way she did it.' He produced a folded sheet from his breast pocket. 'She left a note—here is a photocopy.'

The message was very short.

To the Chief Commander,
Dear John,

   I can't go on here now without Felix. I want out and I am taking my own way. Better to marry than to burn, was said, wasn't it? But sometimes you have to do both.

'She didn't sign it,' said Coffin, 'as you see, but it appears to be in her handwriting. The original has been fingerprinted. Anyway, it was enough to make the CID look at the burned body. The measurements and so match, as far as can be checked at the moment.'

'Wait a minute,' said Phoebe. 'She calls you John. How well did you know her?'

There was a pause. 'Well enough,' said Coffin.

'Oh, my God! No wonder you wanted me on the case and Stella well out of it.'

'Wait a minute, don't get the wrong idea. I met her at a conference on police and security in Brighton; she was unhappy and I wasn't too jolly myself—Stella and I had quarrelled and split up, it was before we married. She was acting as VIP driver and she ferried me around a bit: we liked each other and it could have gone further; I was tempted but I drew back. I had to say to myself: this is not important.'

Phoebe looked again at the note. 'Not to you, maybe, but I think it may have been to her. Well, we've both had confessions to make… Did Felix know?'

'I'm sure not.'

'How many in your force know?'

'One or two may have thoughts.'

'I bet.' She handed the letter back. 'Especially after this.'

'She knew she could turn to me, but I wasn't in time.'

'Did she blame you for her husband's death?'

'No, she knew the job and what went with it.'

'But you blame yourself?'

He didn't answer directly, but went to the front door and opened it to breathe in the hot air. The WPC outside gave him a startled look before taking a tactful step away. Then he turned round and came back. 'I let her down.'

Phoebe stood in the middle of the hall and thought about it. 'You haven't changed as much as I thought you had. You're a nice man but you've got a knack for falling into trouble... I don't think you let people down.'

'Thanks for saying that.'

She took a deep breath. 'You can rely on me.'

It was a small house, not difficult to go over, but they took their time. Coffin started on the ground floor, opening drawers in the pale wood sideboard where they had kept a few bottles of wine, a bottle of gin and one of whisky— both nearly full. There were a few old letters tucked away in a magazine stand, but they were family letters, including a wedding invitation. The furniture was well dusted and polished, nothing there to suggest that two people had died so terribly, 'Bearing up well,' Teddy Timpson had said, and the evidence of this room bore that judgement out.

Upstairs, he could hear Phoebe doing the female bit, opening drawers and cupboards. Then she was in the bathroom, he heard the wall cabinet open and shut.

Presently, he heard her coming down the stairs and they met in the kitchen.

'You ever been here before?'

'No, never.'

'You didn't meet her here then?'

'No, of course not. They weren't married at the time,' he said irritably. 'She hadn't met Felix, I was still with the Met in south London.' Phoebe stood in the kitchen and looked around. 'I want a glass of water.'

Coffin opened a cupboard, took a glass from the shelf. 'Here you are.'

'But you know where to find a glass.'

'Everyone knows where you keep glasses in a kitchen, near the tap. If I hadn't found one there, I would have looked elsewhere. Why do you want the water, anyway?'

Phoebe took a bottle from her bag. 'Aspirin. I've got toothache.' She touched her cheek where a red patch showed. 'Or something. And don't mention the dentist...I will do that when I've settled in, got somewhere to live, got time.'

While she drank, Coffin inspected the kitchen: all the dishes and cutlery were in order: clean and arranged neatly, no muddle. In the refrigerator was butter, cheeses, eggs, two bottles of milk and fruit and vegetables in drawers to keep cool.

'Doesn't look like the kitchen of a woman planning to kill herself...but you can't tell, a swing of mood.'

Phoebe said: 'I've checked over the cupboards and drawers upstairs in both bedrooms and I can tell you that everything there is in apple pie order. Clothes clean and pressed, a pile of clean laundry on a chair by the window. If she kept a diary it wasn't up there, but on the bedside table was a shopping list.'

'So what do you make of it?'

Phoebe took her time. 'The woman who kept this house running, who made out shopping for food, doesn't seem the woman to kill herself in that way. I don't know how or why she wrote that note, but it doesn't match up.'

'I agree.'

'I don't think she killed herself...that's the easy answer. The woman who lived in this house wanted to go on living.'

'There's something else as well,' said Coffin, 'I knew old Albert Waters, I knew that he was always building this and that—it's something of a hobby and obsession with him. But I didn't know he had a stack of wood and was collecting other odds and ends of wood out there... I don't know what Felix knew of him or what he could have told his wife. Nothing, I would guess. So how could she have known where to go?'

'You know what we are saying? I think she was killed. It's murder.'

The word *murder* was out.

'Yes, I believe so.'

'Wait a minute: Did she know Albert Waters?'

'Crucial question. Or did he know her? I don't know. But we'll have to find out.' He moved towards the door. 'Come and see what I found in the sitting room.'

On a table by the window, he had spread sheets from several local newspapers.

'Found these in the wastepaper basket.'

Bits had been cut from each newspaper, what was left was the skeleton of pages.

'It's what we haven't got here that is interesting,' said Coffin. 'The dress shop advertisements were cut out from these papers. Note the dates.'

'Several weeks old.'

'Yes. Felix was alive and working when these papers came out. He cut the advertisements out, so they meant something to him, and I think he told his wife. If he thought it was dangerous knowledge he may have tried to keep it from her but she understood. She sent what he had cut out to me.'

'That's guessing...but a good guess, I reckon.'

'Someone working in the chain of dress shops may be the Minder. You've made a start with Minimal. See what you can get.'

'Without killing myself,' said Phoebe. She thought for a moment, then said: 'I might have seen the manager of Minimal, Eden Brown, at the fire yesterday. I'm not sure, but she could have been there in the crowd.'

'I'm glad you told me that…it's interesting, bears out the connection. Did she see you?'

'Can't say.'

'We'll have to hope not.'

That was her way forward, now he must think about his own. An investigation must now take place stage by stage. At some point, Albert Waters must be questioned again. What was his background and did he know Mary Henbit, either before she married or afterwards? Was she a local girl?

He knew what his next stage must be. Nothing cosy or domestic but the bleak examination of bodies.

As they left the house, Coffin said: 'I will ask for detailed postmortems on the body, and on Felix and on Mark Pittsy. I think there might be something to find out that was missed.'

How much can you find out from a blackened, incinerated body, thought Phoebe, and was that why she had been burned?

COFFIN INSISTED on driving Phoebe back to the lodging house, which he wanted to look at: it was small and cheap but not sordid. He wondered again what Phoebe's real trouble was and why she was so broke.

'I'm going back to Birmingham today to tidy things up there, then I'll be back. I'll probably drop into Minimal and see if I can link up with Eden Brown.' She got out of the car: 'I'm on your private staff for the moment. I've got that. But who will be paying me? Sorry to mention it but it counts.'

She knew what she had to do, she had to follow the suggestion that the killer—the so-called Minder—had a place in the shops that figured in the newspaper advertisements. 'I'll see to it; I have funds I can use. And it won't be for long.'

'And after all, look on the bright side,' said Phoebe as

she shut the car door, 'I might always get killed, I seem to be moving into the danger area. Any advice?'

'Keep your head down and see your dentist,' Coffin said as he prepared to drive away. 'That's the best I can do at the moment.'

'How will we keep in touch?'

'Telephone me, I won't telephone you. Either at home or at the office. I have a private restricted number there.' He scribbled it on a card and pushed it across. 'We are invited to a party this Sunday by Geraldine Ducking—remember her? You made an impression and she wants to meet again. Stella and I will be there. Here is Geraldine's address.' He added another scribble to the card. 'Come if you can.'

'Right.' She knew what she had to do now.

Phoebe went into the lodging house which called itself a hotel when in one of its grander moods and paid her bill. She did not relish going back to Birmingham, to her house in Selly Oak where she might run into Rose, but it had to be done. In her present state of mind, she understood how guilty Coffin felt because she had her own burden to bear. Odd, she thought, you met people, liked them, sometimes liked them too much and fell into trouble and yet you had meant well. Life was a bugger.

She looked at her watch. There were two trains an hour to Birmingham from Euston. She had driven down in a Hertz car but had handed that in. It was still early afternoon; she had time to drop into Minimal.

'Courage, Phoebe,' she told herself; Eden Brown had looked harmless enough.

Still, looks could deceive.

She picked up her overnight bag, then took the underground train to Calcutta Street in Spinnergate.

The shop was open, two customers were just leaving, and Eden Brown was hanging up some of the clothes that had been tried on and rejected. She turned round as Phoebe walked in.

'Oh, you're back. Dress a success? Or do you want an alteration? It was a bit tight on the hips and I could adjust that.'

'No, I'll do that by starvation.' Phoebe had a perpetual struggle with her weight, but it was one she was used to— her body was a friendly foe. 'No, I've come to see if you really do have room for a temporary lodger.'

Eden hesitated for a moment. She could do with the money but her life was complicated, and Phoebe might add a complication. But she liked Phoebe, the woman had style, and style mattered to Eden.

'Yes, OK, we'll try it out. A month on trial, eh?'

'Fair enough. I'm off now to collect my things; I'll drive down in my own car, it's been in dock. Got parking?' Eden nodded. 'I'll come to the shop, get the keys and we'll talk money then. What's the address?'

Eden fished out a business card from her bag, she wrote her home address underneath: 'Here. Got time for a coffee? Come into the storeroom; it's all front, this shop, but I have a little hole at the back between the racks.'

She led the way behind, pushing aside a rack of evening dresses.

'You know it was an Alaïa that last customer left on the floor… Customers.' She was pouring coffee from the flask into mugs.

'Don't you like working here?' Phoebe drank the coffee carefully, funnelling the hot liquid away from her tooth. If it was the tooth, it was beginning to feel more generalized.

'Love clothes, need the money.'

It sounded like an epitaph.

'I used to have my own little couture business…in the booming 'eighties. I had a beautiful customer list and did the designing and cutting myself, but most of my clients lost their jobs or went bust and so, after a pause for thought, did I. I was left with a large, expensive new apartment which I can neither afford nor sell.' She smiled at Phoebe. 'Can you imagine?'

Phoebe realized that Eden was inspecting her, that she had been invited to drink coffee for that very purpose. 'Certainly can, I've had troubles myself.'

'Who hasn't?' The brown eyes were shrewd. 'What's the job? The new one?'

'It's a PR position,' said Phoebe carefully. 'I kind of oil the wheels between a lot of institutions.'

'What does your boss sell? Or make?'

'He's in security,' said Phoebe after a moment's thought. The telephone rang…Eden answered.

'So you haven't seen her? Thanks for ringing back.'

'I'm concerned about a friend of mine, I haven't been able to get in touch with Agnes for days. I think she must have gone away.' She sounded worried.

'I know you'll think I am mad but yesterday I went to look at a fire, there was a body on it, although someone said it was a man.'

'And was it?'

'No, it was some poor woman, a suicide, her husband had died so she was following him. I thought that was awful.'

'How did you hear?'

Eden laughed. 'Oh, local gossip. There's a woman who sells newspapers down by the tube station, she knows everything. Ask Mimsie Marker, she always knows.'

'I'd better be off. I'll see you tomorrow.'

As Phoebe left, she heard Eden going back to the telephone. She moved forward quietly to listen.

'Agnes: this is the third message I have left on your answerphone. Please ring back, dear.'

So it had been Eden at the fire, and Eden had not seen her.

Good.

FROM EUSTON STATION, Phoebe made her first call to the chief commander on his special line: 'Listen, I'll be brief, the train goes in ten minutes. I've been to Minimal. If the woman Eden is deep in anything criminal, she doesn't know it. But I think she's beginning to suspect it. She is a deeply worried woman. I'm moving in. See you on Sunday.'

'What's the worry?'

'It may be something from her personal life: she is concerned about a friend, one she can't get in touch with.'

'Male or female?'

He would put it that way, a bit clinical. 'Woman, called Agnes. Or it could be the shop, I can't believe it's making a profit. The clothes are expensive, high fashion, they won't sell around here.'

'Possibly not.' They would if Stella found them. Sonia Rykiel, Valentino, Kenzo, Ralph Lauren, and the one they all called Yves—nothing else, he was beginning to know the names. 'Agnes doesn't mean anything to me, but she might fit in somewhere.' Phoebe had an efficient card index in her memory where the name Agnes would be filed, ready to be pulled out on demand.

He was tired, and ready to leave early to meet Stella. With her usual vitality, she had put in a day's work at the St Luke's Theatre complex, beginning with a business discussion at the theatre named after her; she would lunch there, nibbling a few sandwiches (I don't need to slim now, dear, Spain absolutely emaciated me), and drinking the dry white wine that they all drank there. Then she had planned to go on to the theatre workshop which was having casting problems, the consequence of the artistic ambitions of the new producer who wanted to be visual, dear, visual, the English theatre is too wordy, dear. After an attempt to settle quarrels, which would only break out again tomorrow under a different name to all the performers' secret satisfaction, she would go on to the new drama school. Life was said to be peaceful there, but that could only be because the new intake was still feeling shy and in awe of their tutors. When this wore off, there would be trouble there too: it was the way life was. Healthy, really. A quiet company, a quiet production, a quiet college, was probably moribund. Stella and confession time.

When the telephone rang again on his private line, he considered ignoring it, but it might be important. Phoebe again, or Archie Young. He was glad to hear Stella's voice.

'Listen, I'm too tired to cook.' She didn't sound it, there was life in her voice. 'So I've booked a table at Max's. He's going to give us that nice little table where we can see the window and hardly anyone can see us. So we won't be disturbed. Got something to tell you.'

'Oh, what?'

'Wait, love. Be patient.' Not one of his skills and certainly not one of Stella's. 'Meet you in half an hour.' That meant an hour at least, time was infinitely expandable to Stella, who regarded punctuality as an overrated virtue. 'But you'll like it. See you there.'

He looked at the clock and decided to do some more work. He opened the file on the inquiry into the leakage of drugs and criminal monies into the City banks. The latest report was technical and detailed and drew a diagram of how the money entered the system.

There seemed no doubt that three banks in the Second City were important channels and the money was being funnelled into them by numerous small businesses. There were the names of the shops again.

Minimal, Dresses à la Mode, KiddiTogs, Feathers and Fur.

There were others in the two new shopping arcades which had recently sprouted in his city. Both had been built by Ashley Dent, who had also been responsible for a lot of redevelopments in the old Docklands.

He had made money out of it, although possibly not as

much as he had expected since the recession had begun to bite, but he had been generous to local institutions like the St Luke's Theatre complex and the two universities.

Reading the report, Coffin could see that suspicion was beginning to cluster round his name.

He had met Dent once, at Geraldine's, come to think of it, and he didn't seem like a murderer, very tall and gently spoken, although you could never tell.

He must know he was being investigated, but he would have first class lawyers ready engaged to defend him, and he would probably get away with his fortune intact.

He might employ someone to kill three people, but the motive didn't seem to be there. It didn't match.

No, there had to be another reason behind the killings.

Someone was being protected but it wasn't Ashley Dent. There was something more personal, sharper, wickeder behind it all.

Coffin returned the papers to their file, noted that he was expected to attend a meeting on the SUBJECT (inevitably it was beginning to assume capital letters in his mind) in a week's time. He put the file away in the small safe to which only he had access, and considered telephoning the incident room, or telephoning Archie Young or Teddy Timpson. But his interest was not always welcomed and was sometimes counterproductive. They kept information back, or let it drift along so that it was late news when he got it. For none of this did he blame them: he would probably have done the same himself in their place.

He looked at the telephone, willing it to ring. Silence. Then there was a knock on his door. He was protected by at least one secretary and several assistants but they had left.

A head poked round the door. 'Can I come in. All right?'

'Archie, glad to see you.'

Archie Young looked surprised; the two men had a good, friendly relationship but he didn't usually get such a welcome. He sat down and did not ask if he could smoke. This room had been a No Smoking area for some time now.

'I heard you'd asked for postmortems on Henbit and Pittsy.'

Coffin nodded.

'Glad you did. I might have done it myself if you hadn't. I've been worried for some time about those two deaths. And I'm not the only one. There's been a bit of talk. It didn't seem right. Two of them in the same few weeks.'

'What's being said?'

Archie Young considered: 'They were known to be working on the banking case, although you weren't supposed to talk about it. The bodies were gone over for the inquests and both were found to have a lot of drink inside them. So the idea of accidental death was acceptable…at first, till people started thinking… But they weren't drinkers, either of them.'

'I've asked for results as soon as possible.'

'We're all a bit edgy at the moment with this report on the reshaping of all police forces. Men don't know where they stand.'

'Sometimes these reports come to very little in the end.' He wasn't sure if he believed that this time and he had the idea that he might be one of the officers eliminated. He had always had his enemies, and this might be a prime chance to get rid of him. He would be made redundant to make way for another head for the Second City force with another title and less freedom of action.

'Hope you are right. Want to go on working myself.' He stood up. 'Said my bit. Off to a concert tonight at the Festival Hall—my wife is educating my ear.'

Coffin picked up his bag. 'I'll come with you.' They walked towards the lift together.

'Pittsy and Henbit were friends,' said Young. 'Trained together. What one knew the other would know too. They wouldn't talk, but Henbit might tell his wife: Pittsy wouldn't.'

'I put the request for the PMs through Timpson,' said Coffin. 'I think it would be best if it wasn't talked about.'

He had put Phoebe like a ferret down a rabbit hole, but if word of the PMs got out, he might have put her in danger.

He had felt hot all day, no surprise with the temperature in the eighties, but now he began to sweat.

STELLA WAS WAITING for him in Max's, which was both a pleasure and a surprise. She was wearing a pale cream shift over tight trousers and chattering away to another woman, another actress. He didn't know her name, he had never seen her before either on the stage or the TV screen but he knew her for a member of the profession. He had learnt to recognize them. 'It's how they present themselves,' he would have said, if asked. 'They don't hold back. They have a pro'ey face', as Stella would have said. It was partly the make-up, always well done, even if they said: 'Only just got out of bed, dear, not even run a comb through my hair', they always had though, carefully disarranging it. But it was also the clothes: there were two types here, either they emerged from Browns or Harvey Nichols weighted down with carrier bags and bills of several thousand pounds to present hopefully to their accountant as necessary expenses, or they strolled around in jeans, shirts and boots. The woman with Stella belonged to the latter group.

Stella saw him, smiled and held up a hand. It was a beautiful gesture of welcome, deserving of a larger audience. The other woman stood and began to move away.

''Bye, Liz.'

'Who was that?' asked Coffin, seating himself.

'Liz Caldecott. She's a doctor.'

'You've destroyed an illusion.'

'Which one was that?' She poured him some wine. 'But she used to be an actress.'

'It's left its mark on her,' said Coffin, with relief—he was not losing his skill. The wine was very cold and delicious, he sank back in his chair with pleasure, cool for the first time that day, because the sensible Max had invested in air conditioning in his restaurant. 'What are we eating?'

'Something cold, I left it to Max.'

'What is it you've got to tell me?' He wanted to know, get it over, he was always terrified she would say: This is it, all over, I'm off.

'Later, after we've eaten… You're tired, I'm tired.' She didn't look it, her eyes were bright and alert. 'After food we shall both be better. But you're worried, I can tell.'

'There's a lot going on.'

'If this was on TV, I would say: Want to talk? And you would, but I have always thought that a particularly corny piece of dialogue.' Nevertheless, she sat with her eyes fixed on him.

'It's a hot summer. Heat doesn't suit this community.' Tension between the rich and the poor in the Docklands was always there but it was aggravated now by the fact that the poorest of the poor were not white and British, but from India, Pakistan and Africa. The native working class British were not being welcoming hosts; in fact, the bulldog breed was showing its teeth. Coffin had to keep the peace and offend no one while doing so, a quite impossible task. 'We haven't had a full scale riot yet, but we've had some nasty little brushes.'

'But that's not it?'

'Let me tell you a story, as if it was a play script, but you don't have a part in it and please God never will. It starts with money—dirty money—being fed into banks in the big old City of London around Threadneedle Street and cleaned up, but some of it is coming to banks here… City of London police and a special unit from my force are dealing with it...the money is not my problem. Or not directly.'

Stella looked at him intently. 'Go on, I follow so far, it's not difficult.'

'But two of my young detectives, two of the best, have died. Supposedly by accident.'

'I know that look on your face: you don't think the deaths were accidents.'

'No, and I'm not alone. But that's not all: now the wife, the widow, of one of the men has committed suicide, or we are meant to think so...'

'But you don't?' It was hardly a question, she could read his face.

He shook his head.

'I don't think I like this story.'

'It gets worse... I put in someone of my own, which means, I have to tell you, that I don't trust even my own officers.'

'I should think your person would be in a hot spot,' said Stella. 'She'll be in danger.'

'She? Why do you say that?'

Stella gave an elegant shrug of her shoulders. 'Like you, dear, I watch and listen. Let me make a guess: it's Phoebe Astley.

'Oh well, it was easier than that... She came in here, you were with her, you were noticed... You think people don't tell me things like that.'

He had to admit that Stella had a strong way of springing her traps. Only it wasn't a trap. She reached out her hand to grip his. 'You're a nice man, and you feel responsible for too much and you try to be responsible for too much. Don't worry about Phoebe, I reckon she can look after herself.'

Max appeared bearing a silver dish from which he insisted on serving their chilled, creamy soup himself, chattering away as usual. When he had left them Coffin took his chance. 'What is it you were going to tell me?'

'Ah...well, I'm going to put my flat on the market and move in with you in your tower. It's silly having two homes, expensive and wasteful. Besides, I want us to be like an old married couple.'

'Do you think we will ever be like that?'

'In some ways, yes. Not old and bored with each other, never that, but comfortable.'

He wondered what had happened to her while she had been away; Stella had never been one to seek the easy relationships.

'Don't laugh at me.'

'I wasn't laughing, I was just thinking how lucky I am to have you.'

'I'd lean across the table and kiss you if Max was not moving towards us with our salmon mousse.' When Max, still chattering away, had left them to eat, she said: 'Cheer up. I know you're having a bad time. I'm trying to help. I know the death of Felix Henbit goes deep, you liked him.'

'In some ways, I saw him as myself when young.'

'Yes, that's always painful.'

'And I liked Mary too. She was a friend as well. Or had been,' he said carefully.

Mary Edwina Henbit, aged thirty-two, brown eyes, with soft hair and a kind heart who had killed herself so terribly.

'I see.' Stella moved her fork through the salmon mousse. 'This is good, isn't it? Perhaps a shade too bland.' She looked at him. 'When was this...that she was such a friend?'

'Before we married, well before. And before she even knew Felix. I just wanted to tell you, that's all. And it was nothing much.'

'You didn't take her to bed, you mean?'

'As a matter of fact, not... Why are you laughing?'

'Eat up and enjoy the pink champagne that I have ordered and that Max is just bringing us. If confession is good for the soul, do you want me to tell you everything I have done in my wicked, wicked life?'

'No,' he said quickly. 'Thank you, but no. Stella, I'm having a bad time but I'll live through it. I get the feeling that something happened to you while you were away. Is there something you're not telling me?'

'Later. Let's go home early and talk to each other in comfort, we don't do much of that.'

'Stella, now!'

'Don't look at me like that. I'm all right, I'm not ill, but on the flight to New York, I...'

She was interrupted by the sound of the telephone in Coffin's case. 'Ignore it,' he said. 'You go on.'

'No, what I have to say is important, serious. I don't want to talk against that noise...we can talk later. Answer it, please.'

Against his will, Coffin lifted the telephone. 'Hello...Archie.' He listened quietly, as he did so, Stella saw his face change.

'Thank you for telling me. Keep me in touch, please.' He put the telephone away and sat quiet for a moment.

'What is it? Are you called away?' Life with a serving police officer had made Stella used to disappearing acts.

'No, no need for me to leave... It's another detective but not one working on the banking case...his car exploded.'

He looked at Stella. 'It alters everything.'

It had grown hotter and hotter outside in the street while they had been eating. Inside in Max's air conditioned rooms they had not been aware of it.

The summer sky had darkened as heavy clouds rolled in from the west. A distant roll of thunder rippled round the room, but was too soft to make an impact on the noisy crowd.

Stella heard it though and felt cold.

FOUR

'HOW DOES IT change everything?'

Stella was hurrying beside her husband, trying to keep up with his pace. He didn't answer, frowning as he walked. She could tell how preoccupied he was because his normal good manners had deserted him. Instead of waiting for her to catch up, or adapting his stride, he was marching forward, dragging her with him.

A flash of lightning, swift and jagged, bolted across the sky. One heavy raindrop fell on Stella's face. 'Damn!' She put her hand up to her head.

A dozen or so great drops and then no more.

'Oh, horror, a dry thunderstorm, that's the worst sort of all. It makes you feel that the gods are sitting up there in Valhalla, throwing thunderbolts at us. Next act, the end of the world.'

'What did you say?'

'Nothing. Talking to myself. Tell me what you meant when you said: this changes everything.'

'Perhaps I'm wrong,' he muttered. 'But if this detective, who was not working on anything sensitive, whom I do not know except by name is hit, then the idea is wrong that only a special group of men were being targeted—it is *any* detective who attracts attention. Or seems an easy target.' He took two big paces. 'It could be anyone next.'

'Does there have to be a next?'

'It looks like a campaign.'

'But it does mean it's not so much your responsibility.'

'Stella, it's always and for ever my responsibility, that's what the job is.'

Stella did not answer. How sad, she was thinking, he's

got this terrible job sitting on his shoulders like some awful goblin. But I can't ask him to leave, resign, do anything else—it is life.

Only not my life? The memory of her travelling companion to New York shadowed her mind.

'Isn't life too short to take all that on, my love?'

Something in her voice got through to him. 'Wait a minute, Stella.' He drew her into the shelter of a clump of trees in the small triangular garden which edged the old St Luke's church where he lived in the tower, his apartment known as Number one, St Luke's Mansions. 'What was it you were going to tell me? About yourself?'

Down the road, a car drew into the kerb outside St Luke's Mansions and stopped.

'Come on, tell me now, Stella, before we go on.'

Stella had seen the car too. 'There's a car just parked,' she said in a nervous voice.

'It's all right. No threat there. It's Archie Young, he wants to talk to me. That's why I want to hear from you now, before we go in. If we wait till we get inside then it will be all police talk. I can't sit through it without knowing about you. You come first; I know that sometimes it doesn't seem like it, but it's true.'

Stella was silent.

'Believe me.' He put his arms round her.

'I believe, just getting my breath.' She assembled her thoughts, then plunged in. 'On the flight to New York, there was a fellow passenger across the aisle that I talked to a bit. A nice man, business, you know. Younger than me, told me about his wife, she was an actress, that's how we started to talk. He recognized me, he said I'd done good work. I was glad to hear that because between you and me, Spain was a bit of a pill. I definitely did not do any good work there and it's not going to be a good film. And I hadn't heard from you, you know, for ages.'

'I wrote.'

'Meagre letters.' Thin, she had thought, half starved letters, not the sort to nourish a person.

'I sent my love.'

'Oh sure, in proper writing. Neat, clean. It ought to have been jagged and rough. A few smudges wouldn't have come amiss.' Tears, idle tears, she wouldn't have minded some sign of those; he had been too calm by half about her absence. 'Anyway, it was good to be admired. It sort of got under my skin.'

'I see.' What was she leading up to? Along the road, he could see Archie Young standing by the car.

'I went to sleep, I was tired. Then I was woken up by terrible noises from across the aisle...it was the way he was breathing. It was his heart...there was a doctor on the flight, young chap, he did his best. I'm sure he did his best, but my friend died. He was my friend by then, I felt he was... He died and I didn't even know his name.'

'He knew yours,' said Coffin, awkwardly, stupidly because he must say something. Archie was walking towards them.

'Yes, sure. But I thought about his wife, who was waiting for him back in Berkshire. She didn't know he was dead. She might be eating her supper, watching television and he had gone...so I made up my mind, that when I got back, I would not be such a separate person. Giving up my own place is a start.'

'Darling Stella.'

'But you've got to help. I need you.'

Archie Young was almost up to them, waving his hand and saying there you are. Damn you, Archie, for coming just at this very moment.

'The other side of the coin,' said Stella in a careful voice. She had her back to Archie, not seeing his approach, 'is that now I understand better how you are divided into two. I can live with that.'

From the citadel above there came a flash and then the

battery opened up. This time there was rain and Archie Young moved forward at speed.

'Not safe under that tree,' he called.

'Not safe anywhere.' But Stella sounded happy and Coffin's spirits rose a little. Came through that one, he thought. In their life together there would be more battles, more chasms to jump, but it looked as though they might do it hand in hand; he thought they were really coming together. Some couples seemed to do it at one go even as they took their marriage vows, but for him and Stella it was more of a long negotiation.

Stella patted Coffin's arm, as if she was saying, well, goodbye for now, but we part on good terms. Her body language was always good, but Coffin never forgot that she was an actress. 'Hello, Archie, nice to see you. Come up, I know you two want to talk, so I'll keep out of the way, but I'll make you some coffee first.'

'Thank you.' Archie Young's response was cautious: no one admired Stella as an actress more than he did, he was her long time admirer but as the husband of a powerful woman himself (whom he acknowledged to be that shade brighter than he was), he knew how to behave: carefully. 'Nice to see you back.'

He had said the wrong thing. 'I was never really away.'

'Ah.' He wondered what she meant by that, but his was not to wonder why. 'Of course, it was me really,' he said humbly. 'Off on a course. That felt like being away, I can tell you. Hard work and terrible food.'

The three of them were walking in a companionable way towards St Luke's Mansions.

Archie Young studied Coffin out of the side of his eye. The chief commander was walking along, just slightly behind them, but in step. He seemed deep in thought.

'Nice place to live in, you've got here.' Archie and his wife had a decent suburban semi: clean but not tidy, no one could call his Alison a homemaker, although she was a good cook.

'Want to buy one? I'm giving mine up.'

'Is that so?'

'Moving upstairs,' said Stella. She put her head on one side. 'What about it?'

'I don't think your husband would care for it,' Archie said. 'I think he sees all of me he wants.'

Stella laughed. 'I'll go ahead and make the coffee.' She looked over her shoulder. 'Wake up the sleeper behind us. I think he's gone into a trance.'

'Sorry,' said Coffin, catching up. 'I was thinking. What was all that about?'

'Just saying hello. Stella's gone to make some coffee.'

'Come on up, there's a lot to talk about with this new incident. Stella won't stay around, she'll be tactful.'

No easy thing being the boss's wife, thought Archie, knowing that his Alison would want to stay around, join in, but Alison was a fellow professional, although mercifully not in this force.

'I was remembering what happened two years ago.'

'I wondered if that would come up. Thought the same myself.'

Two years ago there had been a series of four attacks on police officers within as many months; none had died, although two had been seriously wounded and one crippled. The man responsible had been caught.

They stopped at the foot of the staircase up to Coffin's apartment, Stella had left the door open and the cat had wandered down to look at them.

Coffin bent to pat Tiddles's head while his thoughts ran on: and if so, I've got it all wrong about Henbit and Pittsy. Nothing to do with the money and banking business, but a return to the other affair—a rerun of the attacks on police officers. Perhaps I've thought up a whole fantasy and sent Phoebe in to investigate a case that is not there.

'I remember the man,' he said to Archie. 'Edward Adams, wasn't it? Sent to Broadmoor, wasn't he?'

They had paused at the top of the stairs where the smell of coffee reached them.

'And he's still there; hasn't escaped or gone for a home visit.' Archie Young's feeling about the liberal regime allowed certain prisoners in certain establishments was cynical. 'But he had brothers and uncles and aunts and cousins and they were all near as batty as he was. It was a personal thing too: they thought the police were after them. And to tell the truth, so we were, since they were behind half the petty crime in East Hythe and Swinehouse.'

Coffin went round switching on lights. Outside, the rain was heavy now, beating against the windows. High up in his tower he would see the flashes that lit up the sky and got ready to hear the thunder. The two phenomena were coming very close together, which nursery lore told him meant the storm was overhead.

'Have you been thinking this all along?'

'At the back of my mind: but I knew you had other ideas.' Not that Coffin had ever said much.

'You read my thoughts.'

'Well, sir, you did leave certain signs around.' It seemed an occasion for politeness and formality and not to presume on old friendship. The chief commander had never been explicit in what he thought, but Archie had got the clear impression that he suspected someone who had close contact with him.

'And, once you asked for PMs on three bodies, well...I think Timpson is wondering a bit too.'

'Any news on the PMs?'

'Nothing. It takes time. And we had to get exhumation orders; that takes time too. Good job the two men weren't cremated.' He frowned and sat back in his chair, recalling that Mary Henbit had cremated herself.

Stella returned with a tray of coffee on which she had

with generosity added a bottle of brandy. 'I can see you are going to be late at it, so I am off; I've got bills to pay and letters to write.' She waved a hand from the door, it was a good departure, well choreographed.

Tiddles, who had followed her in, jumped on a chair by the window and fell asleep.

'He doesn't mind the thunder,' said Coffin. 'But the dog's terrified and is probably hiding under the bed.'

'Who is doing the autopsy?'

'Dr Bickly, I don't know if you know him, he's a new appointment at the Lane Grove Hospital, but he also assists Jim Matherson.' Jim—Big Jim to all who knew him—was the Home Office pathologist, a much overworked man in this criminous city. 'He'll do a good job. Everyone says he's conscientious and gets into everything. Mind you, he'd have to with what they throw at it. The other day, the Met sent him four different legs, just the legs, and asked him for sex and race. And he did it too, not too hard as the legs were thin and pale… It was the toms that got cut up round King's Cross, their legs, the Met already had the rest of the bodies. No, he's a clever man.'

'Who is going down there to watch?' The postmortems would be done in the police forensic building in Swinehouse. It was not a beautiful building, being bleak and new, but it was efficient as a workplace and very much better than the old building it replaced which had been a Victorian workhouse. 'I'm glad I don't have to do it any more.'

'Timpson is going himself. I believe he's always sick after it; it's not a thing you ever get used to, but they say that Bickly manages so well you don't feel too bad. Not like Big Jim who likes to see chaps keel over.'

'Good. So about today? First of all, who was it?'

'DC Frank Talmadge, he's with the CID team out at Swinehouse.'

'What happened and how? You've told me the outline,

now fill me in. Exactly what happened and how was the man killed?'

Archie was apologetic. 'Sorry, I gave you the wrong impression, he isn't dead. Or he wasn't, he may be by now, because he was badly enough hurt.'

Coffin relaxed a little. 'That's a relief. I hope he pulls through. Apart from anything else, he may be able to tell us something.'

'If he remembers anything.'

'True.' In any act of violence, the victim's brain often mercifully wiped out the actual event. 'So what did happen?'

'He was driving home, took a left, the car went out of control and hit a wall. Then it exploded.'

'That way round? It didn't explode and then crash?'

'Be nice to know that, but we don't. The forensic team are working on the car to see what they can discover.'

'What about eyewitnesses?'

'Well, there was only one, an elderly woman out with her dog who said it all happened so fast, she couldn't tell which came first.' Archie shrugged. 'And we all know how unreliable eyewitnesses can be.'

He looked at his watch. 'There's plenty of media attention, as you can imagine. Switch on the TV news and see what they've got.'

They were shot at once into the action. There was the street corner; the brick wall had collapsed into a heap of rubble, the windows were out in the house next door. The camera panned across to where the car was being moved, white uniformed experts were superintending its removal to a transporter. A woman stood at the door of the house that had lost its windows. She was saying what a shock it had been.

A reporter's voice asked what she had seen.

'I didn't see anything, I was out the back.'

'What did you feel?'

Archie Young groaned. 'Stupid question, what's she going to say? That it made her day?'

'I went to look, I was shocked. I—'

Coffin was leaning forward to see more clearly. On the screen the car was now being lifted tenderly in the air. It swung for a second before it righted and was drawn slowly out of sight.

'Did you see? It looks as though the rear end was more damaged than the front? That's odd, isn't it? The front hit the wall and ought to look worse.'

'They both looked bad to me.'

While they were talking, the picture changed to that of a prominent politician: he was complaining about the police.

Coffin switched off the set. 'Just give me a minute. I need to think.' He went to the window where the night sky had cleared. Without his noticing, the storm had played itself out, all was quiet. Behind him, the dog had emerged from the bedroom to make advances of an unmistakable sort to the cat.

'I may have got it all wrong,' Coffin thought. 'The picture may not be what I thought it was. I might have set Phoebe to investigate a crime that doesn't exist, while the real crime has been taking place unnoticed.'

He bent down to stroke the cat who had easily discouraged the dog.

'It's possible I have been guilty of imposing my view on events without real justification.' The moon came out from behind a cloud, shining on the distant river, he could just see a gleam. 'I must let things tell the story. They will if I observe with open eyes.' It was what detection was all about: observing, recording, taking your time and not drawing up a picture too soon.

He corrected himself: sometimes it was necessary to put together an early picture just so that you could knock it to bits and start again.

'I might have to do just that,' he said as he turned back into the room.

'Didn't quite hear that,' said Archie.

'You weren't meant to, just me telling myself to be careful. Not to get things wrong.'

'We all do that sometimes.' Archie yawned, he was tired and surely the chief commander must be too? He got to his feet.

'I think I just have. I saw one picture of events while it is possible it was something else altogether.' He looked at Archie who was yawning again. 'I'm going down to the hospital, and I'd like you to come too.'

The superintendent followed him without protest, aware that he had no choice, but he did allow himself another hearty yawn. It was fortunate that Alison was away or he would have felt obliged to telephone her with the message that this was going to be another late night.

THEY DROVE DOWN Calcutta Street, where Eden had been working late. She had gone out for a quick meal at the Indian restaurant three shops down the street, and then gone back to finish her accounts. As Coffin drove past, she had just locked up and departed; one minute later and he would have seen her leave.

He slowed down when they passed the shop. 'I'm interested in that shop.'

Archie was surprised. 'Pricey stuff. Alison had a look and said all she could afford was a pair of tights.'

'I've heard it's like that. Too expensive for this area, I'd say, wouldn't you?'

'Yes, I'm surprised it's still there.'

'The stock changes regularly too.'

You *have* been watching it, the superintendent commented inside, but he did not say so aloud, although the note of inquiry in his: 'Really?' was not lost on Coffin.

'This shop and some others like it are almost certainly one of the channels through which dirty money is fed.'

This was no news to Archie Young, who had heard all the speculation. It was true that the investigation had been kept under wraps but that did not mean there wasn't talk. As a matter of course, he kept himself informed.

'I was case building.' Coffin speeded up and drove on. 'I was building up a nice solid little case there, in which the shops somehow had a connection with the death of Felix Henbit and by extension Mark Pittsy too. But now it looks different.' He drove on, leaving the shop behind.

ONE SECURITY LIGHT was left on at the back of the shop, and a spotlight on a carefully chosen dress and jacket in the shop window. It looked attractive, possibly too attractive, but she had decided that if she was ramraided (as had happened to the tailor at the end of the row of shops) she did not care. She had other worries and one of them was embodied in the absent figure of her friend Agnes Page. Twice she had picked up the telephone to ring the police, and once she had considered a private inquiry agent. But each time she had put the telephone down and gone biting away at her worry like a cat with a sore paw.

THE HOSPITAL in Swinehouse was a new one, built within the last two years and, money being short, was none the more beautiful for that. But inside was a different story. It was well planned with the curving corridors creating islands of privacy, the rubbarized floor quietening all noise. Unlike many hospitals there was a sense of tidiness and quiet.

'You saw the press?' The superintendent hurried to catch up with John Coffin.

'Yes, three of them.'

'One from the local press, one from the *Sun* and the other a freelancer chancing it,' said the knowledgable superintendent. 'Seen 'em all before. One's called Rivers and one is called Hill and I can never remember which is which. I don't think I ever heard the name of the freelance.'

'The tall one is Hill.' Coffin too had seen them before. 'And the freelance is called Frome; I knew his father and you did too—he was one of us.'

Archie stopped dead. 'Good Lord, yes, Bill Frome, he was...' he went silent.

'Yes, he was shot dead. And his killer was shot dead too. End of story.' Part of the violence and turmoil that could hit his bailiwick any time. 'Not for the family, though. I kept in touch...' He looked back at the trio. 'They didn't try to speak to us.'

'Did it on the way out... ''What can you tell us, superintendent? What's the latest news?'' They hope they'll get the very latest. News that the chap's dead.'

A small group made up of two nurses and a doctor were standing in the corridor outside the small room where the injured policeman lay. The doctor put out a hand. 'Can't go in there, sir.'

Coffin explained who he was but it seemed to make no difference. 'He can't talk to you, and if he could, then I wouldn't let you ask questions at this stage. The chap's hanging on and he needs every ounce of strength left in him for that purpose.'

He was one of the new wave of doctors who, on the whole, did not like the police.

But Coffin was one of the old breed of policemen who did not give way. 'Is he unconscious?'

'Not all the time, he comes and goes.'

'I'd like to see him. He may know me; he may wish to say something.'

The nurses said nothing, but were clearly enjoying the scene. They were on the patient's side, he must be protected; they were on the doctor's side, for he was professional too as well as being very handsome. They appreciated his dark curly hair and blue eyes, but on the other hand, Dr Green was exceedingly bossy, showed no sign of inviting either of them out for a drink, and John Coffin certainly had something.

'You can take a look.' Dr Green opened the door a few inches for Coffin to see into the room.

Frank Talmadge was wired to several machines and drips were fed into his wrist and down his nose. His face was bruised and swollen; Coffin could not make out eyes or mouth. A nurse stood across the room, dealing with one drip, and his wife sat by his bed with her hand near but not touching his bandaged fingers.

'Satisfied?'

Mrs Talmadge looked up, she recognized John Coffin with a nervous smile. She was a well-trained police wife, knew who he was, knew he was important to her husband, but she wasn't sure where her duty lay at this moment.

Then she stood up and came to the door towards Coffin. She was a small woman and he was a tall man. She looked up at him, expectantly, hopefully.

Coffin shouldered his responsibility. 'This is bad, Mrs Talmadge, but I'll see that you and Frank are looked after. He's going to be all right, I'm sure of it, but whatever happens we will look after you.'

This was more or less true, he said to himself, with reservation. But he had made her a promise and would see it through.

'His legs,' she whispered. 'They said he might not walk again.'

'You can't be sure of that yet,' said Coffin, with more conviction than he felt. 'Wait. Don't cross any bridges till you come to them.' He felt ashamed of himself for this dreadful platitude—he was always crossing bridges himself before he came to them, and building them too. 'What about the children? Is someone with them?'

'My sister... He was hurrying home to the boy's birthday

party. I told him not to drive fast but he'd be in a hurry. Bringing the fireworks. Eddy had asked for a bonfire and Frank always spoilt him.' The tears were falling now.

Coffin just managed to avoid looking at Archie Young, even though he heard the superintendent's sharp intake of breath. 'Fireworks?'

'Just a few: rockets and catherine wheels and coloured rain, that sort of thing; not too many because they cost so much now, don't they?'

They might have cost more than you think. 'Where would he have put them?'

'Oh, in the back, I expect; he'd be careful, he smoked you see, so he wouldn't have them in the front. No, in the back.'

'Did he keep anything else there?'

Mrs Talmadge was vague, her mind slipping back to her husband's bed. 'Oh, just what everyone does. A rug, a few tools. He was careful, thought ahead, he always kept a gallon of petrol, just in case.'

Coffin put his hand on her shoulder. 'Go back to him and try not to worry.'

As they left, the two men were silent at first, then Young said: 'Looks as though it was his own fault. Blew himself up.'

Coffin didn't answer as he drove away, back to the police station in Swinehouse. Don't carry fireworks near petrol in the back of your car, was in his mind. 'Let's see what they have got to say back at his station. There should be some news.'

In Swinehouse, the police kept a low profile, this being politically wise in a district of many races. But the building itself was new, if unobtrusive, you might have thought it a hostel of some sort if it had not been for the police car parked outside. Inside, late as it was, three men were standing by the reception desk. One was the duty officer, another was a fire officer who seemed to be commanding the conversation and directing what he had to say at the third man: Teddy Timpson.

The chief inspector looked at Coffin without surprise, no one was surprised when the chief commander turned up, he got everywhere. They might complain but they got on with it. This call had been half expected, he knew about the hospital visit, he had his lines of communication as did every sensible officer. He was prepared with what to say.

'The fire officer thinks he was carrying something in the back, sir. He skidded, hit the wall and whatever was in the back,' he shrugged, 'went up.'

Fire Officer Arnold held out his hand to the chief commander. 'We met once before, sir.'

'I remember. A train derailment, wasn't it?'

'It was, nasty affair… Well now, by the skid marks, I reckon he took the turn too fast and the road was oily with the rain. He hit the wall…he may have been smoking, and by the smell he had petrol in the back.'

Coffin confirmed this judgement. 'He did have, and also he had some fireworks in the boot, his wife told us.'

'Poor silly fellow.' Arnold shook his head. 'Driving too fast in the rain; people never learn.'

The Swinehouse duty officer, much outranked by everyone there, kept a silent tongue. He of all the three men knew that his colleague could also put away a pint, and that although they couldn't take a breath test while he was unconscious, both the blood and urine would tell a story. He hoped that they would all go away soon and leave him to think things out.

'Would you like some coffee, sir?' he said, by way of a gentle hint.

Coffin refused. 'Thank you, but no. Archie, I'll drive you back to where you left your car.' An accident, after all. Back to where he was before.

'Outside your place,' Archie reminded him. It seemed a

long while ago. Life had piled on the agony a bit since
then.

As they stood there, the telephone rang on the station
officer's desk. 'Excuse me, sir,' and he answered it quickly.
Never do to seem slack.

'Yes, ma'am, yes, that message has reached me already,
it's been passed round the whole area but there's not much
we can do: if an adult wants to go missing that's up to
them. Unless there's reason to believe there's been violence... Yes, I have a note of the name: Agnes Page.'

'What's that?' asked Coffin.

'Woman called Agnes Page seems to have walked out
on her friends. Friend, actually. She'll turn up.'

That name again. 'Who's worried about her?'

'A friend...' the sergeant consulted a note. 'A Miss
Brown. She seems to think we can flush her friend out.'

EDEN BROWN thought no one was listening to her cry for
help. She walked up and down the big living room unable
to sleep. Insomnia was hard for Eden who had prided herself on sleeping easily and happily. She had been happy
with her own couture business but when that had folded
and the man who had lived with her had concluded that he
ought to go in search of a younger and richer girl, misery
and insomnia had come hand in hand to keep her company.

The windows of her room overlooked the river, as did
the balcony on which, in happier times, she had drunk wine
with her lover. The rain was beating down on it now in
harmony with her rotten mood. She had not been joking
when she offered Phoebe Astley a room. Not for ever, perhaps not even for very long—things must look up; but she
needed the money. And even more, she needed company.

Where was Agnes? Had she gone off of her own will or
had she been taken. Women did get grabbed, taken off,
hidden, there had been several notable cases.

Come home, Agnes, and relieve the mind of your friend.

HER PLEA WAS NOT forgotten or overlooked because both Phoebe Astley and John Coffin were interested. As he drove home, he was wondering where the missing Agnes (if she was indeed missing) had gone and why. And also how she fitted into the picture he was beginning to draw up.

He could hear Archie Young talking away about what he called the Swinehouse hierarchy and the need for a bit of reform there, but his thoughts went back to his own scenario. What had happened to Felix Henbit and Mark Pittsy and Mary Henbit, and where did Eden Brown with her missing friend fit into it?

Did they or didn't they?

'I wonder when we will get the postmortem reports?' he asked.

Archie Young, who by now was feeling sleepy, did not answer.

The storm had passed, the rain dwindled to a fine mist, and in the morning it would be another fine hot day.

Archie collected his car and drove away, leaving behind a thoughtful chief commander.

It was already tomorrow and Coffin did not know where he was going. He had the uneasy feeling that Agnes was going to be very important indeed. Who was this Agnes, who was not to be seen but who was putting her footprints all over the case?

He thought for a moment: Suppose in the beginning, there were two girls, young women really, who somehow got involved in the banking dirty money to clean syndrome?

Supposing one of them wanted out? Would that be dangerous? And to whom?

As he reflected, he added the thought: Depends who spoke to her and to whom she answered. Like Detective Constable Felix Henbit, who might then have spoken, or Detective Constable Mark Pittsy. Or the other way round.

And then someone violent and vicious had got the message.

So two men might have been killed and Agnes run away.

And whichever way you looked at it, Mary Henbit was an innocent victim.

He parked the car. Was he beginning to put together a complete picture now? Was he getting it right, that was the question? There was a bit of rightness there, he sensed it, but perhaps not all there could be.

STELLA LYING wide awake asked herself exactly what was her place in Coffin's life. It seems as though I can easily be forgotten.

She had the remains of a long quiet evening on her own, not exactly what she had planned. She had cleared away the coffee that the two men had drunk, she had fed Tiddles and walked the dog.

Then she had gone up the winding stairs to the big bedroom where she had sat down at the dressing table which had crept into the room when they married as the first announcement of her arrival.

She took off her earrings, noticing without surprise that one of the little butterfly screws that kept the pearl in place behind her ear had fallen away and was lost.

The third this week, she said to her reflection. There must be a creature in this place that is collecting.

Then she put herself to bed in the big bed where she had hoped to be joined by someone other than the small furry creature that soon crowded in beside her.

She heard her husband walking up the stairs, and she was not pleased to hear him say, quite loudly, 'Bloody Agnes!'

FIVE

'I APOLOGIZE.' He had said this once already and would probably say it several times again; he had an idea that he might be obliged to go on saying it for the rest of his life.

'You could have telephoned.'

'I'm very sorry that I didn't.' As indeed he was, and he knew he was going to go on being sorry.

'But you forgot me.'

'Not exactly forgot, Stella. And I have apologized.'

'And I have accepted it,' Stella said with dignity, with the air of one whom to do less would be beneath her. So might Cleopatra have spoken to Antony. Or, Coffin thought, seizing a more sinister comparison, so might Lady Macbeth have spoken to Macbeth.

'And I have carefully prepared and brought up to you this delicious coffee with the brioche I went out to buy specially at Max's so it's quite fresh.'

Stella sat up. 'Did you take the dog?' she asked briskly.

'I did take the dog, and a bloody nuisance he was too.'

'Yes, he always is, one quite loves him for it.'

Coffin knew to keep silent here; he had the definite feeling that things were loosening up a bit, the harrow was being raised, just marginally, from his neck.

He arranged the tray on her lap. 'There's the post, some letters for you.' A bill or two for him but that was only to be expected, and only fair. Part of the punishment.

'I am sorry,' he said. 'It was bad manners.'

'And unkind.'

'Yes, that too.'

Stella leaned back against the pillows. 'Is that the cat there?'

Coffin looked down where Tiddles was leaning against his legs. 'Yes.' Were they both in disgrace?

'Check his magnet he wears on his collar to get in the cat door. I've lost three golden butterflies from behind my earrings and he may have them stuck on the magnet.'

Coffin bent down to run his hand round Tiddles's collar; Tiddles looked puzzled but pleased at what he took to be friendly attention. 'No, nothing gold...two rusty nails and a pin.'

Stella, while sipping her coffee, was opening a large envelope that had come in her post. 'Oh,' she was pleased. 'Harry Trainer has sent me the script of his new play; he said he thought Anna might be right for me.' She was quickly flipping over the pages and counting.

'I'd love to buy you a flight of golden butterflies,' said Coffin humbly.

Stella looked at him. She had already worked out that Anna appeared on nearly every page. Good, very good.

'Unless you think golden wasps more appropriate,' said Coffin, no expression in his voice.

Stella was quiet for a moment, then she burst into laughter. 'We did a good bit of dialogue there.'

I'm over that hill, Coffin decided. Thank goodness.

Stella poured some coffee and buttered a brioche. It was a starvation day really, but it didn't do to discourage one's husband too much.

'I don't know if it's of any interest to you, but in your sleep you were muttering the name of Agnes. Distinctly Agnes. Who is Agnes?'

Coffin was silent, he hadn't realized the case was so much on his mind: a bad sign.

'Not another name for Phoebe?' Stella was half laughing, half serious.

'I hope not.'

'So? Let's go on with the conversation.'

'I don't know who she is. Or what she is. I've had moments of doubt whether she is a person at all.'

'All the Agneses I knew were women.'

'It may be a code or a cover of some sort.'

Stella was genuinely interested: 'Why do you say that?'

'I don't know, I just have a very uneasy feeling about Agnes.'

'Put the idea away,' said Stella with decision. 'She's got to be real with a name like Agnes. Not like Deirdre or Desiree or one of those misty Celtic names; Agnes what?'

'Agnes Page.'

Stella drank some more coffee. For a moment she was silent. 'Do you know, I think I've heard of her. Perhaps I've even met her.'

'You might have done. If she's with us at all, she seems to have some connection with a chain of dress shops called Minimal.'

'I believe I did go in to one once. Let me think about it.'

'Have a go.' Although his wife's entrance into a case was not always attended with good fortune.

Stella put down her coffee cup. 'Yes, I bought a silk shift dress, quite nice but I don't think it will wear... You're taking this case very personally.'

'It *feels* personal somehow,' said Coffin with feeling.

Stella looked at his face, he was tired and drawn. All the anger she had felt—justified anger, she told herself—drained away and she said simply: 'Do you want to talk about it?'

'I'll tell you, be glad to.' He removed the breakfast tray so that he could sit beside her on the bed. 'I've told you a bit already.'

Stella nodded. 'I know about Felix Henbit.'

'Two of my young detectives who were working on a special case, a dirty money mixed up with a bank affair, both of them killed. Then,' he looked at the little gold carriage clock on her bedside table, 'yesterday I got news that a third man had been injured when his car exploded.'

'Was he working on the case?'

'Good question. No. So that seemed to change the picture, and we had to ask if the attacks were just aimed at policemen in general and it was coincidence that two of the men had been working on the same case. Detectives have plenty of enemies and Archie Young reminded me of at least one family that might be capable of it.'

'So?'

'It looks as though the latest victim was really an accident and his own fault at that. He was carrying fireworks, and he was driving too fast.'

'So he wasn't murdered?'

'Probably not...' He thought about it. 'No, almost certainly not. Anyway, he isn't dead. Not yet and with luck he will pull through.' He might not be able to walk because he might not have legs to walk on, but he would be alive. Not a happy man, you could bet on that, but a breathing one.

'But the other two were?'

'Probably, yes. We're waiting for second postmortem results; we know they had both been drinking heavily which was out of character and I want to know more.'

Stella nodded, she was polishing her nails with a soft piece of chamois leather while she gave most of her attention to him, although there was a current underneath considering the new Trainer play, the part she might get and whether he would let her have it at the Pinero Theatre. A short, pre-West End run could do marvellous business. But he was so wedded to the National and there was no denying this was one for the Olivier stage.

'So you think that somehow or the other, but you aren't sure how, that they were both murdered?'

'Yes, and now I think Mary Henbit was killed too. I don't think she climbed on to that funeral pyre: she was put on it.' Alive, half alive, dead, he didn't know. But he would know, the postmortem results would tell him something.

'That makes me feel sick. Why? Why kill her?'

'Felix must have told her something and the killer must have found out. I'm guessing, but Mary must have got in touch with the killer; I can't think of any other way she would be in danger. Unless...' Another thought came into his mind, but he pushed it back for the moment.

'What about the other wife?'

'No trouble there. She's all right, but I am arranging for her to be talked to, so that she is on her guard, and we'll keep an eye out.'

'Phoebe?' asked Stella without malice. She had given up, temporarily, being cross about Phoebe, although she might take up the challenge again later.

'No, I shall do it myself.'

'You are not in a very trusting mood, are you?'

Coffin looked at his wife, he knew he could trust her, even trust her tongue, she knew how to be discreet when she had to be.

'It could be one of us.'

'Ah.' She stopped buffing her nails. 'Anyone special in mind?'

'No. No name, no face.'

'But what's the motive?'

'I'm guessing again. At first, I thought that someone was protecting the money dealers...that may be there, as a subsidiary motive, but now...now I think the killer is protecting himself.'

Stella frowned now. 'But from what? What's the threat?'

'This person dare not be linked with money laundering.'

Stella could be intelligent. 'So not a known criminal but someone of good character and good position who doesn't want to lose it nor risk going to prison.'

Coffin felt he couldn't have put it better himself.

'And you think it's someone you know?'

Coffin nodded.

Stella thought about it. She knew her husband very well, had seen him change from a callow, eager, clever youth into a thoughtful, perceptive man. Intuitive, but always logical. 'Do you have a special reason?'

'I do, as it happens. I don't know how much it means, I don't know if Archie Young would set much store by it, but to me it is running up a flag... Before he died, Felix got a message to me, asking me to meet him at the Crown and the Unicorn. It's not near here, just off Leicester Square; it is not used by any of the local squad. The message said he wanted a word on the quiet. I took that to mean he had something not for any local consumption. He never kept that appointment: I did, he did not. I know now that he was dead or dying while I sat there waiting.'

'How did he get that message to you?'

Coffin hesitated.

'Not the mysterious Agnes?'

He laughed. 'No. His wife. She came round to St Luke's Mansions and gave me a note.'

It might have been why she died. It was a thought that Coffin found hard to bear.

'I wish she hadn't died like that,' he said aloud.

'It's very strange. Why choose that spot? She didn't live near there, did she?'

'Nowhere near. That's a very good question and one I keep asking myself.'

'Who owns the bit of land?'

'It's local council land, once allotments, now running wild. Due for redevelopment. But a man called Albert Waters seems to have proprietary rights over it.'

Stella looked at him, she could convey much in a look. Now it was all question: 'Did they know each other?'

'Albert says not. He may not be telling the truth, we shall have to ask him again. Does he know the killer?'

'The killer may know him,' said Stella.

'There has to be a connection, doesn't there? Thank you, Stella, Albert Waters could do with answering a few questions.'

'Do you think that one person is responsible for killing all three people?'

'I do think so. I called him the Minder to Phoebe. He's protecting someone, either himself or a figure behind him.' He moved over to Stella. 'I'd better get off.'

Stella roused herself. 'I'm getting up. I have a busy morning at the theatre.' She wrapped her robe round her. It was a new one that she had bought in New York, silky, rose-coloured. 'Is this too young and frivolous for me? No, don't answer...' She moved to her dressing table, studying her face in the glass. It didn't look too bad, on the whole she was pleased with it; her face had stood up to life well.

'I resolve not to be jealous of Phoebe.'

'You need never be.'

'Did I say that aloud?' She knew she had, and on purpose too. 'Well, I always wonder.'

'Don't. Please don't.' It was like a knife she was twisting in him. 'You'll see her tomorrow at Geraldine's, you'll know then. Pick up what the relationship is between us. Just professional.'

Stella smiled at him, then started to clean her face. 'You're not vain, are you? No personal vanity.'

Coffin was awkward. 'Got my share.' He went over and kissed her cheek. 'I'm off. To make all my chaps' lives a misery by asking questions they can't answer or don't want to.'

At the door, he turned round. 'Thanks for letting me talk this over. There really isn't anyone else I can be quite frank with. I can say things as they come into my mind and know you won't find them ridiculous. And right or wrong, won't say anything or tell anyone. I value that, Stella.'

The door banged behind him, and Tiddles the cat departed too. He hadn't taken the tray and as far as she knew he had had no breakfast himself.

But that wasn't her job and she wasn't that sort of wife; that wasn't what he wanted from her nor what she had to offer. He trusted her.

And she trusted him. On the whole, with definite reservations. He was a man about whom women clustered.

Phoebe, Mary Henbit (oh yes, she had drawn her own conclusions there) and now this mysterious Agnes. Agnes who might be and might not be.

She had almost finished dressing when the telephone rang.

'Hello?'

A woman's voice answered, not one she knew. 'Phoebe Astley here. May I speak to the chief commander?'

'I'm afraid my husband has left for his office. Have you tried there? This is Stella Pinero.'

'I know. I recognized your voice. Heard you on television. Seen you on the stage, for that matter.'

'Have you?' Stella was pleased.

'Yes, once at the National and then you came to the New Theatre in Birmingham. *The Rose Tattoo.*'

'Oh, so I did. Wasn't it dreadful? We never got that play right somehow. We were all dreadful. I'm sorry my husband is not here. He's only just left.'

'I'll get in touch. I just wanted to tell him that I had fixed up somewhere to live.'

With Eden Brown. It would be interesting but temporary.

'I'll tell him. We ought to meet, you and I. Come to coffee in Max's. Near the theatre.'

'I know where it is...but I'm supposed to be working... I'm not sure if the boss—'

'Your boss, not mine.'

'OK,' said Phoebe with a laugh. 'But not today. Later.' She was not going to be managed by Stella.

'We're going to meet tomorrow at Geraldine's party.'

'Are we?' Phoebe seemed surprised; she hadn't yet decided to go, but she gathered she was expected to be there. Politics of the district, she supposed—Geraldine was someone you had to know. She was certainly someone you did not overlook. She must remember not to wear the dress of which Geraldine had the red version. Just in case. 'I don't know where to go.'

'Oh, you'll get a message,' said Stella easily.

She had a deep and attractive laugh, Stella decided. Sexy, too...

Stella went off to the theatre, taking the dog with her, wondering what her husband was doing.

Her group of friends and fellow actors welcomed her with enthusiasm. Stella was popular, recognized as firm, just and fair. Also, even more important, as a star attraction to this venturesome enterprise. The new drama school, the theatre workshop and the mainstream Pinero Theatre in the old church needed all the help it could get.

Stella responded with happiness to the cries of joy that greeted her. 'These are my favourite people,' she said to herself. 'There's no one like theatre people. They are my people.'

She threw her arms wide as she walked through the foyer of her own theatre. 'Darlings...come and have a drink in the bar. All of you.' Darling on Stella's lips when greeting her own kind lost none of its rolling vibrance.

'Bar's closed,' said a sad voice from across the room. 'Max hasn't opened it yet.'

'We'll force him to open it.' Stella knew she had a key.

'It's all right,' said her new stage manager, 'I know where a key is and we'll chalk the drinks up on the board.'

Do you know that, my love, thought Stella, and you so recently with me? I shall watch you *and* the bar takings.

But for now, she smiled and led the way in.

Not all the casts of the three productions were here, of course, just those who felt sociable or had been given notes and wanted a talk either with their producer or a sympathetic soul. But enough people crowded after Stella to make a party of it.

'Right, Tony, you do the drinks as you know the way.' Tony Bright had come with radiant praise from his first job at the Lake Theatre, Brampton, but perhaps he would bear watching. He was competent, though, she admitted, as she watched him handing out the drinks.

To Rachel Fisher, her new assistant (people came and went fast in this world, moving on after one production or so), she told the news that she had seen Harry Trainer's script and meant to put in a bid for first production. Rachel's cries of interest were strong and loud.

'It's a secret so far,' Stella hastened to say. 'Just between us, must see what Harry says first.' But she did not intend there should be much secrecy—she knew the benefits of advance publicity as well as anyone.

Harry might be angry, but he would come round.

Stella felt full of energy and happiness. She was sipping some wine, not really drinking much, she was full of her own happiness which was intoxicating enough. This was her world but she would make John Coffin welcome in it.

She settled herself at a table by the door where everyone could see her and greet her and held court.

Eleanor Farmer and Phyllis Archer were making their way to her. They were shy of pushing their way through the crowd that surrounded her. Not the most famous of their profession, nor the most talented, they were modest about claiming friendship with the great. Afterwards, they might gently admit that, yes, they did know Stella Pinero, had worked with her once or twice, a lovely lady.

Stella knew them and waved. She liked them, hardworking, professional, loyal girls. Troupers. No greater praise could pass her lips.

'Good to see you. Got a drink? Oh, yes, I'm so happy

to be back. Lots of plans. Stay around, I'm sure there'll be a place for you two.'

Eleanor wore a very short pleated skirt in bright blue, her eye make-up matched it; Phyllis wore her new red suit for the first time—it was her lucky colour, bright cyclamen, more pink than red. She had been right to wear it today.

Stella remembered where she had heard the name Agnes. 'Phyllis, tell me about Agnes. You know her, don't you, darling?'

Phyllis looked surprised but was willing to oblige Stella Pinero. Both of the girls had been in work for six months without interruption now, the St Luke's Theatre complex had brought them luck. Six months clear, and now possibly the chance of more. Little travelling either, so for both no need to take a lodging anywhere; Ellie could go home to her husband and Philly could return to the man she was living with and his two dogs. 'Well, I do,' she began.

COFFIN TOO was conscious of the names circulating in his mind. What was Phoebe doing, how was she getting on with Eden Brown, and where and who was the mysterious Agnes?

Phoebe was, in fact, unpacking her possessions in her new lodging and talking to her landlady. Eden was doing most of the talking while Phoebe listened, making mental notes. Just a load of misery, she decided, about how bad sales were and how anxious she was about the future. Nothing specific.

Eden looked thin and unhappy. She offered Phoebe a cup of coffee which Phoebe refused, then Eden excused herself, saying she had left her Saturday girl in charge of the shop and had better get there quick.

Phoebe completed her unpacking, then took the opportunity to make a quiet survey of the flat. She didn't get much good from it. Eden was either a very cagey lady or else she destroyed her personal records as she went along. Phoebe did this herself.

There was a desk with one locked drawer at which Phoebe looked wistfully but she could not start her stay here by forcing drawers. There was also a personal computer which might contain personal files and this too was locked: Phoebe knew she could not get into it. An expert could without doubt, but she put this thought aside for future use.

She took some more aspirin for her burning toothache, more of a jawache now and decided to take a tour of all the shops in the chain: Dresses à la Mode, KiddiTogs and Feathers and Fur.

She didn't think she would pass as a young mother but she could always claim to be shopping for a godchild.

John Coffin expected results and she had better come back with something.

THE CHIEF COMMANDER was back to routine, which did not really suit him. He had the usual number of letters to read and answer, reports to skim through and two interviews that he could not cancel. He never did put off appointments, experience having taught him that they only had to be gone through at a time that might be even worse. Routine was a bore, but he had trained himself to be efficient about it because in the end it was what your life relied on. It was the bedrock. He himself frequently had flashes of illumination, but he knew very well that more cases were solved by the plodding inquiries of detectives asking questions and making notes.

What you did need in addition was sharp cross-indexing, and here the Home Office computer network into which all forces were linked was invaluable.

But he was thankful, deeply so, that he had trained assistants to feed his computers and then read them back; he did not know their language.

He went into an outer office where screens moved and winked, looked at them, then returned to his room.

For a moment he went to his window to look out; the big double window was open to the sky on this hot day, so that he could breathe in the usual London air of pavements, petrol, and people. A thick brew built up over the centuries, and only changing smell when horses went out and horseless carriages came in. How Victorian London must have smelt of dung and sweat; he preferred what he had, and true Londoner that he was, found it agreeable.

One of his secretaries came in to say that Chief Inspector Timpson would like to talk to him on the telephone. Or he would come in.

'Telephone,' said Coffin at once. He liked Timpson, but the rumour was (and Coffin heard all the rumours, no matter what people thought they kept quiet) that the man had both money troubles and woman troubles and a personal element might always enter into their conversation which he would rather keep clear of for now.

The telephone rang and he answered quickly. 'Hello.'

'Sir, I knew you wanted to know about Albert Waters.' Timpson was keen. 'I've questioned him myself. He says he did not know Mary Henbit, did not know either of them. Not by name or by sight. Blank denial…and I'm bound to say we can't flush up any evidence that he did.'

'Neighbours?'

'He's not close to anyone so there is not much scope for digging. But he has never been seen with anyone that fits either of the Henbits' description.'

'That might not mean much.'

'No, he could meet them anywhere, although it's hard to see why. Nothing seems to connect him to Mary Henbit. We'll keep on digging, of course. There are the Henbit neighbours and friends to question, but I'll be surprised if we pick anything up.'

'Thank you.'

He made a resolve: he would get to Albert Waters himself.

He went back to his desk and his In trays and Out trays and the one he called Forget It. There was always a pile in that one.

WHEN THE TELEPHONE rang again, it was on his private line. Phoebe, he thought, as he picked it up. She might have something. She was always quick at reporting.

But no, not Phoebe.

'It's Stella... You wanted to know about Agnes. You've got it all wrong... I've found out. Agnes is a shop, a dress shop. Agnes is a place, not a person.'

Well, that gives me something to think about, decided Coffin. Add that to Albert Waters and it was quite a bundle.

The strange thing was that his spirits were rising: he liked a puzzle.

THE HEAT ROSE during the day and it began to rain again, but Coffin slogged on, seeing various people, dictating letters, sitting on a committee.

One of his secretaries left early, his assistant seemed to have disappeared on some ploy of his own. Coffin took the hint from life: he slipped on a raincoat and left, telling no one. They would find him if they had to, they always did. But a man must take some freedom while he could.

He walked, the distance was not far, and his code name was *Walker*.

It was possible that Albert Waters would not open the door to him, but he would be at home, he was said never to go away.

The street was empty and quiet with cars parked at the kerb; the fence fronting on the rough ground with the gap through which they had all crowded had been boarded up. Coffin fancied he could still smell smoke but that could have been imagination. He walked straight up to the fence where he ran his fingers along the top, they came away with a black smear on them; then he sniffed smoke. So the ghost of the fire was still there and might be there for ever.

He walked past Albert's house where the curtains were drawn close, but he thought he saw a slight movement as if Albert was there taking a discreet peep out. 'Of course, you are, old man, I'd do the same myself.'

The Tower of Babel in the front garden, which had clearly been based upon a ziggurat, was looking dejected. The storm had passed over it and done it no good; it had been designed for drier, warmer lands. It was also possible that Albert was a poor builder.

Coffin banged on the door. No one came, but the curtain on the upper window moved an inch.

'I know you are there, Albert,' he called out. 'Come on, you know me, let me in.'

Distantly, a voice called back. 'Why?'

'I want to talk.' That was evident, but Albert liked things spelt out.

There was a pause. 'What about?'

Coffin lost patience. 'Oh, come on, Albert, you know what about. Open up.'

A shuffle of footsteps, then the door slowly opened about two inches. 'You can't come in, we'll talk here.'

'No, we won't. If you won't let me in, walk round to the pub and I'll give you a drink.'

Albert considered the offer. 'The Grenadier on the corner? That's my local.'

'I know it.' And a dubious place it is too, Albert.

'I'll get my coat. I'll just close the door.'

Coffin waited patiently again as Albert disappeared to emerge after a considerable interval wearing a raincoat and cap. 'Lost my teeth,' he explained, showing a row of gleaming dentures by way of proof.

They walked together to the Grenadier, where the bar-man gave Coffin an old-fashioned look, and where the publican's wife presently emerged to give the chief commander a long stare. She was a youngish woman with orange-red hair which matched her lipstick, but not her shiny brown eyes.

Albert knew her: 'Hello, Ena,' he said. She acknowledged Albert with a brief smile which did not take in Coffin. She was stiff and muscular and could have been a grenadier herself.

He wasn't welcome there and he knew it. If he had been in Albert's shoes he would not have chosen to come in here with a top-ranking policeman, but everyone has their own tariff of risks they are prepared to run.

Coffin brought Albert the Guinness he preferred to drink and took a light beer himself. He was glad to sit down, it had been a long and difficult day and he was tired.

'So, Albert, you say you don't know Mrs Henbit?'

'Never heard of her.'

'So you have no idea how she came to an end up on your patch?'

'No.' Albert took a draught of beer and looked away.

'I should have thought you would have noticed anything odd that was happening on that particular bit of ground. Your ground in a way.'

'I don't own it, Council does. And other people use it, a gypsy caravan got on it once, then moved on. Bunch of kids camped out there. No, it's not just mine. And I was in the back garden trying to get into something else. I started building an ark once.'

'Yes, you told me.'

'It didn't work,' said Albert briefly. 'I didn't know enough about ship building.'

Coffin didn't think Noah had done, but he'd managed. He left that point and went on to what really interested him. 'Still, I am surprised that you didn't notice anything.'

'I was concentrating. It just shows you don't know anything about how a man feels when he creates something. You concentrate, don't see anything.'

I may not know much about creativity, thought Coffin, but I know something about when a man's lying.

'Why are you down here anyway? I know who you are, you're the Big White Boss, the top brass; what are you doing going around asking questions of the likes of me? I'm not important.'

'I'm interested,' said Coffin.

'Oh, I've heard about you and your interests. When you get interested, things explode all round.'

'Who told you that?'

'Oh, I've got friends.'

'I am certainly interested in why a fire you had started was used. I mean, how was it known about?'

'Could smell it, I suppose. It's not the first fire I've had there, I have 'em regularly. Not every week, I'm not saying, but often enough. I do a lot of building work, you see, and there's debris. I clear up as I go... Then those campers left a lot of rubbish, I burnt that. Why don't you ask them what they know?'

'We will when we find them.' So that was where Albert was pointing the finger? Clever old boy. He must find out if they had ever existed and if so, what Timpson was doing about them.

'I like wood, you see. I need a lot, use a lot, I think about wood. You can do anything with wood if you are gentle with it.'

'Is that so?'

Albert leaned forward. 'There's a tree on that ground that I'm watching as it grows. I've got my eye on it. It's sycamore and when it's ready, I shall have a limb or two for my own use. I shall be making a coffin. I call it my Coffin Tree.'

He looked at Coffin with a mixture of malice and mirth, his teeth in a crocodile grin. Coffin was used to not being liked, but it was the first time he had felt the impact of such strong malice.

'Whose coffin will that be?'

Albert shrugged. 'My coffin, your coffin. Who needs it first. First come first buried.'

Definite malice, Coffin thought, and found it interesting. Somehow, he got an arrow in. 'Two people were seen around the bonfire,' he said. 'We have a witness.'

'My lovely neighbour. What could she see? Shortsighted old bat.'

And that might be true, Coffin thought. You've got all the answers, Albert, but I've still got the questions.

He bought Albert another drink and went away. As he looked back, he saw the man looking at him, and he picked up something from that look.

'You're frightened, my old boy.'

HIS FEET DRAGGED with fatigue as he walked back to the office, wondering what Stella was up to, and what state their relationship would be in when they next met. He ought to do something about that meeting: ring her up, go round looking for her. Tell her he loved her. Do all three, that might be wisest.

He did not think that Albert Waters had murdered Mary Henbit; it was even more unlikely that he had killed Felix Henbit and Mark Pittsy. But Albert had shown unmistakable signs of anger and unease.

That meant something.

He was surprised and not too pleased when he got to the office to collect his papers and get back to St Luke's Mansions and Stella, to find a message from DCI Timpson, asking for a meeting: he had something the chief commander would want to hear.

Timpson was at the end of his telephone line in the incident room. The room itself sounded quiet as if not much was going on there, perhaps they were all asleep.

'We've had the postmortem reports on all three bodies. In the case of the two men there was a substantial amount of sedative in the stomach.' Timpson could be heard turning a page and then reading from it: 'Chlorpromazine diazepam...'

'I thought there might be something of that sort.'

'It's a well-known sedative. You can get it in liquid form so it could have gone straight in the whisky, which they'd also had, and they would never have known. The taste would have been masked... The drug would have made them docile; you could say it made them easy to handle.'

'Easy victims...so it was murder?' Coffin felt relief to have it out in the open.

But the chief inspector had not finished with him.

'The third body, the burnt one, what there was of it, presented different problems...the prolonged, intense slow heat destroyed the soft tissues...seems there are some tests that can be used. But the path lab isn't hopeful.'

'I can understand that.' He sensed that Timpson was holding something back.

'The heat shrank the legs, the whole body was badly distorted...'

Coffin frowned; he wondered what was coming. 'Come on, out with it. I know there's something.'

'The skull was so badly burned that it was hard to establish the features, but the teeth survived... The teeth do not match the charts for Mary Henbit.'

'The body is not that of Mary Henbit.'

SIX

WHEN HE GOT TO ST LUKE'S Mansions, climbing the stairs to his high, light sitting room, there was no sign of Stella. But she had been there. A coat was flung over a chair, her big pale leather handbag, half opened as if she had dragged something out in a hurry, was on the floor, and she had been drinking tea, the cup was on the floor too.

He felt relieved: she was back, this was her home, the cup declared it. He touched it, still warm, she couldn't be far away.

He sat down in a chair to think about what was going on in his sprawling, violent bailiwick. He knew that at any one time there would be an act of violence of some nameless sort, he might never get to hear about that attack, the victim bearing his wounds in silence, but it would have happened. Several robberies of greater or lesser importance, a ramraid on a shop, some domestic violence, rape and incest and the odd missing person. They all happened. Some crimes would be cleared up, others would never be solved.

But his mind would not leave the present problem alone, he worried at it. If Stella came in again, he could talk to her and get his mind off it.

Presently, he took a pad of papers from the desk by the wall and started to make notes.

Why was this business special? It did matter to him, because Felix, whom he had respected as well as liked, whom he had seen as a man of the future, had been killed.

There were three murders now to investigate. Felix and Mark, and this unknown woman. Who was she? Was she in any way connected with the deaths of the other two? It had looked almost certain to be Felix's wife, but now...there might be no connection at all.

He went to the window to stare out at the night sky where the clouds had rolled away from the moon, then he looked down towards the city, *his* city, which was certainly not sleeping.

Coffin turned back to his pad of paper.

Let's assume, he wrote, just for the sake of argument, that it was murder. This, in spite of the confusing evidence of a woman being seen climbing up on the pyre or being pushed by another person. The informant seemed to change her story on each questioning. She had seen something, but what? Lying, fantasizing, or just mistaken?

Evidence for that, he said to himself, is that Albert Waters says she is, to use his own words, as blind as a bat.

Was she worth questioning again?

He stood up and began to walk round the room. Inside him, the silent dialogue went on, and he wished Stella would come back to be an audience.

If the victim on the fire had been murdered, was there any reason to believe that the killer of Felix and Mark was her killer? 'Not till we know her identity,' he said aloud. 'We have to know who she is.'

And if she was not the burnt body, then where was Mary Henbit? Was she still alive?

And if everything hung together and it was one case, with one killer, what was the motive?

'My starting point,' he said aloud, 'is that the money laundering in this area was being done through a chain of dress shops. I selected two men to work on it and report to me; I thought it good for their careers, but it now looks as though because of this work, they died. What does that make me?'

Rhetorical question, needing no answer; he felt guilty.

But he knew why he was taking it so personally. It was

because only someone close to the two officers could have known what they were getting close to.

Or if not known, then guessed.

So he had to suspect his own force.

The door below banged with that particular force that only Stella gave it; he went to the door. 'Stella?'

'Yes, who else? I've been shopping. And for food. You were short of everything from coffee to butter. Not to mention bread and animal food. I don't know how Tiddles and the dear old dog have managed.' Stella was the dog's patron, because he had once saved her life. And from something even nastier: rape. They were allies.

'Max helped out,' said Coffin humbly, watching his wife run up the stairs; she was carrying two big carrier bags, and clutching her purse. Even in a light cotton dress, with a soft coat over it because it might rain, she looked charming.

'That must have cost.'

'Not too bad, we all ate the same. If I had fish, then they had fish, and if I had pasta so did they. Max made a special price.'

She was level with him now, so that she could see his face. 'You look terrible, what's up?' She put down the bags of shopping. 'I had to go all the way into East Hythe to find some late night shopping…they close up early round here. Sleepy lot.'

'Not always,' he said ruefully.

'I ought to have left the shopping in the kitchen.' The sitting room in Coffin's tower was at the top of the staircase, with the kitchen, where the view was not so fine, two floors below. He had not put a lot of thought into his kitchen; Stella was working on it, money would be spent.

Coffin reached out. 'I'll take them.'

'No, give me a drink first and then *I* will cook.' She smiled. 'I promise you something good.' She sat down in the big chair that faced the windows. 'Wine, I think. Thank you… So, what is it? Is it me? Or sister Letty? Or your mother's memoirs? Perhaps you've found a new horror there?'

He laughed. 'No, nothing like that.'

'It's the usual then? The job? Why don't you give up and retire?'

'I might do that. Don't think I haven't thought about it. But not until this business is cleared up. I feel betrayed.'

Stella said: 'By anyone in particular?'

He sank back into his chair and ran over the names in his mind.

'Let me think.'

Stella nodded without speaking and sat quiet; she slipped off her shoes, sipped her wine and waited. From the look on her husband's face, his thoughts were not happy.

These were the men in a position to know what Felix and Mark might have turned up: Chief Inspector John Fisher, in charge of the team; Chief Inspectors Bill Edgar, who kept the records, and Teddy Timpson who had been one of the team for a few months; and Sergeants Hillingdon and Thwaite.

Edgar, Hillingdon and Thwaite had done the most work and been operational in the fullest sense. The other men were there as padding (although it didn't do to call it that) and to liaise with officers of similar rank from the Met and the City of London police, or the nameless men sent in by the Old Lady of Threadneedle Street.

One of these men, God help him, might have been involved and protecting themselves or the person who had been dragged into it.

He didn't want to believe it, but it could be so. This was why he had called in Phoebe Astley. And might have thrown Phoebe to the wolf. There might be wolves, but he preferred to think there was just one hungry wolf.

Because Felix Henbit had been interested in Minimal, he had sent Phoebe to sniff around Eden Brown and the shop.

Then Eden Brown had walked into the frame, asking the police to look for her friend Agnes Page. Find out about Agnes, he thought, because Stella says she does not exist as a person, and Eden Brown seems to think she does.

'Anything I say in this room, you must keep to yourself.'

'You know I will.'

'Well, first: the woman who was burnt is not Mary Henbit.'

Stella drew in her breath. 'That's a relief. So who is it?'

'We don't know.'

'And Mary? Where is Mary?'

'I don't know that either.'

'But you are afraid?'

'I am afraid,' he agreed.

'But we do have a missing woman: Agnes Page, though you say she is not a woman but a shop.'

Stella put down her wine, her face was full of animation. 'That's what the girls said: Agnes Page was a dress shop, several dress shops, in fact: one in the West End, one by the Tower of London, and one down here in the Second City. They think there might have been others but Ellie said she used to buy her bras in the one in the West End. They were not really expensive and you felt good in one.'

Coffin said bluntly: 'There's a woman who keeps calling the police saying that Agnes is a woman and is missing.'

The cat came into the room, looked at Coffin and then Stella, and leapt on to Stella's lap. She stroked the furry head. 'I'm puzzled. Does it matter? Is it part of this affair?'

'I think it might be.' He added: 'Also, I've had a talk with an old man who I think is lying.'

He's really worried, decided Stella. She accepted all the facts he had thrown at her, if it was helping him, good. 'All this matters?'

'To me, desperately.'

Stella had no hesitation. 'You've got plenty of action

men: get them to sort out what Agnes is, a chain of shops or a woman.'

She stood up. 'I'm going downstairs to cook supper.'

Coffin rose. 'I'll give you a hand with the bags.'

'Don't bother... You get on with it up here.'

'Thanks Stella. You have helped.' He realized with happiness what comfort and relief Stella would bring: she opened his mind up again when it had been painfully bogged down.

'And what about the old man, the one that was lying?'

'Albert Waters? I shall leave him to sweat, because I think he is frightened as well as lying.'

Stella stood at the door in silence for a moment. 'You really are a hard man.'

'Yes, sometimes. I have to be; it's the job.' He went over to kiss her, she turned towards him and lifted her face. For a moment they stood closely together, then she said 'Supper,' and drew away.

He heard her talking down below to the cat, who had, of course, left with her, and reprimanding the dog who was barking softly. What a joy it was to have her—darling, darling Stella.

Just at that moment, the doorbell rang loudly. Stella ran down the stairs to open it and he stood listening. He could hear a woman's voice and Stella replying.

Since Stella was an actress, her beautiful deep voice travelled well; he heard words of thanks. 'It's so good of you. Oh, my husband will be very pleased.'

A lighter voice was answering, whose words he could not hear. But Stella again. 'Oh, do come upstairs and show him.'

Coffin groaned. Oh, Stella.

He stood up again, waiting. If he didn't sit down, then this unexpected caller might go soon. He wanted a quiet few hours with his wife. Alone.

He could hear Stella still talking as they came up the

winding stairs and then she came into the room, ushering before her a young woman in tight jeans and a white shirt. She was smiling nervously but it was an engaging, hopeful smile, so that Coffin found himself smiling back.

'This is Ellie,' said Stella, 'and she's got something for you.'

Ellie gave Stella a shy, hopeful smile, as of one who dares to call a star a friend.

'Stella said...' another look and a smile at Stella, 'she said you wanted to know about Agnes... Well, I found this in my bag.' Ellie swung her big shoulder bag in front of her, opened the zip and began to dig inside. Even a brief glance showed Coffin that it was loaded with possessions: he saw a hairbrush, a spray lacquer, a box of tissues, an apple, a packet of clean tights, and a bar of chocolate. Ellie stirred the mixture around and came up with a small piece of paper. 'I found this at the bottom of my bag,' and she held it out.

'Thank you,' as he took it, and congratulations, he thought, it must be quite a feat to find anything in that bag.

He looked down: it was a handwritten bill for six brassieres and briefs. The billhead said: AGNÈS TROUBADOUR.

Ellie surveyed him with satisfied pride, like a cat who had produced the best kitten. 'I knew I'd shopped there.'

The address was Number three, Treddle Street, W1, and another address in Knightsbridge and Kensington—three shops in all. 'French,' said Coffin, noting the accent on the name.

'I'm not sure how French,' said Ellie in a doubtful voice.

'Not very French at all, I should think.' Coffin was studying the address: 'Treddle Street. That's one of the little streets behind Regent Street, isn't it?'

'Yes, I was in a show at the Haymarket at the time so I did a bit of shopping up there. You see, she had quite a few shops then, they came before the Agnes Page shops in the Second City, but I knew I recognized the style as hers, the shops had the same look.'

The bill was dated almost a year ago, much crumpled with a smear of lipstick on one side. Coffin wondered about the archaeology of the contents of Ellie's handbag.

'Thank you very much, this is useful.' Was it? He wasn't sure but he wasn't going to snub this nice young woman.

'I expect you think it was a great number of bras I bought, but you see, it was the year bosoms went pointed; she had such lovely cone-shaped bras and I got them for nearly all the cast.'

'They are all the same size,' said Coffin before he could stop himself. Stella glared at him: some things you do not say.

'We are all 36B. We always are.' Ellie was earnest. 'Some of us may pad a bit.'

'Handwritten bill, that's unusual.'

'Ah, that was the shop, you see, it was meant to be old-fashioned. There was a padded sofa and a lovely smell of potpourri, and the bills were written out with a quill.'

'Someone spilt ink on this one,' said Coffin, looking at various streaks and smudges.

'Yes, she got it all over her fingers too.'

'Stay and eat,' said Stella, as he had known she would. But to his relief, Ellie said no, she had to get home, she was having some friends round.

Stella showed Ellie down the stairs, giving a clear signal to her husband with those eyes which Kenneth Tynan had called the most expressive orbs on the London stage.

'Get on with it,' she had said earlier, and her gaze now said she meant it.

So he telephoned Timpson, who was still in the incident room but on the point of leaving. He sounded grumpy at being caught there when he might, with better luck, have been safely at home, so missing the call altogether.

'Find out who Agnes Page is, the name keeps surfacing.

Identify what the name means. It might be a shop.' Then he added: 'If she exists at all as a person and not a shadow, she might be the burnt body.'

'That's a new idea.'

'It just came to me,' said Coffin falsely. 'The name has come up as that of a missing woman. We may have found her.' The bill that Ellie had given him lay in front of him. 'It may be worth checking at a shop in Treddle Street.'

'Sir.' Timpson was gruff. 'Fine, I'll see if we can pin the two together... But what about the deaths of Henbit and Pittsy. If it's murder, then who is taking it on?'

'I shall oversee it,' said the chief commander. 'Archie Young will be in charge, and will keep me in touch. But I want your team involved. I see these cases as all one.'

As he put the telephone down, he wondered grimly how Timpson was taking the request, and whether it was one he had been fearing?

STELLA HAD GRILLED a steak and prepared a salad; she liked to grill anything that could sit flat under the flames because she could watch it cook. Boiling an egg, however, where the cooking went on in a silent manner inside the shell, presented a problem she never mastered. So she never boiled eggs.

As they were finishing the meal, the telephone rang. Stella reached out a hand for the portable which lay on the table between them. 'Hello? Yes, he's here, I'll hand you over.' She gave Coffin a quizzical look. 'It's your friend Phoebe.'

He knew how to field that one: 'Your friend too... Hello.'

'Listen, am I expected at this party tomorrow?'

'Yes, Geraldine's. You've got the address?'

'I don't think I can come.'

'I'd like you to. She's an important lady. Well worth knowing.'

He was very conscious of Stella watching him across the table.

'How are you doing with Eden Brown?' There was a pause. 'Is she listening?'

'Could be,' said Phoebe in a quiet voice. 'And the answer to your question is fine.' But her voice suggested caution.

He kept his voice low: 'She seems to be anxious about a friend called Agnes.'

'I can confirm that.' Eden had been talking to Phoebe for almost two hours about Agnes, with more emotion than detail.

'There was confusion at first whether Agnes was a real woman or a chain of shops.'

Eden would weep for a chain of shops, probably more than for a woman, Phoebe thought.

'But I now have addresses for three shops called Agnès Troubadour. I think they might be worth investigating.'

'Do you want me to?'

'Timpson will be sending someone, but you could take a look.'

'See you tomorrow then,' said Phoebe. 'I'll try to be there.'

'Her voice sounded odd,' said Coffin as he turned to Stella.

'How odd?'

'Thick. She might have been crying.'

PHOEBE WENT BACK to Eden; she herself had not been crying but Eden certainly had. Eden was in her bedroom, full length on her bed, with her face buried in the pillow.

Phoebe sat down beside her on the bed and gently touched her arm. 'Come on now, it can't be that bad.'

'I'm frightened. I might be going to die.'

Death, thought Phoebe, I've been doing a lot of thinking about that myself.

'What about Agnes? I suppose she does exist?'

Eden jerked her head round. 'Of course she does. She's a person.'

'Why are you worried about her?'

Eden didn't answer, then said: 'I told you: I can't get in touch with her. And the police won't help. They say adults are allowed to go missing.'

'That's true.' Phoebe nodded. 'It's a way out that some people take.'

'Tell me about her.'

Eden shook her head: 'I don't know much, she was a business acquaintance.'

'Oh, come on, you don't cry for your bank manager. What was it with Agnes? Did you love her?'

'I'm not a lezzie,' said Eden with an angry jerk.

Phoebe gently withdrew her hand. 'Are you frightened for yourself or Agnes?'

'You don't understand.'

'I understand about fear all right,' said Phoebe, who was frightened herself.

PHOEBE WAS NOT the only one who was frightened that day, nor was Eden.

Albert Waters was frightened and wished he had not made that joke about the Coffin Tree to the chief commander.

'I think I'll telephone him. He's my man.'

FEAR WAS SPREADING like a disease. It *was* disease, a malady of the mind.

THE INCIDENT ROOM dealing with the burnt body had quietened down for the night. Not much helpful information had so far come in, but what there was had been collated and passed around to the investigating team. The collator was just finishing up, talking softly to a young detective still typing up a report.

Timpson felt that he was caught in what military tacticians call a pincer movement, and the chief commander was doing the pinching.

If Henbit and Pittsy had been murdered—something he had been very unwilling to concede—and if Mary Henbit had been the body on the pyre, then it was one case, and he must extend his inquiry.

But now, apparently, the burnt female body was an unknown woman and not Mary Henbit, the nice woman whom he knew. A relief but also an added puzzle.

So the two cases were not connected. Not in his mind at least. But he could see that the chief commander still thought the three dead people were tied in a packet.

If I am investigating the deaths of the two detectives, then I want more men.

And if you are going to send us off looking for a woman called Agnes Page, then I want still more.

'But I won't get them,' he said aloud. His head began to ache. Life was on top of him at the moment. He dreaded to go home to find what new bills were waiting for him. He frowned as he walked to his desk.

· He was not a stupid man, he had been a policeman a long time, and he could read the signs with the best. He had seen Coffin look at him, and he had felt himself look back.

Rumours were going all round Swinehouse and East Hythe; Coffin might think that men were not talking but they were, he had heard the rumours that the Big Man suspected one of his force.

He was not a man who talked freely to his fellow officers, and he was taciturn with the young detectives who were on this team. They didn't like him and he knew it. They liked Archie Young, who could be jovial and friendly while never losing his grip, they respected and even feared the chief commander, John Coffin, and took pains to keep out of his way.

He looked round the room, he needed to talk to someone. The collator, who was a curly-haired girl, was keeping her eyes down, while the young detective was putting on his coat ready to go.

He had one confidant, his own brother, Frank. He put on his coat, collected his car from where it was parked—he would telephone Frank. Not from home, but from the nearest call box.

'Hello, Frank.'

'Ted? How are you, boy?' Frank was a happy man who ran a small garden shop where he was content to sell seeds, bulbs, potting mixtures of various strengths as well as cut flowers. He was always poor but he and his wife had reared three highly successful children. The brothers were alike in colour and build, but Ted had the muscle.

'I think he's on to me.'

'I told you not to get mixed up in it, you should have steered clear.'

'Well, you know why, I needed the money. You're lucky, your wife doesn't demand new clothes all the time and dinner out every week.'

'Take my advice, tell your wife and tell your boss man.'

This was not advice that Timpson wanted to hear.

THE NEXT DAY was Sunday and was the day on which Geraldine was holding her party.

Although it was Sunday and the shops would be shut, this was a murder case and the investigation was not closed down altogether. A young detective constable was sent off to find the shop in Treddle Street.

DC Darby took the trip to Treddle Street lightly, regarding it as a morning out. Also, it being a Sunday, surely he would earn points for being so punctilious?

He had rung a friend in the Met and discovered that the

shops in Treddle Street ignored any trading rules and remained open on a Sunday if they wished. There was also, he was told, a thriving Sunday street market round the corner in Peckery Street if he felt like a detour. Goods on the whole worth a look at but to watch his wallet. Darby decided he would buy his girlfriend a present if he saw anything she might like. He was very fond of her, but not good at expressing his feelings.

He walked down Treddle Street from the Regent Street end. He soon saw the shop because the name Agnès Troubadour was inscribed in gold on the shop front. But the glass was dirty, the window empty and the door boarded up. It was not the only empty shop in Treddle Street, several businesses had gone broke in the great recession. Next door to Agnès was a sandwich and coffee bar which was open for business.

He ordered some coffee and made his inquiry of the man in the white overall. 'What happened next door?'

'Went bust, that's what.'

Darby drank some coffee which had no clearly defined taste but was hot. 'Tough on the owner. What happened to her?'

'No idea, I wasn't here then, this was a shoe shop. If you want more sugar, then it's on the counter.'

Until then, Darby had not noticed that the only thing his white frothy so called cappuccino tasted of was sugar.

THE PARTY AT GERALDINE'S started slowly. They were what she called 'her Sundays', held on the second Sunday of the month, unless she was abroad or work prevented it. People accepted with alacrity, you met an interesting mix of people: actors, writers, lovely models and prominent businessmen, as well as the odd academic: Geraldine cast her net wide. She provided good drink and tasty food which you helped yourself to and then moved around the room

with your plate. Nothing was formal and the flow of movement and conversation was everything.

John Coffin got regular invitations but he did not always
accept as a matter of policy: it did not do to get too close
to someone like Geraldine.

On this occasion, he got there before Stella who had gone
to the theatre to take a call from New York about a new
production. 'We'll meet there,' she had said cheerfully. 'I'll
try not to be late and don't you be.'

Geraldine had been one of the first residents in the converted warehouse, even before it had become fashionable,
so she had had first choice. She had chosen the whole top
floor and had got an architect to make it over for her into
a living space, with a platform for her bed. Not much privacy but a lot of free air. The furniture was sparse, but
what there was had been designed for exactly the spot
where it stood or lay and was expensive. An air of spon-
taneity but nothing by chance. Coffin thought it exactly
mirrored his hostess's character.

When Coffin arrived, the large light room overlooking
the river was already crowded. He saw several people he
knew, including Sir Ferdie who was holding court across
the room. Phoebe slid into the room behind him. He got
her a drink, and let her look around the room.

'Nice place. She must be rich.'

'I suppose she earns a lot.'

'And spends it too.'

Phoebe looked flushed, one cheek was slightly swollen.
'It's this tooth,' she explained. 'I must get it fixed.' She
took a long drink as if it would ease the pain. Coffin, who
knew the strength of the cocktails that Geraldine mixed,
watched her with some alarm; he himself was drinking
white wine.

Presently he saw Stella crossing the room towards him.
Geraldine moved to get her drink. 'Champagne, Stella?'

'Yes, lovely.'

'I'll bring it to you.'

Stella kissed her husband on the cheek, and smiled at Phoebe. 'Nice to see you again.'

Always remember, Phoebe said to herself, that she is an actress.

Stella turned to Coffin: 'Oh darling, there was a phone call for you before I left: a man, I think he said his name was Waters, he wants to see you. Something to tell you. I didn't quite know what to do, didn't turn him away, of course, but I suggested Inspector Timpson, I hope that was right?'

'I'll see him,' said Coffin. 'I know who it is, I'll go round tomorrow.'

Geraldine pressed a goblet of champagne into Stella's hand. 'Come along then, Ferdie,' she said. 'I can hear you padding behind. You want to talk to Stella.'

Sir Ferdie did pad, thought Coffin: he walked softly but heavily. Watching Stella with Ferdie, he drew Phoebe into the window. 'What do you make of Eden Brown?'

'She's in trouble,' said Phoebe; she too was watching Stella with Sir Ferdie. 'I think he's a bit of a shark, that one, but your wife seems to be getting on all right with him.'

'She likes to flirt.'

'That's an old-fashioned word.'

'In some ways, Stella is an old-fashioned lady.' And of course, she knew that a light, flirtatious manner was what Sir Ferdie wanted. He was well known in academic circles as a womanizer who rarely followed through.

'I need to see Eden.'

'I think you should.'

Coffin went over to his wife. 'Is it all right if I leave you here?'

Stella took it well, she might complain later but she never let him down in public.

'I'll look after your lady,' said Sir Ferdie with a courtly bow.

Stella smiled. 'I suppose it's work.' She surveyed the room, over by the window was a well-known writer, closer to hand was a TV presenter. 'There are people here I would like to speak to. Don't worry.'

She was perhaps less pleased to see who went with him.

'Stella didn't like us leaving together,' Phoebe said in the lift.

Coffin was easy, he knew his Stella, she might enjoy a scene afterwards about Phoebe but deep inside she trusted him.

EDEN'S APARTMENT was a cheaper image of Geraldine's place: it was in a converted factory, but a very small one and the conversion was not so well done. There was the one large living room with the huge window and balcony overlooking the river, but already it had a tired look. The carpet on the floor came from the Indian continent but was from a factory and not handmade. The walls had been colourwashed by Eden herself, who had left them streaky.

Phoebe let them into the small hallway. 'Wait here, let me prepare her for you.'

Coffin walked to the window to look out. There was the Thames, cleaner and emptier than it had been for many generations, there were even salmon swimming in it somewhere.

Phoebe was soon back. 'She's putting on some clothes. She knows you're a copper but she doesn't know exactly who you are. She wants to talk.' She dropped her voice. 'Don't be too rough.'

Phoebe would always see a side of him that Stella never would; but he nodded. A nod meant nothing and he needed Phoebe's support.

'I suppose she now knows what you are?'

'Not exactly.' Phoebe grinned. 'She thinks you're my boyfriend.'

Eden was taller, thinner and blonder than he had expected, but about the right age: early forties. The age when you've had a success and lost it and are struggling. Failure is hard to bear then. You'd do anything to get back again. He could understand that she would be ready to do anything without asking too many questions. Just the sort of woman some criminals would be looking for, and no shortage of them, he thought sourly.

He looked in her eyes which were vacant, as if all emotion was retreating backwards into fear. She was jelly, squeeze her and she would give him what he wanted.

He didn't even have to squeeze very hard.

'I know I've got to talk to you, Phoebe is right, she seems to know the world better than I do. I thought I did, I was the big successful career girl but I know now how wrong I was.' She bit her lips. 'When my own business went down the drain—I had a small design and couture business, and my boyfriend left me, he was only in it for the money and when I couldn't go on paying for his smart suits and cars and weekends away, he upped and left. I was broke and suicidal...'

'I don't think you would ever have killed yourself,' said Phoebe, 'but I know what you mean.'

'Anyway, it didn't come to that. I met this woman at a dress show. I tried to keep in with the world, you see, and I was applying for jobs, I'd seen her around so I was willing to talk. She told me the same thing had happened to her but she had been introduced to this venture capitalist who was willing to put up money; he worked through a bank—she thought he might do the same for me.'

It was fine at first, she went on, and she thought her life had started again, but very soon she realized she was nothing more than a manager and one who had to obey the rules, and it didn't take long for her to start wondering.

'Then I began to worry; I think I'd known all along really but I didn't want to think about the idea that mine and Agnes's shops were set up on criminal money and used to launder large sums.

'Then Agnes became frightened and hinted that she knew about murders and was frightened for herself.' Eden shivered. 'Now she's gone and I don't know where. Her shops are neglected, her chief assistants don't know where she is.'

'Who is Agnes Page?'

'I don't know. I don't think it's her real name, I don't know who she is or where she is.' Eden shuddered. 'But she knows where I am, and so do our hirers... I don't know if I am right to talk to you, I may be risking my life.'

Coffin said: 'Have you got a letter or something she handled?'

Eden thought about it. 'She never wrote to me... Wait a bit, she left a compact here, and I never gave it back to her.'

Coffin held out his hand.

'I'll get it.'

While she was out of the room, Phoebe said: 'Confirms what you thought.'

'Confirms that the two men had been murdered, but I already know that much. I don't know who killed them or what part this Agnes woman played. I want to know that, and I want to find her.'

'Right,' he said, as Eden came back into the room, holding out a small powder compact in a suede case. 'Good, thank you.' He took it carefully. There might be fingerprints. 'Thank you. I'll be in touch. Don't worry too much.'

Phoebe showed him to the door. 'Stay with her,' he said. 'She needs watching.'

Phoebe held back. 'I've done part of what you wanted. I want a few days' private time.'

'Why?'

'Private, as I said.'

'You can be a nuisance, Phoebe. Stay with her tonight and give me a call before you go off.'

As he went away, he was not unsatisfied.

He had the bill from Agnès, a powder compact and the corpse had a finger.

When he got home, Stella was already there; she gave him a reproachful look.

Coffin laughed and hugged her. 'I wasn't worried for you. Perhaps a bit for Sir Ferdie.'

'He said he was going to get an honorary degree for me,' said Stella with a satisfied look. 'It'll be my first one.'

'Don't touch it,' said her husband promptly. 'He'll want his price, no free lunches, you know.'

'So how's Phoebe?'

'Phoebe's doing very well,' he answered sturdily. 'I think this affair may be about to fold up and Phoebe will have played her part. Tomorrow I will wait to see if Albert Waters telephones me and if not, I will go and call on him myself. He interests me, and what he has to say could tell a lot.' He felt full of energy and hope; the mysteries would be cleared up. Phoebe was out there working on it, she had always been a great digger into the background: she'd asked for 'personal leave' but he thought he knew better: she would be working. Dangerous, may be? But there was no point in worrying. 'Come on, change out of that party gear and put on jeans and soft shoes. We'll take a long Sunday afternoon walk. I'll drive us to Greenwich Park and we'll walk up the hill to the Heath. With any luck there will be a fair on and you can ride on the roundabout.'

SEVEN

THE SUNLIGHT had been golden on the hill in Greenwich Park as they walked up the grassy slope with its dells and hillocks to the top where General Wolfe stood looking out across the old palace and the Seamens' Hospital which had been old when Wolfe was fighting the French in Canada.

Half way up, Coffin paused to look back at the city in sunshine. 'Looks beautiful.'

'And peaceful, everyone enjoying their Sunday afternoon.'

'But it isn't, it's a battlefield down there.' He held out his hand to her. 'Come on, we'll help each other up the hill.'

They got to the top, then sat there, slightly breathless. Coffin smiled at his wife. 'Worth it now, isn't it?'

'Yes, more or less.' But Stella smiled too. 'Remember when I played in the old Greenwich Theatre? And you were very very young.'

'So were you. We both were.'

'Somehow I think I was older than you, girls are. It sort of happens and I'd been around about.' She looked at him from under her eyelashes.

'So you used to boast. I have to tell you that I never quite believed you.'

Stella picked a blade of grass, drawing it through her fingers, then beginning to chew it. 'I did exaggerate a bit.'

'I wasn't all that experienced either.'

'I knew that too. I could tell. But I loved you even then.'

'I did know, dearest Stella, I knew. But you could be a real little bitch.'

'I was so young and ambitious...you were too.'

'I know.' He was sad. 'Two for a pair. We wasted years. But we did both have the careers we wanted, even if it cost. And now life has given us a bonus. Perhaps we don't deserve it, but we've got it.' He put his arms round his wife and kissed her.

'You can be very nice,' she said. 'And very sweet and very honest...and it's usually when you are about to be truly terrible.' She put her head on one side. 'So what is it this time?'

'I don't think I am.'

'You don't always know, I've noticed that, you surprise yourself.'

Coffin considered: she might be right, he could feel something brewing up inside but he had no idea what. 'I'm not in love with Phoebe, nor about to fall in love with her.'

Then he said: 'I think what I've got inside is anger. I feel violent. I want revenge.' They were his men, those dead policemen, there was possession to fuel the anger as well as the pain of loss.

Stella was silenced for a moment, absorbing what he had said. 'You're very Shakespearean.'

'No. You haven't got it right. The wrong writer: I'm Dickens or even Wilkie Collins.'

'I don't mind being Cordelia or Lady Macbeth but I won't be Little Nell.'

'Shakespeare for you, Dickens for me.'

Stella stood up. 'That's settled then. You can choose between being Inspector Bucket or Sam Weller. Let's walk on. Let's go to the old Observatory and stand on the Greenwich meridian. I'll stand on one side and you can stand on the other, so we shall straddle the globe.'

The world having been satisfactorily encompassed, they walked across the Heath from which the rioting peasants, supporters of Wat Tyler, had threatened the City of London, but on which a fun fair now caused the only noise. They ate dinner at a fish restaurant overlooking a quiet pond where ducks swam and small boys sailed their toy boats.

'Did you ever sail your boat there?' asked Stella as she forked up her salmon mousse.

'No.' Coffin gave a quick glance at the privileged child who was guiding his battery-controlled boat round the pond. 'No, I never had anything like that, but I had a little wooden canoe that I used to shove up and down the gutters when the weather was wet enough.'

'Oh, you poor deprived child.'

'I was all right,' said Coffin, who had never pitied himself. 'I had a good time, and I learnt a lot of my craft on the streets of London. I learnt how to hide when I had to, how to tell a good lie, and how to know a good lie when I heard one. If you don't take that in with your blood when you're young, you never do and you're lost.'

'Neglected, starved but learning to be a good copper?'

'No, I was never starved or neglected exactly. And if no one loved me very much, then I didn't love them.'

Stella, child of a comfortable middle class home who had been cherished and even spoilt, knew what he had missed. 'And that's what you have had to learn.'

'Well, I do love someone now, and it's you. And the cat and the dog, that's enough for me.'

'I never know when you are being serious or not,' Stella complained. 'Or whether to believe you.'

'Yes, you do, you know better than anyone. And if other people don't, that suits me very well.' He poured her some wine but did not take any more himself; he was serious about drinking and driving, unlike some of the London coppers he had trained with years ago and unlike some of his men now. 'I'm sure I was a monstrous child, I daresay we all were, Letty, William as well, and I don't blame Mother for leaving us all behind one after the other.'

His mother was celebrated, as he knew now that he had read her diaries, for loving and moving on, leaving behind children, but sometimes husbands or less regular partners. She was a prime example of what Bernard Shaw called the undeserving poor.

They drove home to St Luke's Mansions in affectionate silence. That night, in bed, with his arm across Stella in a protective way, he reflected that it had been a goodish day.

He had enjoyed Geraldine's party, he had been amused to see Stella flirting with and perhaps tormenting Sir Ferdie, who deserved it; then he had gone with Phoebe to meet Eden Brown to whom he had offered a certain amount of protection, although she would be advised not to depend too much on it, and he had his conviction about the deaths of Felix and Mark.

He would find out about Agnes whoever she was; he thought Albert Waters had a lot of talking to do.

He turned on to his back, studying the ceiling while he considered his problems. He had two.

One was Phoebe.

The other was Chief Inspector Timpson.

The image of Phoebe seemed to impose itself on the ceiling: he saw her face, usually good humoured and controlled, but this was not how he had seen it this morning. Then she had been tense and secretive. Yes, that was the word: she was hiding something. And she had been crying, her face looked puffy. But he trusted her to be still on the job.

He considered. Perhaps puffy was not quite the word. It was swollen.

Phoebe's face faded away, and was not replaced by that of DCI Timpson. There was no impulse to summon up his image. The ceiling remained blank while the worry increased.

The cat was sleeping on his feet at the bottom of the bed, and the dog was snoring on the rug by his side, with the intention of climbing on the bed too once Coffin was deeply asleep. He would also try for a good spot on his master's feet. If he succeeded in dislodging Tiddles then the cat would move up to sit on Coffin's head: feet and head, these were the two prime places.

He shifted his feet but the cat did not move. 'Get off, you brute!' He managed to slide his feet away and swung out of bed.

The problem of Timpson was going to prevent sleep for a while. He had pushed it to the back of his mind for too long, but now the anxiety had broken the crust and come crawling out.

There were rumours going around about Timpson: no one had said anything to him, he was supposed not to know, but he did know, he knew everything, it was his job to know.

In this eccentric tower home, the living room was on the top floor where it got the best view and the sunniest light, the bedroom was underneath with the kitchen below that. Coffin crept up the stairs and sat by the window which he had always found to be a good place for thinking.

He caught a distant sound of music, coming from who knew where, it came and went on the wind like the music of spheres. One of the marvellous things about London, he mused, however late the hour there was always someone around; you were never the last to put out the light. In fact, the light never went out, it was never a sleeping city.

What was the rumour about Timpson?

That he was on the take. That he mixed too closely with certain criminous elements, that he was far too friendly with one or two, and that he did favours. Money passed hands.

Coffin knew this was being said, and he knew that very soon now he would have to take action, he would have to question Timpson. Unofficially first, in one of those mock-friendly interviews that set your teeth on edge, and then, if that did not go well and get straight answers from Timpson that cleared him, launch another set of questions in an official way.

He thought about Timpson, the solid citizen, the family man with a wife who was a teacher and two children, both of whom must be at university by now. He had only good reports of the children, no trouble there. So why was good citizen Timpson so short of money?

He was not anxious to find out why, although he would have to, but he would have to find out what he was doing about it.

He walked to the window, as he so often did, to look out: no lights to be seen but on this summer night there was already that pale lightening of the sky that spoke of the dawn.

It was already tomorrow: the day on which he must decide what to do about Timpson.

First, take him off the case because he might be the killer.

Then suspend him while an inquiry was mounted.

'Damn it all,' he said aloud.

The sound of distant music had died away but through the silence, he thought he heard a noise.

Downstairs, in his own house, was movement.

St Luke's Mansions was known to be where he lived, and on this account got protection and surveillance because he was someone who might be attacked at any time. Over the door was a video camera which recorded all comings and goings, although those most frequently photographed were Tiddles and the dog. Even Coffin, who knew them intimately, had been surprised how often they went in and out through their private and personal exit flap. The security expert who checked the establishment had recommended doing away with the flap, but Coffin who had to live with the animals had ignored the advice.

He turned to the screen to look: the usual empty night scene, no parking was allowed near his door, but on the picture there was a retreating back: a man and by the way he moved, not a young man. He thought he knew that back.

Downstairs there was a folded sheet of paper in the letterbox. The message was in pencilled large letters.

I am coming to you tomorrow. Not saying when, not safe. I will come in my own time, you wait.

No telephone, you are listened to. Who have you got who listens?

The letter was blotched and smudged as if the writer had been crying over it.

The missive was not signed, but it didn't need to be, he knew it was from Albert Waters.

And there it was again, that suggestion that someone about him was not to be trusted.

It was not going to be a night for sleeping.

He climbed the stairs to the bedroom where he slid into bed beside Stella who moved her hand in sleepy welcome. Tiddles was still there, having expanded quietly into all available space, and the dog had a spot at the bottom. Coffin considered kicking them both off but decided that life had to be lived on the terms offered.

'Have you thought,' he said aloud to her, 'that there have been too many stories about the Second City police lately? Well informed stories at that. And have you thought that the source is inside the force and that just might be the hard up Chief Inspector Timpson?'

Stella did not answer.

That was what was nice about marriage, Coffin decided, you could ask your wife a question in the middle of the night which she would not answer and you would not mind.

IN THE MORNING he did what had to be done: he sent a message, polite but neutral in tone, asking Chief Inspector Timpson to call on him. Then he ordered a check to be made on Albert Waters's house. 'See if he is all right. Talk to him.' Then, with a shrewd assessment of Albert's reactions, he added, 'Better send a woman.' He wanted to add: the youngest and prettiest you've got, but that was not PC and dangerous talk these days. 'And tell her to let me know what she finds.'

Then he got back to routine matters, which always seemed to drag in money and resources these days. He had a handsome uniform which he hardly ever wore, and was one expense on the Second City force which he would most gladly have sacrificed. But it seemed that when you met the Queen you had to wear the ceremonial gear, and he had a royal visit coming up next month.

Planning for this visit had taken up a great deal of his time for the last year: committee after committee, some local, some in at the Palace with the Household officials. Everyone was invariably polite but uncompromising: you did things their way or not at all. He did not anticipate any serious danger to the Queen on her visit: the inhabitants of the Second City were monarchists and enjoyed a royal show if they didn't have to pay for it, but Coffin knew that danger could come in from outside. But apart from the usual horrors attendant upon any production of this sort (and you had to think of it in terms of theatre), there was no special problem.

His office was quiet, but noises from the building filtered through to him: loud voices, someone coughing, the constant ringing of telephones.

He worked on for a while, then he raised his head from the file of papers. Last week he had been with Stella to a student production of *Pygmalion;* it had not been a good production, the Professor being particularly unconvincing, but the right words now came on his lips.

'I am a patient man,' he quoted. 'But where the hell is Timpson?'

He picked up the telephone and demanded of the CID unit where was the chief inspector. There was an interval before his call was answered.

'Sorry, sir,' said an apologetic voice, 'this is Inspector Marsh here, we seem to have a problem about that… We can't say where he is just at the moment. He called in with a message saying he was going out on the job.'

'Going where?'

'He didn't say, sir, and he hasn't been in touch since.'

'No idea where he's gone?'

'I tried the forensic laboratory, sir, but no go.'

'What about the incident room?'

'I am in there, sir. Your call was transferred.' Marsh sounded uncomfortable.

There's something wrong here, and he knows it, Coffin decided.

'Give him my message when he does arrive.'

'Yes, sir.'

The voices from his outer office seemed noisier; he went to the door to see what was going on. Outside was a Detective Brenda James. She had a determined look on her face.

'I was told to report to you, sir.'

His secretary was flustered: 'I didn't think you wanted to be disturbed, sir.'

'This is all right. Don't worry. I do want to hear. Come in and tell me.' He looked at his secretary. 'Coffee, please?'

Inside his own room, he sat Detective James down. 'Here's the coffee; help yourself to sugar and milk.'

Brenda James, unused to such polite attention from her macho colleagues, took her coffee and stored up the moment.

'So what did you find?'

'Well, sir, he's an old…' she hesitated.

'Go on.'

'He's an old bastard,' she said with conviction.

THE YOUNG WOMAN detective had parked her car well away from Albert Waters's house, not wanting to draw attention to herself, then she had walked slowly round the corner to where he lived.

It was a quiet morning, children were at school, husbands or boyfriends at work, and most women putting the weekend's laundry through the washing machine. It was a sedate domestic street which did not like trouble and had seen enough of the police.

Both instinct and training warned Brenda James to be cautious. She walked a few yards past the house, then turned back. She allowed herself a moment or two's study of the Tower of Babel which was slipping to one side as if it would soon tumble down. Not one of Albert's better buildings, she decided. She had never called on him before but she had gone past his garden when she was still in uniform and walking the beat; she remembered a fine Leaning Tower of Pisa (she supposed it had been that, it had certainly leaned to the left) which she had admired. There had been Nelson on his Column too, she seemed to remember, not such a success.

She opened the gate and rang the bell.

No answer.

She tried the knocker and when this brought no reply, she backed away down the garden path to survey the window.

'You from the social?' The speaker was Albert's next-door neighbour.

'Sorry?'

'Social worker… He's had one of those call already.'

'No, I'm not.'

'Just thought you might be. Insurance then?'

Brenda kept silent.

'There must be insurance after what happened. He's in a bad mood and you can't blame him after all this. It was a horrible business.'

'Horrible,' said Brenda, who felt she must say something.

'Oh, you know about that do you? Thought you must know something in spite of you pretending not to...' As she shut her door, the neighbour said: 'If you're not the social, and not the insurance, then you must be the police.' She shut her door with a triumphant bang, aware of having scored.

Brenda James went back to the door, she abandoned the bell and applied herself to the knocker.

'Come on,' she called. 'I know you're there. Let me in.'

All she got in return was silence. But she knew someone was there, she could sense it, hear soft rustling. Old devil, she thought, he's playing me up.

She banged the door and rang the bell. More than once. Still silence. Then a movement behind the door.

A husky voice called out. 'Fuck off!'

'SO I LEFT, SIR,' she said to John Coffin.

'Quite right. You did all you could. Thank you. He was in good voice, anyway.'

'He was that,' said Brenda with conviction.

Pleased with his courtesy, delighted to have had such a contact with the chief commander, whom she only knew by sight, and with the satisfied feeling that she must have done her career a bit of good, she returned to the incident room. What she really planned to do as soon as a suitable moment came was to get a cup of tea in the canteen and let her colleagues know where she had been.

Coffin worked on. No Timpson, no Albert Waters. Bad thoughts fill a vacuum. He was having bad thoughts in plenty.

When people don't do what you expect, then you do what they don't expect. If necessary, you go where you are not wanted. So he tidied his desk and left his office. He walked slowly down the stairs. He knew the word would soon go out: *Walker* is on the prowl.

In mid-afternoon, the canteen was not crowded, but there

were more men and women there than he would have expected: small groups around the room, heads down, talking quietly.

It was not a place he went into often, it was their territory, not his, but occasionally he strolled in with someone like Archie Young.

He was noticed instantly and the conversations died away. Then, as he took a cup of tea to an empty table in the window, the talk started up again.

But not naturally, the conversations had changed; whatever they had all been discussing before they had stopped. He could tell. And that told him something: they had been discussing Timpson. The absent Timpson.

One by one, men got up and drifted off. He was careful not to look at them.

Presently, Archie Young came hurrying in, and that told him something too. Archie had been warned and summoned. Word had gone out to him that *Walker* was out and he had better get down there and do something about it. It was known as a damage limitation exercise. Archie came up, and was friendly. 'Hello, sir, can I join you?' He sat down. 'Don't often see you down here.'

'I thought I'd just look around.'

'Ah.' Archie put some sugar in his tea, reminded himself that he was, in a way and as far as it could go in their circumstances, a friend of the chief commander. 'Ah,' he said again.

'Oh, come on, Archie, you can say more than that.'

'Well, does it need saying, sir? Would you be down here if it did?'

'Timpson.' Coffin let the name drop into the conversation like a stone.

Archie Young was silent for a moment. There was such a thing as loyalty to your peers. You did not drop a man in it.

Not until you were sure he was deep in the mud anyway and wouldn't get out.

About Timpson, he suspected that he was in trouble, and behaving foolishly.

'He's a silly fellow,' he said sadly.

'Go on.'

'He's got a girlfriend, and he got into debt.' The one thing followed the other. 'And he's been selling stories to the press. Mind you,' he added cautiously, 'this is only talk, I don't know of my own knowledge.' By which he meant, this is not official and I shall deny having said anything.

'How's it done?'

'I suppose he meets the contact in a pub and passes over what he's got. If anything. Probably safer that way. No telephone calls or such.'

'Who's the contact?' For a moment, he wondered if it could be Geraldine. But there were a lot of information hungry journalists.

Archie shrugged. 'Haven't heard a name.'

'How did you hear about this business?'

'Hard to keep things quiet,' said Archie simply. 'But of course, it's just canteen talk, none of it may be true.'

'And is that all?'

'As far as I have heard,' said Archie cautiously.

'I won't ask you how long you have known of the stories going round.'

Archie had the strong feeling that his status as good friend had gone several degrees down. The truth that you cannot ride two horses at once was being made painfully clear to him.

'Timpson was in charge of the combined investigation into the deaths of Henbit and Pittsy. I suggest you take him off it and assume control yourself.'

'Already done.'

'Good. Timpson should have initiated a forensic study of a bill and a small powder compact. If any discoverable fingerprints link up with the burnt body—there was a hand and finger—remember, then you will have the identity of the dead woman.'

'He did do that; I checked.'

'I am not sure if that will settle exactly who the woman was; I think she may have had layers of identity, but we shall know what she was calling herself to certain people at certain times.'

Archie Young looked round the canteen which was almost empty, all the tables near them had cleared with speed. It was like being Typhoid Mary, he thought.

'You're not suggesting that Timpson had anything to do with the money laundering or the murders...if the two are connected.'

'I am sure they are, and as for Timpson, I don't know, but he could have been involved.' Someone close to him was, if his own suspicions, now fuelled by Albert Waters's hints, were true.

There was silence between them as they both considered the horrors of bringing Timpson before a disciplinary court. Apart from its effect on morale in the force, the publicity in the newspapers and TV would be enormous. Coffin knew that however scrupulous he was in setting up the tribunal, the words 'kangaroo court' would come up sooner or later.

And he had his own reason for not wanting hostile publicity just now; he kept this reason to himself.

It was still very hot weather, a heavy moist heat that was unpleasant. The sky was grey with low mist.

Coffin broke the silence. 'Well, I'm off.'

'Yes, I'd better get back. I'll let you know as soon as the forensics are back.'

Across the room, a trio of uniformed women constables had established themselves, they were very conscious of the chief commander, but were keeping their heads down.

One of them looked up as another woman came into the room. 'Hi, Brenda, join us?'

Brenda James nodded, she took up a cup of tea, debated a chocolate biscuit, but she might put on weight and so she turned it away. As she did so, she saw the chief commander and Superintendent Young.

The disquiet that had been bubbling up inside her all day burst forth. She marched across to their table.

'Sir, about what I said this morning…it wasn't the way he spoke that upset, not the language, I've heard worse. Hell, I talk like that myself sometimes, we all do, it was the way it was said… Horrible… And it wasn't just that.' She stopped.

Coffin prompted her. 'Yes?'

'I've been thinking about it all day… I don't know if it was him speaking. The voice wasn't right… I think someone else was there in the house.'

Coffin stood up. 'Thanks for telling me, you've been useful.'

HE HAD WAITED all day to hear from Albert Waters, but he had waited too long. When alerted by Brenda James's anxiety, he went to the house, he rang the bell and knocked only once.

Then he knelt down and peered through the letterbox. No one there. It was then he walked round back of the house, looked in the kitchen window and saw Albert lying in his own blood.

And all the time, there was another body rolling over and over in the Thames, moving with the tide.

EIGHT

INTERIM REPORT, Coffin said to himself, sitting in front of his typewriter and ignoring Stella's cry that the dishwasher had lost its memory and was pouring hot water over the kitchen floor.

He didn't believe this, he knew an actress's cry for attention when he heard it.

ALBERT WATERS died because he was going to tell me something. He was knifed in his own kitchen with one of his own knives. The killer did not bring the knife with him, which might tell us something or it might not.

What Albert was going to tell me must have posed a great threat to the killer or such drastic action would not have been necessary.

That suggests to me that it bears upon the deaths already being investigated. Perhaps Albert knew the murderer and was about to name him.

But I've always known that about Albert, he reflected, leaning back in his chair. Or at least since I met him to talk to: that he had a secret inside him that he wasn't going to let out.

He may not have let that secret out, in fact. I suspect, or indeed, I am sure, that for Albert to know the killer, then there must be a great deal about Albert that I do not know.

He would probably dig out Albert's secrets, it was what the police were good at. It was probably easier to dig out a dead person's secrets than a living person's. The line about taking your secrets to the grave had a certain easy falseness to it.

You of all people should know that, John Coffin, look at the case of your mother. She had secrets, lived a very secret life, but she couldn't forbear writing them all down and sending them out into the world when she was gone.

Even now, he never used the word dead of his mother. She might turn up.

The death toll was going up, the Second City was getting more publicity than he wanted. So far, he himself had not come in for any criticism, but that could come any day.

He had some information: he had found Albert's body at a few minutes after five o'clock. The first, quick medical opinion was that Albert had been dead some six hours. He breakfasted, and he had eaten well, and his breakfast was still largely undigested. So it looked as though he had come back from his nocturnal visit to Coffin, gone to bed, and got up to eat breakfast. His bed was still unmade, but he might have been a careless housekeeper. The kitchen and bathroom were clean enough but untidy.

There was no sign of a forcible entry, thus Albert had let in his killer, whom he probably knew.

Or the killer had a key, which again suggested that Albert and his murderer were known to each other.

WDC James's visit was entered in her notebook as taking place at an hour before midday.

So that when Brenda James called on him, it was probable that he was already dead or dying, thus the voice that had spoken to her must have been that of his killer.

There were no 'musts' in detective work, Coffin reminded himself, but he was prepared to accept that one.

Would Brenda recognize the voice again? He had asked her and she seemed eager to try, and yet doubtful at the same time.

Stella wandered into the room, dropping into a chair where she could watch him.

'How's the dishwasher?'

'Pig!'

He laughed. 'I know you, you see. If it had been really leaking, I would be down there like a shot.'

'I bet.'

'Well, on to the plumber, anyway.'

'I just wanted company.'

'I know. You think I'm obsessed with these murders.'

'Taking them to heart too much.' She curled up in the big chair, voicing her complaint. 'I hate it when you go all silent and withdrawn like that.'

'I know. I wouldn't do if I didn't have to.'

'It's this business, isn't it?'

'There are complications, Stella.'

'It's not Phoebe Astley?'

'I'd like to know where she is, but no, it's not Phoebe, not in the way *you* mean.'

'She's hanging in there, though,' said Stella. 'I'm psychic, remember?'

Thank goodness you are not, thought Coffin. I have troubles enough.

'Have you sorted out the Agnes problem? I mean, I did help there, didn't I?'

'You did. Yes, I think we have. I'm waiting for confirmation.'

'That means she's dead, and if she's dead, then she's the woman that was burnt.'

'Good guessing.'

As if on cue, the telephone rang. Stella stretched out a hand. 'I'm expecting a call to finalize a contract... No, it's for you.'

'Archie?'

'Yes. Just to let you know that Timpson called in to say he would be back tomorrow.'

'Did he say where he'd been and why?'

'I don't think we will get much of an answer to that one. If I had to guess, then I'd say he was walking the streets trying to get up the courage to come back... He might even have been thinking of jumping in the river.'

'I'll see him tomorrow.'

'Yes, he expects it, I got the impression he would be glad to talk to you.'

One of my least pleasant jobs, thought Coffin. His eyes rested on Stella who had taken up a magazine but was probably listening to every word. She was wearing a pleated silk trouser suit which looked expensive. No wonder she was interested in a new contract. With whom and for what?

'And there's a provisional match on the fingerprints on the letter and bill with the one finger on the burnt body. It was a forefinger on the right hand...it seems this was the woman known as Agnes Page.'

As one problem was solved, another turned up.

The burnt woman was Agnes Page. But there was a query hanging over her head.

Albert Waters who probably knew the answer was dead. So that was a new problem.

And there was still the old one of the mystery surrounding Mary Henbit. Where had she gone, and why? She was not in hospital, she was not in prison, she was not with her family, of which there was only a married sister who did not seem too worried. Both the parents were dead. It is difficult to disappear entirely but she had managed it. Four dead bodies so far, going back to Felix Henbit and Mark Pittsy. And behind it all, the business of the money laundering.

Money came into it, and was the motive for murder, but more and more he was coming to think that this killer had a sharp personal motive.

To ADD TO HIS troubles, next morning, just as he was leaving, he took a telephone call from Geraldine, whom he suspected of smelling blood, offering to do an article on him and his years of office.

He said no.

And still no word from Phoebe, just an hysterical message from Eden Brown to ask where she was.

NINE

ALTHOUGH THE WEATHER had been hot and dry, the recent heavy storms had made the Thames run fast and turbulent, not like the placid river going about its business as it should. The grey-green surface was flecked with scum, underneath you had the impression that the current was running fast. The Thames in such a mood can be treacherous and mean; it is not an easy river as all bargemen and tugmasters who have to navigate her know, sometimes to their cost. On that morning, bits of debris and rubbish such as only the Thames can collect were swirling round in clumps as if they were growing together in some form of vegetable life.

Coffin knew as soon as he went into the headquarters building, that it was a bad day; he could feel it, almost smell it. They were a close lot these policemen, he knew how they felt, he had been like it himself in the old days when he had been one of them. Now he was not one of them, far from it, and he could arouse hostility with ease. They knew about Timpson, and they were gathering about him in support. You got into the stockade when one of your number was threatened, it was a primitive male instinct; you took the animals and women and children with you, that was instinct too, and he did not know what took its place in the present situation, but it just might be their motor cars, he had seen at least one copper carefully double-locking his car and then going back to look. It must be frustrating not to be able to get your car inside the stockade.

But you could confront the enemy and they were doing that, in their own way, not direct confrontation, careers were on the line here, but quietly; he probably would not enjoy going into the canteen today. Not that he was planning to.

Timpson was waiting in his outer office. He was standing by the window, with his back towards the door. Coffin could tell by the slump of his shoulders how he felt. If it's any comfort, he thought, I feel lousy too. My breakfast is not sitting easy in my stomach any more than yours is. You have a problem but it is mine also.

He nodded to his secretary, who knew what it meant and quietly departed. 'Coffee, sir?'

The chief commander nodded. 'Bring it in to my room for both of us.' He looked towards Timpson who had turned round and was looking at him now, silently. Coffee was not going to cheer him up, but he appreciated the gesture. He was down the drain but was not going to be kicked as well. Well, yes, he would be, but the chief commander was signalling that humanity was still in place. He followed the chief commander into the room but he did not sit down until asked.

'Sit down, man.' Not the most cordial or friendly of invitations but the best Coffin could manage at that moment. He couldn't treat the man like a naughty child, it was all too serious for that and he was angry, but he wouldn't bully him.

All this time, Timpson had not spoken, now he did. 'It's been difficult,' he said.

Difficult? Coffin thought, is that what you call it? I think I've got another name for it. Like bloody dishonest lunacy. He bit back the words that rose to his lips. 'You'd better tell me.' There was no sympathy in his voice, it was not an invitation to kiss and make-up.

Timpson recognized it, and what there was of colour in his face drained away. Normally, he was a florid, cheerful-looking man, now he was grey and pinched as though the flesh on his face had shrunk.

It probably had, Coffin thought: the man looked as though he hadn't eaten or drunk or slept for some time.

'When did you last go home?'

'I don't remember. I think it was the day before yesterday.' He didn't look as if he knew when yesterday was. Not a day that he wanted to remember, anyway.

At this point, the coffee came in. Coffin poured a cup. 'Sugar?'

'No, thank you.' He took a mouthful, and then drained it as if he was very thirsty but had not known it until that minute. He hadn't shaved either, Coffin thought, or at any rate, very roughly and probably in the washrooms below. He felt the first real touch of sympathy for Timpson that morning. It must be bloody, sitting there, facing the boss with your chin half shaved. The hand that had come forward for the cup didn't look too clean either, the nails were grubby. Timpson had normally been a man who set store by an immaculate appearance. He had been drinking too, Coffin could smell beer on his breath. Well, he had to have been somewhere if he wasn't at home, and he no doubt knew a friendly publican. Or the man, sick at heart as he must have been, reluctant to go home to face his wife (what about her, by the way?), might have just sat by the river with a can of beer with the rest of the dispossessed of this city. The Timpson he remembered had not been too sympathetic to the down and out, maybe he would be now. But somehow he doubted it, the thing about misery and guilt was that it turned you in on yourself. He ought to know: he had had his own dose of it in his time.

'Well? Let's have it.'

'I needed the money, I had debts—I don't want to talk about how or why, I don't want to drag someone into it that doesn't deserve it, she isn't guilty of anything. I'm not going to blame her for what was my fault. I was offered a deal and I took it.'

He sat silent.

'You'll have to do better than that. Who offered and what and for what?' He had a pretty good idea, the information handed over had to have been on the banking investigation, and possibly, anything on the death of the two policemen, that would be about it, but it had to be spelt out.

'I've known Peter Billson of the *Trumpet*...' This was the name that they gave to a well-known daily. 'We were at school together. We had the odd drinks together occasionally.'

And he dredged the waters for any information you might have and would talk about. You've probably been a bit free with him before, only this time it was more important and not free. You fool.

'I never passed anything of importance over, believe me.'

'We will have to go into that.' It had to have been of some importance to be worth anything to the *Trumpet;* Coffin knew the editor and he was not a man famous for his generosity. 'I shall want details, and you will have to make a statement. That's not what this talk is about.' Timpson knew how it went as well as anyone. 'This is just to tell you that you are suspended, that there will be an inquiry.'

Timpson nodded. There was no need for him to utter a word, nor did he.

'Of course, you will be represented and supported.' Not quite a kangaroo court, but something pretty close to it; he knew it and Timpson knew it, and the men downstairs knew it which accounted for their mood.

'How did you find out?'

'You just looked so guilty. And of course, stories about what you were up to have been going around. Did you think they wouldn't be?'

This was not quite true, Coffin had his own quiet intelligence service within the force, spies you might have called them, informers in criminal circles, but he knew he had to rely on information coming to him, so he had his contacts. Archie Young was one, but there were others, and of both sexes.

'And what made you come forward?' Not goodness of heart, he thought, or the straight desire to clear yourself; you're the sort that would hang on until the bitter end, because you would hate to admit you were ever wrong. I've known your sort before, and they were always cocky and self-confident until life caught them out and then they would go on swearing black was white as long as they could. You are one of the brazen-it-out breed, so why not now?

'Geraldine Ducking…she asked me for a drink and when she got me there she sprang it that she was ready to publish an article on corruption and the press…naming me.'

'You believed her?'

'Yes, she showed me what she'd got…photographs, tapes of telephone calls, photocopies of receipts… I never took cheques, it was always cash, but I had to give a receipt of some sort so we made it look like I'd settled accounts at shops and wine bars… I don't know how she got them, but I'd signed this and that, she had photocopies. Oh, she had done the job. And she hates the *Trumpet*.' Timpson fell silent. He seemed to be looking into the pit that had opened before him.

That bloody Geraldine, thought Coffin, she's dangerous. I wonder if this is why she's been courting me and Stella? Not because she loves us so much but because we could be part of a story.

'She rang me yesterday, wanting to talk again.'

'Keep away from her.'

Timpson muttered something about never wanting to see her again.

You might have to, Coffin thought, we both might have to, but we shall have witnesses with us. She would too, of course, Geraldine was no fool, so there were not going to be any quiet little meetings in bars. He was surprised that

Timpson had not taken more precautions; he was fundamentally a stupid man who had been too pleased with himself.

'I didn't…know…have anything to do with the killings,' he hesitated, struggling to get the words out, 'to do with the deaths of Pittsy and Henbit.'

Coffin felt cold. The man should not have said that. He looked in his face, hoping to see something wholesome and reassuring there. But no. Just a shifty sense of guilt. It was the sort of remark that commanded suspicion. Rolled him nearer the precipice.

Coffin stood up. He wanted to say, get out, get out of my sight, but he restrained himself. Probably read it in my face, he thought. 'That's it for now. You can go. You are off the case, of course.'

As he shuffled to the door, Timpson said: 'Geraldine said I did have knowledge…'

'I told you: keep away from her.' Coffin suddenly felt weary of it all. 'That's the best advice I can give you.' Except drown yourself. Then he thought of the river and thought that the Thames did not deserve Timpson.

Even when the door had closed behind him, the room did not feel empty of Timpson, he still seemed to be present. Coffin went to the window and threw it open, a breeze blew in and he hoped that Timpson blew out with it.

He went back to his desk, feeling that events were moving all round him, more than he knew as yet, which was the way things always happened when they were big events.

The interest of the media was intense by this time, newsmen from all round the world were encamped outside the incident room from which only guarded statements were being made. There was pressure on Coffin, so far resisted by him, to appear and make a statement. He was so televisual, he was told, to his fury.

Eden Brown had been told of the forensic tests, she knew

that the burnt body had been identified as that of Agnes
Page, but she had not been asked to view the remains. Agnes's flat was sealed and would be examined. Her shop had
been visited and the young assistant, ignorant and puzzled,
who had been trying to keep things going, had been questioned. The reports would all, in due course, rest on Coffin's table.

He had an engagement to go to the theatre with Stella
that night, but first he had some other business. He prepared
himself for it in a wry mood. He tidied his hair, inspected
his nails, and brushed his suit. He was half ashamed of
himself for doing this, but it also amused him. This was
John Coffin here, who had been a poor boy on the London
streets and had come this far, but he was the same inside
and he knew it. This surface sophistication was skin deep,
one scratch and he would bleed.

He was interrupted by a call from Geraldine.

'I want to interview you, please. Soon, now if you can.'

'No, Geraldine, no interview.'

'I'm interested in what's going on.'

'Leave it.' His voice was hard. 'There's nothing for you
here.'

'I am the avenging angel, darling,' she said with a laugh
in her voice. 'And I think you have a stinking mess on your
hands down there.'

Much as he had liked Geraldine, and respected her
achievements, he did not care for this mood of hers, which
he had met before.

'I can't talk to you now and I am not going to be interviewed, believe me.'

'You can't stop me writing about you and your colleagues.'

'I could probably drop an injunction on you.'

'But you won't do that.'

'I might. If I feel I have to.' He did not remind her that

she was on a committee of his which might involve her in a dichotomy of interests. Hold that back for now.

One of the strengths of Geraldine Ducking was that she knew when to back away. They continued talking for a few minutes more, during which her tone changed to being quieter and less aggressive, and she ended on a friendly note.

'I really admire Stella. I think she's about the best actress on the London stage just now and I love the way she looks.'

'Thanks, Geraldine.' He thought she was trying for tact.

When Coffin put the receiver down, he sat there for a moment thinking. That was another thing about Geraldine: she did provoke thought, she stimulated you.

The important thing about detection, he reminded himself, is that you must see the obvious.

The other most important thing is that the vital clue may only be presented to you once and you had better see it.

He had the feeling that already the vital clue had been shown to him and that he had *not* seen the obvious.

He stared at the blotter.

He was interrupted by his secretary. 'Lady Eastham and Colonel Lee are here.'

Coffin stood up. 'Show them in.'

No greater contrast with Geraldine Ducking could be imagined. Lady Eastham was tall, thin, well-groomed and dressed in a discreet linen suit, she carried white gloves. At a first glance, Colonel Lee seemed a match, equally thin, tall, restrained and well-bred. It was only at a closer look you saw that in fact he was not tall and was sturdily built rather than thin.

Coffin had done his homework so he knew that the Eastham earldom was both old and respectable, it went back to one of Queen Anne's more successful generals, but was not rich. Lady Eastham had been one of the Queen's senior ladies in waiting for some years; she was known to be good-humoured and reliable. Colonel Lee had served in the Guards in the Falklands and was now retired: he was a royal equerry. They were both here to oversee the arrangements for the Queen's visit.

Coffin produced maps of the road system which the royal cars would have to go through, and plans of the buildings which would be visited by the royal party.

Eileen Eastham was efficient, she told what was required, checked that everything was in place, explained that she had to tell the drivers the exact position of the entrances and doors so that the car could drive up where the door would be opened in the correct position for the Queen to make her customary graceful arrival where the welcoming party stood. If the car door opened on the wrong side you were in trouble. Colonel Lee was making notes on the security arrangements.

'Everything will have been double-checked with dogs by my security men here, two days beforehand,' Coffin assured him. 'And I shall have men stationed all round of course as usual, and on roofs.'

All three of them knew that in addition there would be careful searches by the Queen's own security men, and no doubt by other units as well: some operations were so secret you did not mention them even to those close.

'It all seems in order,' said Eileen Eastham with a friendly smile. She too had done her homework and knew who John Coffin was and what his career had been. 'But I expected no less.'

Coffin thought he could read in that smile a sentence or two about him: You left school as a lad, did your National Service, did well but were not an easy recruit, joined the Metropolitan force, and now you are where you are. How hard you must have worked.

Coffin had his own thoughts: I have worked hard, and I have had some strange experiences that have educated me. He smiled back.

'Good show,' said the Colonel. 'You run a tight ship here.'

Coffin knew what he meant: We don't want any riots or street fighting or any scandals before or for some time after the Queen's visit.

'It's a good set of people here. You can rely on them giving Her Majesty a warm welcome.' I have people here who don't like the police and people here who don't like the army, but then a standing army has never been popular in England and for that matter nor have the police, but provided I keep a low profile and you don't wear a military uniform, they will all be out on the streets cheering. It will be a public holiday in the schools so that will make for popularity too. Anyway, in certain junior circles these days, I wouldn't count on them coming out waving flags. More likely to stay at home and watch the visit on television. But the Queen was probably well used to all this and did not mind at all. She might even have preferred to be at home watching television herself.

So he smiled cheerfully at the equerry, and offered a reassuring handshake to a man who was trying to do a good job. I am fighting a war here, he said to himself but it is a war against me. I don't know the face of my enemy yet but I feel his breath on my back.

He walked to the car with them, stood talking for a moment, realizing that he liked them both, especially the cool Lady Eastham, and then he made his way to the incident room where the investigation was now upped in status to a MAT inquiry, taking precedence over all the others currently being pursued by his CID and enabling it to draw first on men and resources.

The room was half full, with men crowded round one desk; they all turned round as he came in and fell silent; he knew what that meant.

They had been talking about him. So the battle had moved to here too? But Archie Young emerged from the heart of the group and he realized that he had been wrong.

'Think we've got something, sir, on the Agnes Page case. In the first place, it wasn't her name, of course.'

'I never thought it was.'

'No, seemed likely it wasn't. Just her business name, but she let the Eden Brown woman call her by it. I guess she liked her bit of secrecy, and perhaps didn't trust the Eden woman too much, or thought she wasn't likely to hold her tongue. Jessop found papers that gave her name as Agnes Gray. It was her married name, he found her passport. She travelled a fair bit.' He paused.

'So?'

'But except for the passport which a police dog sniffed out in a roll of newspapers, the flat was cleaned out. No personal papers at all. That's interesting in itself.'

'Jessop thought the passport was hidden?'

'He did, he did. He's shrewd, is Jessop, and he made up his mind that the whole place had been searched, and that the woman had thought it would be. The passport had been quite cleverly hidden. The passport was in the newspaper but it had been put there deliberately, no accident. He was sure of that, done on purpose.'

Coffin could tell from Archie Young's voice that he had something else to tell. 'Come on, let me have it. I can tell you've got something.'

'He found a list of telephone numbers pencilled on the wall by the telephone. Most were business numbers. He will be calling on all the firms to see what he can get, of course.'

'Of course.' It was like squeezing a tube getting anything out of Young at the moment, you had to keep pressing.

'But there was another number partly rubbed out. He was able to get it back... It was Albert Waters's number... They knew each other. There's a connection.'

Coffin had the feeling that an important fact was fleeting past him. So what, he thought, I'll catch it later and hang on to it. But it might be that this was the important bit of evidence he must become aware of at once. See the obvious, he told himself. Don't look for the elaboration.

So what was obvious here? One murder victim knew another murder victim. There was a relationship.

'Find out exactly what the relationship between those two was,' he ordered.

'Working on it,' said Archie Young. He was a little annoyed that the chief commander had thought he had to tell him. 'But she hasn't left much around for us to work on.'

'She expected trouble; Waters didn't. I think he was taken by surprise even though he had telephoned me and sounded frightened. He didn't think whoever was coming for him would come so quick. He didn't have time to destroy papers. Go over his house. You'll find something there.'

With luck, he said to himself, because everyone needed luck and he thought they were due for a piece.

'Will do.' Young was already turning away. Even he was touched by the slight resentment towards the chief commander. Or perhaps he just wanted to show his colleagues that this friendship of his with Coffin (about which he was careful not to make too much show), would not, could not, corrupt his loyalty to his own. They were watching him from across the room where the green screens flickered and the telephone still rang at intervals. 'I'll get on to it.'

Coffin looked at his watch. He was due to be with Stella in just over an hour, but there would be time. 'I'll come with you.'

A look flashed across the superintendent's face, and he read it aright: it was not pleasure.

ALBERT WATERS'S house smelt smoky and cold even though the day outside was hot.

'A damp little house,' Coffin thought. 'No wonder he spent so much time outside doing his building.'

The whole place had already been looked over by the

police team, and two men were working there still; he recognized them as being from the forensic team whose work, laborious and methodical, always took longer than that of anyone else. They recognized him at once and seemed surprised to see him. And once again that look; they were not pleased. But they stood up politely and waited to see what he was there for.

He did not speak to them, apart from a brief greeting, and let the chief inspector and the detective who had come with him explain what was going on. He himself walked quietly about the house. There were two rooms on the ground floor as well as the kitchen, and each was furnished simply: one as a dining room and the other as a comfortable if shabby sitting room. He already knew that Waters had spent most of his money on his ambitious building; someone had said that he probably wanted to get into the *Guinness Book of Records* for the best home builder. The rooms were not particularly tidy but they were clean enough and the sitting room smelt less damp than elsewhere, suggesting it was the room in which he had really lived. A large television set stood in one corner of the room, next to the fireplace, and facing a battered leather armchair which looked comfortably used. There was a small table by it with a pipe and tobacco on it and a newspaper. Across the room by the window was a small desk.

Coffin looked thoughtfully at the desk but said nothing, knowing that it would be searched again for any signs of Agnes, and for any clue to her contact with Albert Waters; it was not wise to irritate Archie Young by too much interference, he was aware of being already on the edge.

'Not much there,' said one of the forensic experts, following his gaze. 'We've had the drawers out and so have the scene of the crime team. Not much, just a few personal papers and not a lot of them.' He nodded towards a small pile of envelopes and scraps of this and that, newspaper cuttings, old postcards and more than a few bills.

He went out into the kitchen, where the smell of damp was strong. A wet patch on one wall suggested a leaking pipe. There was a bucket with a cloth in it, as if Albert kept it there in case of trouble. Coffin touched the cloth, it was dry and stiff so he had not used it lately. Perhaps it was something to do with his building works, but Coffin thought he could smell disinfectant. He had a picture of the old man on his knees, mopping the floor. He picked up the cloth, underneath the clean smell of pine, he thought he smelt vomit. So someone had been sick? Perhaps Albert himself. There were certainly enough horrors around to make anyone sick.

He opened the kitchen door to take a look at the garden. Not the garden of a man who was interested in flowers or vegetables or a smooth patch of lawn. There was grass but it had a chewed-up look which was clearly the result of Albert's creative building. His latest and last piece of work was hard to make out, all that was to be seen was a wooden frame that might have been going to be anything from the Ark to the substructure for a replica of St Paul's Cathedral. From what he had known of Albert, he guessed that the inspiration was running dry. Maybe even Albert had got bored with pretending.

He shut the door, walked through the kitchen, briefly observed the men still at work in the living room and went up the stairs. Albert had obviously used the stairs as a combination of filing cabinet and clothes depository. On almost every step were old newspapers, folded shirts and pants, dirty shirts and socks—he kept the two separate as far as Coffin could see, but otherwise took no interest in order.

No, that's not the case, Coffin told himself, there is a mad kind of order here, the order of a man who lives for himself, according to his own rules. And this was just about the impression he had formed of the man.

Obviously no wife or woman in the household. Had he ever married? The sort of fact that Young would have turned up, but what was clear was that she was either dead or long since departed.

Melancholy thought, was what Coffin decided, as he got to the top of the stairs. Is that what some men, most men, came to when they were left alone? And if so, would he, if Stella was gone?

That was a thought better not dwelt upon, so he moved on from the bare little upper hall with its pictures of the river Thames of long ago with barges and tugs and battered tramp steamers as much a part of the past as old Albert himself.

He went into one bedroom; empty except for an unmade-up bed. All the cupboard doors were open, so a search had been made here which had tumbled a few dark brown blankets to the floor. The smell of damp was in here too, underlined by the peeling wallpaper by the window. Coffin shut the door behind him.

The second bedroom had been where Albert slept. This room was neater, with the bed tucked in, and although there were piles of clothes on both the floor and the two chairs, yet they were so arranged as if Albert knew how they were and meant them to be so. The police searchers had disarranged them somewhat, but he could see that each deposit had been made up of a complete set of clothes: underpants, socks, shirt and trousers. The jacket on the chair nearest the bed clearly did duty for each outfit. In a cupboard on the wall, a dark blue suit hung next to a grey tweed, but they had the neglected air of clothes not worn for a long while. Drawers underneath had been opened and left open, but they contained nothing except pyjamas, and more vests, pants and shirts from which the strong odour of mothballs arose.

He picked up one shirt and the sleeve of the perished material tore away even as he did so.

Funny chap, he thought, he concentrated on a few of his clothes while letting the rest rot away. Still, there but for the grace of God. Don't finish that thought, hang on to the thought of Stella and their evening at the theatre.

Thus prompted, he left the bedroom to go back downstairs.

Archie was standing in the middle of the room by the table.

'Was there a wife?'

'Yes. He was a widower, seems to have been so for years.'

'Temperamentally suited to it, I'd say. Any children?'

'I don't know.'

'Find out.'

'We are doing, but he was a recluse and a bit of a mystery man.' Archie stood back from the table. 'Here are all the documents we can find, and as you can see, there is not much there. A few postcards that are more than ten years old and date back to when he was working, and they don't say anything much, except it doesn't rain in Spain and the beer is cheap. Or welcome to Sunny Blackpool. There is his passport, which incidentally he hadn't used since nineteen-eighty when he went to Malta for a week, and his birth certificate. Oh, and his pension book where he had a month owing to him. Nothing else. Not much is it, for a life?'

'Too little, entirely too little.' He let his fingers rest on the small pile. He picked up the birth certificate which told him that Albert had been born in nineteen-twenty in Deptford and that his father had been a merchant sailorman, and his mother's maiden name was the unusual one of Pilgrim. 'I think someone, the murderer presumably, has been in and cleared out this house too. What do you think?'

'I think so too.'

'It's interesting and perhaps helpful: because it means that Albert was important, just as Agnes was. It also shows us that the killer was well informed and could move fast. I don't think Albert was upset and anxious until he knew that the body that burned was Agnes Page. I think he vomited then. It may have been the cat next door or his killer, but I guess it was him. The news went straight to his stomach, then he telephoned me.'

'So he did.' Young looked troubled.

'But the killer knew he knew and either knew or guessed he wanted to talk to me. How was that?'

Young's lips tightened. 'Just guesswork, as you say.'

'Some positive knowledge around though: I think Albert knew of the identification of Agnes Page with the burnt body and either he told the murderer himself, or the killer knew anyway. How was that?'

'It was talked about,' said Young uncomfortably. 'The press do get on to things.'

Coffin nodded. 'Too many leaks, Archie, too many leaks.'

He looked at his watch. He had thirty minutes in which to meet Stella. 'Tighten things up,' he ordered, and it *was* an order, not a polite request. 'Talk to the neighbours here and see what they know about him and his lifestyle, and I don't mean the obvious things like his building hobby and where he drank his beer. He's lived here a long time, they'll know.'

'Around here, they'd just as soon not let you know anything.'

Coffin ignored this. 'And fingerprint everything here and at Page's place. If we find a print of hers here or one of his there, then I want to know.'

He walked away to his car, thinking of the strange man who had lived in this half-dead house, thinking too of Stella and glad that he still had her. Hang on to Stella, he told himself, for that is where life is.

It would be nice to know where Phoebe was, that was another worry at the bottom of his mind which sometimes came to the top. A few days off for a personal matter, she had said, but he hadn't believed that: she'd been working and wanted to come back with a big bone in her mouth to surprise him, that was her style. But time was running on. And prolonged silence was not like Phoebe, he would have expected a telephone message or a fax or sudden appearance; Phoebe went in for drama when she was in the mood, he remembered that well.

Stella was waiting for him in the foyer of the theatre; since it was a hot night she was wearing a thin, soft chiffon dress that looked pale and misty. Also exceedingly expensive, which he believed it to be. She had murmured that the designer, a famous name, had made a special price for her.

She greeted him with a kiss, did not mention that he was late and had kept her waiting, but said: 'You haven't shaved.'

'Sorry, I've been busy.'

There was a surge of people around for a moment, greeting Stella, nodding to him; when they'd gone, Stella said: 'You're having a bad time, aren't you?'

'You could say that. Shall we go in?'

'This is sympathy I'm offering.' She moved ahead of him. 'Let's go into the bar. I've ordered drinks, they'll be waiting at my table.' Stella had a special table in a corner which was always reserved for her. 'It's particularly good of me to be sympathetic considering that I've had Eden Brown ringing me up and talking to me about Phoebe Astley.'

'She shouldn't be bothering you.' He could see that she had ordered champagne which must be a good sign. There was no denying he would prefer to keep Stella and Phoebe apart in life and as subjects for conversation, but events seemed to be driving them together.

'Seems she's getting letters for Phoebe she can't send on because she doesn't know where to send them. Also bills. Lots of them apparently. Did you know Phoebe had bills?'

'We all have bills, they're a fact of life.' And Phoebe had given the impression of being hard up. 'I'm sorry it's worrying Eden and I'm sorry she's worrying you, but I don't see what I can do about it.'

He picked up the bottle of champagne, but the bar waiter, one of Max's sons-in-law, hurried forward to open it. Stella gave him one of her sweetest smiles and a marginally less sweet one for Coffin.

'I think you could.'

'No one worries about Phoebe. She can look after herself.'

'I hope you don't talk about me like that.'

'Certainly not.' He was getting into deep water here.

'Good. But I can look after myself too.'

He realized he could not win this battle and should not even be fighting it.

'How I talk about you has no connection with anything I might say about Phoebe Astley. I work with Phoebe, I am married to you. And as a matter of fact, I don't talk about you.'

'Oh.' He could see Stella considering that remark. The waiter had moved away and was smiling at them from a distance. He was clearly one of the ones that worshipped Stella.

'But I think about you. A lot.'

Stella smiled. 'Bless you.'

'Let's stop thinking about Phoebe Astley, and enjoy the champagne and then the play. What is it, by the way?'

'Beckett's *End Game* and then a short Pinter.'

'Ah.' He would have preferred a hearty comedy, but this was a student performance on which prizes and scholarships rested, and serious plays were what student performers always went for.

Stella looked at him with sympathy, she knew his tastes, and held out a hand. 'Hang on to me and I'll see you through the evening.'

He took her hand with pleasure. 'Being with you is all that I want.'

BUT EVEN AS HE SPOKE, Phoebe, eyes closed, was drifting, darkness around her. Pools of darkness moving into deeper darkness. The darkness seemed to move, it smelt.

ACROSS THE ROOM, Coffin was not pleased to see Geraldine Ducking, resplendent in her usual red for battle—velvet this time. He looked away quickly, but it was too late, she waved and started to come towards them.

'Damn!'

Stella turned round to look. 'Oh, Geraldine, good. I like her. How she dresses! That one must have cost her!'

Geraldine was smiling happily, refused any champagne, told Stella she looked a living dream, and said to Coffin, 'I hear you are in trouble.'

'So you've said before.' He thought she had been drinking, there was a glitter about her eyes, and although Geraldine was reputed to carry her drink well, everyone has their limits.

'You can't trust everyone, you know.'

'What does that mean?'

'Well, I'm not talking about Timpson…he's history. But what about your lovely aide, Phoebe Astley. I've heard she's got lost.'

Coffin didn't answer, he saw Stella looking at him gravely.

'I've also heard that she's got bills, needs money.'

Eden Brown again, he supposed, full of information and complaints.

He still did not answer but sipped his drink. 'No comment, I see,' said Geraldine. 'I note that and draw my own conclusions.'

She looked so pleased with herself that Coffin felt a strong desire to deflate her. 'You are wasting your time, Phoebe Astley is working under my supervision.' And God help me, I hope I am right; come back quick, Phoebe.

Geraldine seemed prepared to go on. 'I don't believe a word of it.'

He shrugged. 'Believe what you wish, Geraldine, but print anything and I'll get an injunction to stop you publishing. Won't do you any good, Geraldine.'

'And I admired you, and was going to do an article on your wonderful career,' said Geraldine sorrowfully. 'I'm a working woman and have to get my stories.'

'I'm not one.'

Stella followed Geraldine's departure with interested eyes. 'She was drunk, I think. I've never seen Geraldine that way before. What have you done to her?'

'Nothing. Nothing to her and nothing to Phoebe. I wish she'd leave me alone.'

'You are touchy.'

'At the moment, yes. Forgive me, I don't want to spoil your evening.'

'Is it the murders?'

'In part. Four deaths, Stella, and a royal visit hanging over me.' He didn't tell her about the other thing, because in the present circumstances, it might come to nothing. Lady Coffin, he would like to be able to call her that, let her wear a glory he had given her.

'Are all four deaths connected?'

'It has to be so,' he said with sad conviction.

'But could one person do all four murders?'

'This one could.' Faceless, nameless killer but vicious. 'The different ways of killing are unusual, murderers usually stick to a formula, but this killer is exceptional. Each murder is a new murder to him, and not a repetition. He's not a serial killer, not a mass murderer, not a man obsessed. And that means the motive is solid and real: self preservation, and/or money. This killer does not want to be caught, he is not sending out tacit pleas: Catch me, like some of them. This is a case of personal survival, and no one else considered.' He added thoughtfully, 'He may have had some help, though.'

Stella said: 'What makes you think that?'

'I'm guessing. But I guess that Albert Waters gave some help, possibly without realizing exactly what he was doing. But he did realize when Agnes Page was identified as the body on the fire, and that was when he became so frightened that he was sick, and when he telephoned me. And that was why he was killed.'

THE FIRST WARNING bell for the performance rang: Five minutes, ladies and gentlemen, please take your seats, but Stella did not move.

Coffin stood up. 'Come on, we'd better move.'

Still Stella remained seated. 'They can't start without me, I'm one of the judges... Are you really in trouble, as Geraldine said?'

'She's trouble,' said Coffin with conviction.

'No, but what about you?'

He put his arm under her elbow to draw her to her feet. Darling, darling Stella, her flesh felt cool and sweet.

'I am in a guerrilla war,' he said. 'With little knots of enemies.'

'Will they win?'

'No, you don't win a guerrilla war unless a very strong army comes in to help you, and that won't happen.'

At least, he trusted not. The Home Office, his police committee, some hostile politicians, now that was an army, but, he had to hope it kept out.

'Let's go in, love.'

Stella smiled at him, put her head up high, and walked steadily forward. A little rustle of applause greeted them.

To his surprise, he enjoyed the performance; the students were so keen, so anxious to perform well, and—he had to admit it—so talented, that it would have been a stony heart that did not rejoice with them.

The air conditioning was on high, but it was still hot in the auditorium. Geraldine Ducking was seated two rows behind them, and two rows behind her was where Eden Brown was sitting. She had come because she needed company and a theatre full of people seemed about all she could get at the moment. A seat away was Ellie Farmer and next to her was her friend and fellow hoofer, Phyllis Archer. The girls had had a good evening so they felt happy: they had said, good evening, to Stella Pinero, caught the producer's eye, had a free drink of champagne at whose providing they did not know, but not their own, and found the Beckett play puzzling but had enjoyed the Pinter. The playwright was present in the theatre and although they had not managed to speak to him, they felt lustre had been shed upon them.

They managed to smile and wave at Stella as she left with her husband which gave them pleasure too. Stella had announced the prizewinners Best Actor and Best Actress for the Year at the drama school, then handed over the medals. 'Did it beautifully, didn't she?' said Ellie. 'But she always does. Suppose she won all the prizes herself once?'

'No, I've heard she came in through repertory theatre when there still was one, but she had star quality.' Phyllis admired Stella too, but liked to get her facts right.

On their way out, they found that Eden Brown had somehow become attached to them; they accepted her company easily and with a smile. 'Let's go into the bar to have a drink,' said Ellie, 'although the prices have gone up, haven't you noticed? That Max is getting a bit above himself.'

'On me,' said Eden, buying her place with them.

They all looked around to see who was there, no one they knew, but Geraldine Ducking was drinking at the bar where she made room in a companionable way.

So that made four of them, and Ellie thought that was a nice little group and although she looked around hopefully for the producer or the odd critic or Stella, she settled down, as did Phyllis, to enjoy their post-performance drinks. 'Boiling in there, wasn't it? Needn't have worn a wrap.'

John Coffin and Stella walked home in a friendly silence. They too were hot. 'Shall we go for a walk by the river?' Stella asked, taking his arm.

'No, home I think.' There might be a message from Archie Young. Whatever there was to know, he wanted to know it tonight.

Stella yawned. 'Yes, I'm tired. Think you're right.'

The cat and the dog were both on patrol outside the door of Coffin's tower, it had been a hot evening for them too, but they were now ready to settle down for the night.

There was a message for the chief commander, it had come through on his fax and was backed up by a spoken message on the answerphone.

'Young here, sir. A quick flash on the fingerprints... None of his in Page's place, but hers are all over his house. Don't know what that means, but there it is. I knew you'd want to know.'

Stella looked at him, her curiosity showing. 'So what does it mean? Anything or nothing?'

'Ask yourself: who is likely to have been in his house, made free with everything in it, left prints everywhere and not worried. She wasn't a social worker or a nurse, not that he needed either as far as I could see. So what was she to him?'

Stella considered what she knew of Albert Waters. 'Not his wife or his mistress.'

'So what's left? Someone close, his daughter? We can check... Maybe he burnt his own daughter's body on that funeral pyre without knowing it. That was why he was sick.'

THE LITTLE PARTY in the bar stayed until Max started to close up. It was still very hot, hotter than ever perhaps, but they were in a jolly mood as Geraldine had been generous with her drinks. And Phyllis wondered if there was the chance of some publicity from her. An article? Or even just a mention of a talented young dancer met one evening in the theatre. Or two young talented dancers; she was not selfish and would not grudge Ellie her share.

'Let's go for a walk by the river to cool down. There's one spot where the old Western Canal joins the Thames where you can pretend that you are in Venice.'

'Never been to Venice,' said Eden Brown. 'I think I'd better get home.' She had drunk more than she usually did, with a headache beginning to brew behind her eyes.

'Not been to Venice either, but I've seen pictures. You can imagine.' Phyllis was always imagining places and events; if she ever got an Oscar, or married a millionaire and went to choose clothes in Paris, she would have been there already in her mind many times. She linked her arm in Eden's and drew her along. Ellie did the same with Geraldine, and then she put her arm through Phyllis's.

We must make a nice group, strolling along like on the deck of a great liner, she thought, because she too had her imagination as a prop. People might wonder who we are. Pity there's no camera around.

As they got closer to the river, they quietened down under the influence of the still dark waters.

At last they looked down where it lapped at their feet. The tidal river had deposited a burden at the water's muddy edge.

It took them a minute to understand what they were staring at, then Eden began to scream.

TEN

Eden was screaming and screaming. Geraldine gripped her arm. 'Shut her up,' she said fiercely. 'Give her a slap.' She raised her own arm.

'Whoa there.' Ellie put up a hand. 'She's upset, you don't have to commit battery. I don't like the look of it myself.' She put her arm round Eden. 'Hush dear, turn your face away. Or close your eyes... Is it a head?'

'It is.' Geraldine's voice was grim. 'It's a head, all right.'

Phyllis was staring down, her face was very pale. 'I hope it's no one I knew.'

'How could it be?' asked Ellie.

'It's Phoebe,' said Eden. Her voice was coming in little gasps now as if breathing was difficult. 'I know who it is, it has to be her, it's Phoebe.'

Phyllis was white, the colour of her lips and eyes standing out, she had overdone the make-up and now looked as if she had had a clown face. 'How can you possibly tell? Have you looked? Really looked? You can hardly tell it *is* a face.'

'We have to tell the police.' Geraldine had a grip on herself. 'The sooner it is done the better.' She pulled her mobile phone out of her shoulder bag. She felt a strong temptation to dial the police emergency number and then leave the others to it, but she was a journalist, and Ellie and Phyllis would not fail to mention she had been there. She looked at them. 'We could all go, we needn't stay, I could just dial and report without saying who I was. Or mentioning any of you.'

Ellie shook her head. 'My dad's a policeman. We couldn't do that. Besides, I don't think Eden can walk at the moment, she's going to need driving home.' Eden was leaning heavily against Ellie, her eyes closed, she was silent now except for a small moan whenever Ellie moved. 'Anyway, she thinks it's this Phoebe, and she's going to say that.'

'It can't be Phoebe Astley, but all right, I'll ring straight through to the local station, they know me there. A car will come.' She shrugged. 'You can all go if you like, I daresay Eden could manage if you help her, I'll deal with it.'

'I'm tempted,' said Ellie who seemed to be everyone's spokesperson, 'but we will have to talk to them sometime, and it might as well be now; they are bound to ask and wonder what you were doing down here on your own.'

'The police have long since given up asking what I'm up to.' Geraldine perched herself on a broken bit of wall. 'But please yourself.' She searched in her bag. 'Sit down while I get on with it. Smoke, anyone?'

A patrol car must have been close at hand because before her first cigarette was finished, there were flashing lights at the end of the road, and a patrol car arrived in relative silence.

They were all quiet now, even Eden. Geraldine walked across to the car, murmured a few words, then she pointed to the water. 'Take a look.'

Both the constables got out of the car to stroll. 'You sure what you've seen, ladies?'

'Oh, come on.' Ellie wasn't standing for any patronage. 'What do you think we are?'

'I know who it is.' Eden stirred, stood up straight and spoke out. 'It's Phoebe Astley.'

'Is it now?' The first policeman was staring into the water. 'You'll have to tell us about that, miss, and why you think so... It's a head all right, but I wouldn't care to say who it was.' Or sex, or even what, he told himself. If it was my mother down there, I don't think I'd know her, that's hardly a face.

Swollen, the flesh dark and torn, the hair matted about the face like seaweed, only the forehead and the nose looked human.

'It's Phoebe Astley. You'll have to tell him. He got her to live with me, I didn't know at first but I guessed. She was on a job for him.'

'What are we talking about, miss?' The constable kept his voice polite because he could see she was under pressure. 'Who do we have to tell?' He turned to the other man. 'Get on the radio, Joe, and report this. We need help.'

'John Coffin, your boss... He knows her. There was something wrong with her, I could smell it; he couldn't, he was too close to her. But she was all at sixes and sevens, I'm that way myself so I could tell in her. That's why she went away.'

At the mention of the chief commander's name, the constable put out a hand. 'Stop there, miss. You'll have to tell all this to someone else. All I'm doing is reporting the finding of a head. You save that up for later.'

'There's too much death about,' said Eden. 'I'm frightened it will be me next, I'm so close, you see—too close. I'm bound to get hit next.'

'I'll take her home,' said Geraldine, 'I'll run us all home, my car is just down the road.' She showed him her press card. 'I'm well known, that's my address.'

The young policeman was genuinely regretful, he felt sorry for Eden, for Ellie and for Phyllis, who hadn't said a word but who looked sicker with every minute.

'Am I imagining it?' Phyllis broke her silence with sudden urgent speech. 'Can you smell a dead smell? I can. It's coming up from the water, isn't it?'

'Just the usual Thames smell,' said the constable, 'it's been a hot day, things do go off.' It was an unfortunate remark which he regretted as he saw Phyllis heave. 'Stand away from the river,' he added hastily. 'Come and sit in the car.' But that too, was perhaps not the thing to say.

'Too late,' said Geraldine, hastening to the side of the girl, 'You've done your bit.' If she had been full of wine when they left the theatre bar, she was dead sober now. 'Come on, love, here's a tissue to wipe your face.' She let her fury show. 'My God, when's that other car coming so we can get this over with.' She wished they had never come to the river to find this gruesome object. Death ought to be tucked away and not show its awful face. It was probably some poor suicide who deserved better than being gaped at by all of them. There was absolutely no point dwelling on any other possibility. 'Oh, here's the cavalry,' she said as another police car drew up.

'The sergeant is here now, miss.'

The CID had arrived: one sergeant, and one woman detective, the radio message having conveyed the news that there were four women involved as witnesses, one of whom was hysterical.

You'd have to say two now, thought the patrol man, if not three. No, you could hardly call Geraldine Ducking hysterical; angry, yes. He had taken note of her name and remembered that he read her column when he bought a paper and had finished the sports news. She had a wicked pen.

He left the CID sergeant taking all the particulars while he himself sped away with his companion, having received another call.

'Fast off, Joe,' he said. He was glad to be gone, there were things you didn't want to get mixed up with, especially with how things were with the Second City force at the moment, with all the rumours flying round. He wondered how the chief commander was sleeping?

'I think I'll forget that I heard about this Phoebe woman,' he told himself with a yawn. 'Just never took it in. Not the sort of remark to remember.'

But of course, he did remember and considered it as the night went on and his tour of duty came to an end. Phoebe

Astley and the chief commander? Well, the man had always had a reputation.

GERALDINE DROVE them all home, depositing Ellie and Phyllis at their different lodgings first, and then taking Eden back to her apartment. She parked the car. 'I'm coming up with you. You're not fit to be on your own just yet.'

Eden protested: 'Phyllis is worse than I am, she was sick, I wasn't.'

'Phyllis was sick, yes, but I don't know about worse... I'll see you to bed. Got any sleeping tablets? Right, take two with a glass of hot milk.'

Eden didn't have any milk, hot or cold, she was on a permanent starvation diet, but Geraldine reckoned orange juice would do.

She watched while Eden got undressed and into bed. 'What's this with you and Phoebe Astley?' Whom she also knew but did not intend to say so. 'And John Coffin?'

Eden drank the orange juice; it had gone stale but she could not resist Geraldine's firm gaze... I'd take poison if that woman gave it to me, she thought, the way I am at the moment and the way she is. 'Just one of those things. Forget I said it.'

'Is it likely? I'm a journalist, remember?'

'Then I shouldn't have said it. I was shocked, that's all. Of course it wasn't Phoebe down there.'

'You seemed pretty sure at the time.'

'I was wrong. Still a bit drunk. You don't think it was Phoebe?'

There was a pause while Geraldine thought about it. 'No,' she said, 'I don't.'

'I'm all right now, you can go.'

'That's not very polite.'

Eden closed her eyes. She did not feel polite, she wanted to be left alone. Either that, or to talk her head off.

'You want to talk, I can tell.'

'He put her into my apartment. I didn't realize that at first, she seemed a nice woman who was looking for somewhere to live. She said she was a businesswoman, in public relations. But later I realized she was a policewoman, then I thought he'd put her there to protect me.'

'Why?'

Eden ignored this question. 'Now I'm not sure. She was working all right, but on what? And she was jumpy, nervous.'

Geraldine said: 'You're the one that's nervous. Why were you nervous and needing protection?'

'All right, I'll say: Agnes Page was a friend. Make what you like of that, I'm not saying more.' The sedative was beginning to take hold, her eyes closed.

'Come on, you can't leave it there.'

Eden gave a small, private laugh. 'I can, but I will say that I began to wonder about her, about Miss Phoebe Astley... Letters,' she said dreamily. 'I know a bill when I see one, unpaid too. I can smell them. I began to wonder if she was after money, blackmailing someone.'

'Who?'

Eden let her eyelids drop again. 'Who? Who is there? You name someone.' Geraldine allowed herself an answer. There was John Coffin, already deep in trouble.

What was that word when you were thinking rubbish? Crud.

THE NIGHT HAD PASSED quietly and comfortably in St Luke's Mansions in that tower which Stella as well as her husband now thought of as home. It had taken her some time to give up her own apartment, a dual life with two places to live in suited her very well in some ways, but she had come to realize that if she wanted this late marriage to work then she had to give ground. He was not going to, it hadn't entered his head to move to her place, so she had to be the one.

But once done, she found to her pleasure that it made her happy. She liked the feeling that night and morning, if at no other time (he was a hard man to hold to a schedule), they would be together. It was sometimes her turn to be absent, when she was filming abroad or travelling to raise funds for St Luke's theatre. You had to work hard to stay in the same place in the present climate, and since Coffin's lovely sister Letty Bingham had run into financial problems, it had been up to Stella to see the funding did not dry up. She had a large theatre in the old church of St Luke's, she had the heavy responsibility of the fledgling drama school looking to her for guidance and support. But she was happy, she enjoyed it, and knew she was a lucky woman.

Stella woke up to see the gleaming green eyes of Tiddles the cat staring into her own. The smell of coffee floated up the stairs, she stroked the cat, who was sitting on her chest, and luxuriated in the knowledge that soon a tray of breakfast would be coming up the stairs. Coffin knew how to manage an elegant breakfast: fruit juice, coffee and hot toast. You could train husbands as well as cats. In fact, better, because cats could be remarkably resistant when it suited them, but husbands liked to please. What a splendid thing sex was, thought Stella leaning back on her pillows, it did oil the wheels.

Then she remembered their conversation of last night; she was happy—her life, in spite of dips here and there, was going well—but her husband's life, to which she was now joined, was not so easy.

'I can't be happy just on my own now, puss. If he's worried then somehow I am too. I suppose at last I'm really married.' She considered whether she liked that thought or not; once she would have been through the door and over the hills and far away at any such notion, but not now. If it was part of what made a marriage, then she accepted it.

'I feel almost holy, puss, I don't believe I'll ever be wicked again.'

She began to laugh, her sense of self mockery getting the better of her. 'Now that was a nice little scene I built up there, puss. Straight out of a vintage Bette Davis film: the bad girl reforms. I shouldn't do it, men really are more decent than women.'

The telephone rang and was answered downstairs. When her breakfast failed to appear, she got up, belted on her dressing gown and went to see what was happening.

John Coffin looked up at her as she came into the kitchen, he was still holding the receiver but had stopped talking.

'What is it?'

'Oh, just the usual morning report.' He put the telephone down. 'Let me pour you some coffee.'

'I always worry when you are so polite in the morning.' Stella sat herself where she could see out of the window into the sky, it was still hot with the sky a hard blue, but the clouds were massing. A storm before evening, she told herself. 'You are usually gruffer.' She let him pour her some coffee while she buttered a piece of toast. He'd burnt that a bit, which was more normal. 'Is there anything fresh to worry about?'

'Four unsolved murders, a royal visit and corruption in the force, that's enough, surely?'

'But you are getting somewhere? The fingerprints that show Agnes had been at Albert's house, been there a lot.'

'She was his daughter, I think. But where that leads to, isn't clear.'

'It goes somewhere,' said Stella, spreading honey on her toast, covering the burnt bits with a thick layer and crunching through it. He looked at her with liking and love, thinking that those were not always the same thing and how fortunate a man he was to love someone that he liked. 'And you will sort it out.'

'Thank you for that vote of confidence.' He sat down to drink black coffee. He picked up the paper to study the day's headlines, restlessly aware that the murders in the Second City were still getting the screaming big black banners. And there was another little story, neatly placed beside it but no comment, about the illness of DCI Timpson who was retiring from the case.

He recognized the breath of wind that might turn into a hurricane. He folded the paper.

'Anything there?'

'Nothing.'

Stella never read the papers, other than *The Stage,* except for reviews of plays she was either performing in or interested in.

'Nothing about last night?'

'Didn't see it.'

'Probably went to press too soon. I saw Andy Jacobs there, he'll give us a piece but he's very slow. He'll get it in tomorrow. And there will be the Sundays if we're lucky, they usually cover the prizes—I hope so, it does cheer up the student body.'

'I'm off.' He kissed the top of her head. 'And you needn't keep talking just to cheer me up. I shall survive, I always have before.'

Criticism from his police committee, snide remarks from the press, an attack from the local MP, he had come through them all.

This time, he just might not.

Archie Young had let him know on the telephone that three high rankers were threatening to resign.

The guerrilla warfare was beginning to escalate. Hotter and hotter the fire would burn, just like the fire that had burned up Agnes Page.

He had better get down to his headquarters straight away. No Sir John and Lady Coffin, but an ex-copper on a retirement pension and, a last ignoble thought, with Stella still in star roles and earning in gold.

That would be hard to bear. It had to be admitted: men are nastier than women.

AS HE DROVE to the headquarters, he thought about what he had not told Stella. That name he did not want to mention. He thought about Phoebe.

I put her to this affair like a cat to watch a rat-hole, and she disappeared. With an excuse, believe it if you could, and I haven't seen her or heard from her.

Gone to join the rats, I thought.

And now it has to be that damned woman Eden Brown who calls out her name, and Geraldine Ducking is there.

He had arranged to meet Archie Young in his office on his arrival, but the speed with which Archie appeared as he drove into his parking spot showed him the state of the game.

He nodded as he locked the car. 'Looking for me?'

'I thought a quick word, now...on the quiet.'

'Go on.'

'It's the finding of the head in the river...'

'Yes, you told me. It was seen by a group of women of whom Eden Brown was one. A coincidence that I don't like, but I don't want to be paranoid.' Although he thought he was getting that way. 'And I regret that Geraldine Ducking was there. So?'

'There can't be any positive identification of the head just from looking at it,' said the superintendent. 'But Eden Brown shouted out that it was Phoebe Astley; God knows why, she couldn't possibly be sure unless she's got some information we don't have.'

'Where is she now?'

'Under sedation, damn her. But of course what she said went round with the speed of light. Not slowed down by Ducking.'

'She hasn't printed anything?'

'Only because I kept her under questioning all night. She's shouting for her lawyer, for her editor, for the world...you're included. Top of the list, in fact.'

'I hope you handled her with care?'

'With silk gloves. Except for being so slow in processing what she had to say, she can't complain. She will, of course. But I didn't think you'd want the identification all over the papers.'

'Is there any reason to connect this new body with the other four?' Four was enough to be going on with, surely? 'Bodies do turn up in the Thames; not all murder victims, there's suicide, accident. Why should it be Phoebe?'

'You can't even be sure of the sex or age,' said the superintendent. 'Not for certain, not just by looking... All the same, I think it is the head of a woman.'

'I'm coming to the incident room.'

'Thought you would, sir. They're expecting you.'

'Thanks for the warning, I take it it was one?' Young merely grunted in reply. 'Who's there?'

'The usual team: Jeavons and Eliot and Amy Passant—she's doing the forensics.'

The names were known to John Coffin, but he did not know the officers in person. Well, they were part of a new, highly skilled intake, good at their jobs, he hoped, but so far faceless to him.

'None of them threatening to resign, I take it?' Too young, too ambitious. 'Name me some names, please.'

'I haven't spoken to any of those named,' said Archie Young. 'But I've heard that Eddie Syres, Tom Gambit, and Luke Franks are the ones.'

The old troublemakers, all friends of Teddy Timpson, all near to retiring age. One small unit in the guerrilla war had identified itself and joined the war against him.

'Will they actually go, though? What have you heard on that?'

Archie Young shrugged.

So he thought they would, Coffin decided. 'I could take the initiative, and have a purge on my own account.'

Young looked alarmed. 'You're not serious?'

'I wish I was, but no. I'll step canny.'

'I hope so.'

There was a note in Archie Young's voice that alerted Coffin to more trouble. He's a natural actor, Stella had said once—very expressive voice.

'What is it now, Archie?' They were very close to the door of the incident room. It had been set up in one of the new buildings, and the suite of rooms had been specially created under Coffin's guidance. He had a lot of experience of what you needed when taking on a major investigation and this was both major and multiple; the burnt body of Agnes Page, the stabbing of Albert Waters, and behind it the deaths of Felix Henbit and Mark Pittsy. All linked, he was sure, with the laundering of dirty money in the shops and banks of the Second City.

Mary Henbit was missing, and Phoebe Astley's headless body might be floating in the Thames. He resisted that thought with energy, Phoebe must be alive. He insisted on it. Survive, Phoebe, he said fiercely but silently, our pasts are too entwined for you to go down without taking me with you.

'Can I have a private word with you, sir, before we go in? It's important.'

Coffin had a moment of dreadful insight. 'Not you too, Archie?' he said wearily. 'If you're saying you are resigning too…'

'No, it's not me. You.'

'Now you have halted me. What about me?'

'There's a rumour going around that you have been selling information, that you are short of money because of your sister's bankruptcy.'

'Letty is not bankrupt.'

'It's said she's near it and that puts you and your wife in Queer Street.'

'Where's this coming from? Who says it?'

'It's all over the place. Syres may have started it, he was the first I heard named as saying it was one of his reasons for going. It's canteen talk, sir.'

They were standing in the small courtyard before the Prescott Building, which was the new block named after one of the earliest commissioners of the police force set up by Sir Robert Peel. He had not been a great policeman or great man, but he had been famous for his humane handling of both police officers and criminals—he deserved to be remembered. Coffin had chosen the name himself to ward off the suggestion that the building, already showing signs of its age, although so new, would be named after him. He hadn't wanted to look across to the John Coffin Building every morning of his life.

'It's rubbish, of course.'

'I know that, sir, you don't have to tell me.'

No, Archie Young was loyal, but he had his moment of doubt, Coffin sensed it, even Archie, whom he counted as a friend.

It was a mark of how dirty the game was going to be. But with a surge of excitement, it also told him how close he must be to getting the right answers.

'Who else is saying it?'

'Geraldine Ducking let out that she's heard it. No one's using it, but they will.' After a pause, he added reluctantly: 'I thought I heard Jim Eliot say something too.'

The media would not use it yet, or not directly, but sliding comments and bits of gossip would appear in the newspapers, so that people put two and two together and thought how clever they were. And when he resigned, as it must be intended he should do, then everyone could say: I told you so.

Coffin stood there, thinking. I must be close to the killer:

I don't accuse the banks or bankers, they have nice legal ways of doing you in, this must be a more personal matter between me and a highly personal killer. This murderer is only concerned with himself.

Damn Geraldine... Or was it good Geraldine, who might be doing him a service by alerting him?

'You don't think it started with her? That she let it out to Syres?'

'I wouldn't have thought so, sir. I don't see her talking to Syres...and I thought she liked you. Said some very nice things about you in her column.'

'Yes.' He too had thought Geraldine liked him and admired Stella, but never trust a journalist. He fought the reaction. He had had enough ignoble thoughts for one morning. 'Where is she now?'

'Drinking coffee in my room. I kept her there. One way and another, I thought you'd want to talk to her.'

'So she's been here all night?'

'Not all the time, no. She drove the other two women who found the head home, together with the Eden woman, and then came back here. She'd sobered up enough by then to think about work. I gather that she'd had quite a bit to drink earlier.'

'I saw her at the theatre; I was there myself with Stella, but I didn't notice her drinking.'

'I gather it was later, with the other young women; it was the effect of the Beckett play, they said.'

'I'll see her.'

'She'll want something in exchange for anything she may tell you.'

'Have to think about it.' He straightened his shoulders. 'I'll go to the incident room first. What's new there?'

Whatever there is, they won't want to say, thought Archie Young. They are in a very possessive mood down there at the moment.

'And where is the head?'

'In the university pathology lab. We got Professor Evans out of bed to look at it… He said it was human and recently dead, but it has been in the water over a week, possibly nearer two, and he wouldn't say more. Couldn't. But he has promised to work on it fast, to see if he can see any cause of death and any identification marks. There won't be, of course: we should be so lucky.'

'You're a cynic and a depressant,' said Coffin, suddenly feeling amazingly cheerful. 'I'll see what's going on with Jeavons and Co, and then I will talk to Geraldine. Don't let her escape.'

No one looked up as the two of them went into the incident room which was creating its noise and action. But there were pools of silence, one of which was where Sergeant Jeavons was sitting studying notes of an interview, every so often throwing a remark to the man at the desk opposite him. 'That's Eliot,' said Archie Young quietly.

'I remember him now.' Cocky bastard, but clever, no doubt about that, and an able detective. For which, no doubt, one ought to forgive him much. But not too much, reflected the chief commander. He recalled that the young man's father was the chief constable of a provincial force, and that the son had ambitions.

Not my job, though, he said to himself. Or not yet, and you aren't helping anyone else to it either.

Amy Passant, the forensic expert, whom he knew from a previous case or two, was a sturdy young woman with big beautiful blue eyes. Her nickname, which she ignored, was Bluebell. She was intent on a computer screen which was lined with files of figures; she touched a button, and a graph appeared, she seemed deeply absorbed, but she looked up at Coffin and smiled.

'Thought it was you, sir.'

'Got anything for me?'

'Nothing special yet, I'm working on the Page-Waters case. They certainly knew each other well, traces of her all over the place.' Her eyes looked into the distance. 'I'd like to compare their blood groups... Not my job, of course.'

'They're related?'

'Yeah...kin.'

'Father and daughter, I think.'

'Yeah,' Amy said.

Jeavons and Eliot, alerted, walked over to them. For a moment, Coffin ignored them, then he said, 'So what's this about the head in the river? Any of you seen it?'

Jeavons spoke first. 'No, sir, saw no need.'

'I went down to the path lab, took a look,' said Amy, unexpectedly. 'When I heard it might be Phoebe Astley. I knew Phoebe, we worked together for a bit in the Met.'

Coffin was surprised. 'Did you?'

'Did a college course in Wembley together.'

'So what did you make of it?'

Amy shrugged. 'Couldn't tell. You wouldn't have known if it was your own mother the way the face was.'

'I've been told the face was badly damaged.'

'Hit something hard. After death, they were saying. A ship's propeller, something like that, plenty of stuff around in the river. For what it's worth, I don't think it's Phoebe Astley.'

John Coffin did not answer. No one else spoke. But he could see them looking at him. Speculation about his relationship with Phoebe must be running wild. He could imagine the shrugs and sly comments. He had always come in for criticism from outside as too radical, too popular, but within the Second City, within the force of which he was head, he had been respected and even liked by some officers at some times. But now all this was ebbing away. Times were changing.

He walked across the room towards Jeavons. Progress on the Henbit-Pittsy deaths had almost come to a halt. Routine checks and inquiries were still going on but what was coming in was trivial. Or at least it seemed so, although he had to remind himself that it was the trivial detail that was often important.

Only in the search for Mary Henbit was there development.

Jeavons said: 'A neighbour who saw Mary after Felix's death said that she had told Mary she ought to go away for a break and Mary had said she had an old schoolfriend who made the same suggestion and she was going with her. We're following that lead up. The schoolfriend may be the one called Alice Fraser who sent flowers and a card to Mary when she heard about Felix, we traced her address through the florist. She lives in Devon, in Teignmouth.'

'So what are you doing about it?'

'The local police are dealing with it.' He saw the look on the chief commander's face and put the right interpretation on it. 'If he gets some hard information then I will go down myself.'

Mary Henbit might be a route forward on the case, she might know something helpful, or she might not, but just to find her would be something.

Coffin allowed himself to wonder for a few minutes, what, if anything, Felix might have told her about his work: about Agnes Page, about Albert Waters or some other detail about the money laundering and the personage who was arranging it in the Second City and who must be the killer.

He did not believe there was more than one mind at work, profit and self protection was the motive and had been all along: this criminal was mercenary and ruthless.

He made a quick decision. 'Let Ducking go. I'll see her later. If I need to.'

Then he turned back to work, there was plenty to do, he had not been so attentive to routine matters lately as he should have been. To his surprise he worked well and fast. The telephone was quiet, so that it startled him when it rang.

Jeavons wanted to speak to him, he was polite and eager:

'I've heard from Devon, sir. The mother of Mary Henbit's friend, Mrs Baker—the other girl is married and the husband is with them on the trip. Mrs Baker said Mary telephoned and told her daughter she would like to come on the trip and would meet them in Exeter. She doesn't know more, it was left a bit vague, but Mary was definitely coming to Exeter.'

'So where are they?'

'Touring, but the mother knows the route they planned to take through Devon and into Cornwall; she says her daughter rings up sometimes and she will tell her we want to locate Mary. I'm going to Devon myself so that I can go straight to interview Mary.'

'Good. I am beginning to think she is aware that she knows something dangerous and is keeping out of the way on purpose.' And I couldn't blame her for that with the mortality rate what it is round here at the moment.

Perhaps she knew and was in touch with someone in the Second City. Nothing surprising in that, and there were always the newspapers which had been liberal with details and speculation. He had a pile of cuttings on his desk this minute which did not make happy reading.

'Let me know at once when you make contact.'

'Will do, sir. I'm on my way. The mother said her daughter might telephone this evening—it was her usual time—so if I'm speedy, then I can talk to her myself. And with luck to Mary Henbit.'

'Don't frighten her, but let her know that I'd like to see her. We needn't interrupt her holiday.' Although he would do, ruthlessly, if it seemed right. Nothing to be gained at this stage by not being direct.

And he still believed that she knew something about the circumstances of her husband's death.

In fact, he wanted to question Mary Henbit closely. It should have been done earlier, but then they had all wanted to spare her more pain. But some pains are necessary to give birth to the truth.

He returned to his papers, many of which concerned the royal visit, but his mind was not on the exact itinerary that the Queen would follow, nor the lunch that she would be taking with Sir Alfred in his new university building, as yet not finished but which Her Majesty would nevertheless be opening on that day.

He was not invited to that lunch, although the Queen would be visiting his headquarters and he would be presented at a reception beforehand. Stella got a look in here too, which was not always the case with wives, but Stella was special. It was rumoured that the Queen herself had watched her last TV series. Had it videoed, anyway.

His mind went back to the committee which had appointed Phoebe. He could see them now as they sat round the big table. All faces he knew, some well, some less well, all people whose judgement he had trusted: Sir Ferdie, plump and dapper; Jane Frobisher, her eyes hooded; Professor Edna Halliday—an old friend, I'd trust Edna anywhere, but of course, she has been ill. Geraldine Ducking, attractive and forceful, she was being tricky. Chief Inspector Taylour, no problem there, surely. Superintendent Fraser he hardly knew but he had impressive credentials and did not live anywhere near the Second City. Finally, there was Teddy Timpson, but he had been dealt with.

So why his unease?

There was an answer to that which he should have thought of before; it was buried inside himself and derived from the way he ran his machine.

He delegated, he had to in order to survive.

This committee to appoint Phoebe Astley with a new appointment and also a covert task had been put together by Chief Inspector Timpson.

Coffin had asked him to put forward a list of suitable names from which he then chose the ones that suited him best, being careful, or so he had thought, to choose those who would go for Phoebe.

It was a political act, but perhaps Timpson had been playing politics too. Perhaps he had slipped in a person or two of his own choice. Or someone who had paid him to do so.

Which meant that either Timpson or an anonymous other had speculated about Phoebe's role.

HE THOUGHT about it as he worked on, he had few appointments that day so it was desk work, and when Archie Young dropped in on a routine matter, he said: 'Who would you trust most in the CID at the moment?'

Young had his own questions. 'To do a good job or to keep his mouth shut?'

'Both.'

'If you really want to be safe, then there's me.' He didn't say: And only me, but it sounded like it.

Coffin smiled. 'Friend to friend?'

'Right, and if it turns out a libel or GBH job, I shall expect you to stand behind me.'

'We'll be in the dock together,' Coffin promised him. He went to his cupboard where he kept hospitality supplies and drew out his own special bottle of whisky which Letty had kept him supplied with in the days of her wealth. He had but two bottles left so he hoped sister Letty got rich again soon. He had a certain confidence in this: her telephone calls lately had been very cheerful and there had been some mention of popping over to Rome to see her favourite couturier.

'Let's drink on it.'

As he poured the whisky, observing with pleasure the subtle peaty brown suggesting the land from which it had come, neatly bottled, he lowered his voice and told Archie, friend to friend, as agreed, what he wanted.

'All of them?' Archie was surprised, his thick eyebrows went up.

'It might not be such a bad idea, but no, not all. Concentrate on...' he paused, then lowered his voice still further before he spoke.

Archie raised his eyebrows again. 'OK, I'll keep it discreet.' What a pity he would not be able to tell even his wife. He did not tell Alison everything, but since he regarded her, with reason, as being able to see further into the wood than he himself, he valued her judgement. 'That's a hot couple to take on.'

'Concentrate on those two, but don't forget the others, I may have been stupid.'

Archie Young let the whisky warm his soul. Sir Alfred Rome, what a hard nut to crack... And the other one, well, well, he could but do his best.

'Not circles I have moved in,' he said.

'I don't want you to move in them, Archie. Just dig them up.'

'You could really do it best yourself.' The whisky was making the superintendent bold.

Coffin was silent. He couldn't say what he felt—that somehow the figure of Phoebe stood in his way.

They finished their drinks, did not take a second one, and Archie Young prepared to go; Coffin really needed help on this one, but he wouldn't have it, he was on his own.

'Jane Frobisher has expensive tastes and may need money, Sir Alfred may have a bit on the side, Edna Halliday might have had one lover too many, and as for Ducking...'

'Don't be too coarse, Archie.'

'Drives you to it. No, don't worry, I'll be good.'

Archie Young smiled, he passed his hand over his eyebrows, which now seemed permanently raised.

AFTER HE HAD GONE, Coffin stood looking out of his window. He was thinking of Phoebe Astley. What did she mean to him now? What had she meant in the past?

He thought about that past: he was not proud of it. Phoebe had played her part in one of his more rocky phases when his career might have gone down in the abyss. In that period, he had found support from Phoebe. She might not have said much but she had made him feel his career was worth saving. She had been a mate. And a damned good detective.

Sex had come into it, but only briefly. Somehow, between the two of them, it hadn't worked. His fault probably, a memory had always been there in the back of his mind.

He didn't want to think Phoebe was dead, dead because of a case in which he had involved her.

He remembered that last sight of her at Geraldine's party when her face had looked flushed and slightly swollen. There had been something wrong with her then which he had not paid attention to.

Damn it, Phoebe, be alive still. For my sake. I don't love you, I never did, but you are important to me. As I think I am to you.

Stella wouldn't mind that, would she?

He felt sacrificial, willing to do anything to keep two women happy. He poured himself another small measure of whisky, feeling like the young Queen Victoria: I will be good.

But his life always veered between tragedy and comedy—farce even.

Even as high-flown feelings surged through him, of doing this and not doing that, the door opened and his secretary, the new one, appeared with a flustered and anxious face.

'Sir, there's a dog in a taxi downstairs for you.'

In no time at all, Bob was in his room, with a message from Stella tied round his neck and his taxi fare waiting to be paid.

'The driver says he charges extra for dogs travelling on their own.'

Coffin handed over a note. 'Tell him to keep the change. And bring a bowl of water for this creature.'

Stella had written: *His regular sitter is ill and I have to go out. He needs some exercise or he will smell.*

Coffin looked at Bob who was breathing heavily all over and thought that Bob smelt now. 'Come on, beast. A short walk and that's it.'

As the two of them walked towards the street, heading for Plucketts Park, their paths crossed with that of Sergeant Eliot on his way out to the canteen.

He smiled at Coffin and Bob. 'Nice dog, sir.'

Coffin and Bob exchanged glances of a neutral kind: sometimes they liked each other, but sometimes they found each other a nuisance. Bob loved Stella and knew jealousy.

'You have to get to know him,' said Coffin, 'to appreciate him.'

Eliot decided to chance his arm. 'Something just came in; Agnes Page's birth certificate, it was pinned to the back of old Waters's marriage certificate… She was his daughter all right.'

She was his daughter: Agnes Page was Albert's daughter, the words turned round and round in Coffin's mind as he and Bob walked towards the park.

He noticed that the parking spaces of all three of the officers threatening to resign were empty; all driven off somewhere to conspire against him. Well, sod them! He bent to release Bob from his leash. 'Off you go, Bob!'

Bob never looked back, but ran eagerly through the park, pushing through the bushes, ignoring other dogs, galloping along, all the while giving himself little barks of encouragement.

'I believe you wrote that note about needing a run yourself, Bob.'

IN THE PATHOLOGY LAB the study of the head was going on. It was established that it was definitely a woman. Probably aged between thirty and forty, this had to be approximate, a guess really. Phoebe was that age.

The hair had been washed free of Thames mud, it was a straight light brown. Phoebe's hair was that colour.

The facial bones were fine and thin, not a heavy-boned woman. Phoebe, although sturdy, had not been a large woman.

The eyes, or what remained of them, had been brown. Phoebe's eyes were brown.

The teeth were now being examined. Who knew anything of Phoebe Astley's teeth?

As the delicate, professional fingers moved over the skull, assessing what was there, it began to look as if the original cause of death had been a massive blow to the head.

But this was guesswork again, they needed the rest of the body. Teams of divers were searching the waters. So far, they had found nothing. But watermen who knew the river and its ways, could point out where bodies came to rest: Pickled Herring Creek, Lamots Reach and Tibbins Stretch... Good places to look, they said. The Thames had its little ways, but it was regular in its habits.

She'll be there. At last.

ELEVEN

IT WAS SUMMER, and a hot evening with the sun still shining, although the oppressive heat hinted at rain later, but the park was becoming empty as the evening drew on. It was true that this was an open space far away from the area where murder had been done, yet people were being careful. It was a nasty business, everyone agreed and it was better to look after yourself, the police couldn't be everywhere, so there was almost no one around as Coffin and Bob turned homewards towards St Luke's Mansions.

But Bob sat down, suggesting a rest. 'Lazy devil, thought you wanted exercise?' But Coffin was indulgent, they sat on the grass for a while, enjoying the open air. Bob had his eyes closed but Coffin had plenty to think about. He hoped that Jeavons would soon come through with news about Mary Henbit; it looked as though she had gone off for reasons of her own.

Next, he would be grateful when the headless body was found and some identification could be made. They were floundering at the moment. If she was a murder victim then that was one more to the toll that the Second City was accumulating. He could see the royal visit disappearing over the horizon, and although he was a loyal subject of the Crown, this would cause him no real grief. Nor the Queen either, he imagined, she had plenty of such trips and might enjoy a day off. But he could see his job going over the hill too.

'Come on, Bob.' He pulled Bob to his feet. 'Let's get back.' The grass was pleasant under his feet so they avoided the path by which they had come to stroll through the trees which surrounded a small pond.

A woman was lying in the grass by the pond, staring up at the sky from behind dark spectacles; she sat up as the two of them approached enabling Coffin to recognize Eden Brown.

She took off her dark spectacles. 'Saw you before.' Her eyes when he could see them looked tired and aching. 'Didn't think you would want to speak to me.'

'The other way round more likely, I should imagine. How are you?'

'Still frightened for my life, if you really want to know; there's too much death around me for me to feel comfortable.' Eden put her spectacles in her handbag as she stood up. 'You're not too popular round here at the moment, so I've heard. But I think you are a nice man.'

'Thank you.' It was a strange vote of confidence in the circumstances, but he recognized a lost soul in Eden for whom he could find a fellow feeling.

'In spite of what you did to me. Yes, I know about Phoebe. I believed her at first when she said she did PR work in security, well, so she did in a way, but I soon guessed what she really was. Of course, I didn't know what she was doing, and I certainly didn't think I came into it, but I got uneasy. Especially when Agnes... Even before she was killed. I knew things were wrong, terribly wrong.'

'You don't have to say anything to me.'

'Because it might incriminate me and all that stuff?'

'Not exactly, but if you did let something out that you'd rather not, I couldn't pretend I hadn't heard.'

'They've closed my shop down, you know? Just swept in and shut me up.'

'I thought there might be something like that...'

'It's to do with laundering dirty money. My shop was used.' She looked at Coffin with a question. He nodded in reply. 'You knew, of course—that was why you planted Phoebe on me. Funny, I don't hold it against you, but I do blame Phoebe because I liked her. Women ought to protect women not spy on them.'

'I'm sorry, it was her job.'

'I'm not under arrest or anything like that, but I've been told not to move away and to report to the local station if they ask. I expect they will ask. I've no shop, no job and not much money. It might be a relief to be in prison, at least they would feed me and I'd feel safe.' She gave Coffin a look. 'Or would I? Maybe with all they are saying about the police in the Second City, I might be safer elsewhere.' She dabbed at her face. 'What am I saying? I don't want to go to prison.'

'It won't come to that.'

'Promise me, can you? No, don't worry, I won't hold you to it. I liked Phoebe. Oh, not at first, but soon I did. I trusted her, she seemed strong. But she wasn't really, she just covered up better than most. Because then I saw she was as frightened as anyone.'

Coffin was suddenly alert. 'So what was she frightened about?'

'I don't know. But I wasn't surprised when she went off. I think she was hard up, she was short of money, a lot of bills have started to come in for her. I know a bill when I see one.' Eden slung her bag over her shoulder. 'I'd better go home... I feel better for telling you. You are a nice man.'

'Thank you.'

'She didn't sleep that night before she went off, I heard her walking up and down all night.' She gave a small, bitter laugh. 'I know how she felt: I feel the same myself now. But I wish she'd told me what it was all about. I deserved that much.'

Coffin wanted to keep the conversation going. 'We'll walk your way.'

'I'm all right. I'm not going to top myself or anything.'

'Of course not.'

'You can't take anything for granted. I have wondered about Phoebe; haven't you?' Coffin shook his head at her, unable to say anything, but inside he was saying, *no, no, no.* Eden echoed the shake of his head with a small demurring movement of her own. 'She was really disturbed that last day or so. And I don't think she liked you very much by then…she said it was better to have no friends than false friends…she must have meant you. What did you do to her?'

Having sent off this arrow, which pierced him with an instant sharp pain, Eden waved her hand: 'I go this way home, don't come any further. Remember me to your wife—a great actress.'

That finished it, Coffin thought, as he watched her disappear round a bend in the path and into a clump of trees.

How much of that talk was deliberate anger? Does she hate me that much? Did Phoebe? Do they all?

He must have made a noise, because Bob looked up at him in some alarm. What's up, boss? was in his eyes, and is there anything I ought to be doing about it? Like biting someone or running fast in the opposite direction? Bob was not a brave boy, his life had put stresses on him, so although he would do his duty, he would avoid trouble if he could.

Coffin interpreted the roll of Bob's eyes with accuracy, they had known each other for a long time and he knew Bob's history in which death had played a part. 'It's all right, boy, nothing for you to worry about. Life does get a bit strong, sometimes, doesn't it? You and I both know that fact. Nothing to be done about it. Let's go home.'

BOB WAS PLEASED. Home to him meant food, a bone and a warm comfortable place to sleep. Coffin was less pleased. Home to him these days meant Stella. It had taken him some time to get to this state but he had got there.

And Stella would not be home.

He called in at his office on the way to St Luke's Mansions where he left a message that anything important was to be passed on at once. Especially anything from Devon about Mary Henbit. If Jeavons got in touch with any news, he was to be asked to telephone the chief commander at home and at any hour. Archie Young, of course, investigating Sir Ferdie and the other two committee members, had his own private orders about communications.

Then he and Bob drove home.

He didn't have long to wait. Once in the apartment, he fed Bob and looked around for the cat, but Tiddles was out on his own affairs.

He made himself some soup and a sandwich. Stella had left a note explaining her absence. It seemed to be due to an unexpected chance to star in a TV series where another star had dropped out. Stella always said that she did not audition, but she was willing to have what she called 'a talk' about a prospect of work.

He had brought a file of work home, and he bent over his papers while he ate his sandwich. Tiddles came in through the window to be fed. Coffin worked on until the telephone rang.

'Jeavons here, sir. I was told to ring you.' The line was not good for some reason and there was music in the background. 'Ringing from a pub in Exeter, sir. It's where I am staying.'

'What have you got?'

'Not good, I'm afraid, sir. I was with Mrs Baker, the mother of Mary's friend, Alice Fraser, and she said that her daughter telephoned last night to say that Mary never came. They waited at the appointed place, but Mary never turned up.'

'I see.' He patted Bob's head. The dog could be a comfort sometimes. 'When did Mary telephone to set up the arrangement?'

'When Alice wrote to suggest that she join them, three weeks ago.'

'And did she hear again?'

'No, they arranged where to meet, at the main railway station in Exeter, and the early afternoon train; Alice thought she would hear again, but everything was settled so she wasn't too surprised when she didn't.'

'So it's weeks since she's spoken to Mary?'

'Yes.' He hesitated. 'It seems that the Henbit marriage wasn't too happy. Mary didn't like being the wife of a policeman. And she had a boyfriend. So when she didn't hear she thought maybe that's where Mary was. She even thought marriage was on the cards.'

Coffin thought hard: that could be what Mary Henbit's letter had been about: not death by burning but a marriage.

'She rang the chap, she knows him. Mary was not with him. It looks bad, sir.'

'You'd better get back here.'

'I'm on my way. I'm catching the night train, be there in the morning.'

He was a good man, Coffin thought, and he would learn to mask that brisk, cold manner.

He himself went back to his work for an hour, when he was interrupted by a telephone call.

Archie Young's voice was quiet: 'Didn't want to interrupt your evening but I suggest you turn on the television. Local independent station: Docklands TV.'

Coffin did so at once, he knew when Archie spoke in that tone that you heeded it.

The programme had already begun, he recognized it as a late night news and comment programme that centred on local Second City affairs. He already had that slightly sick feeling when you know bad news is coming, and as he looked at the screen he began to feel worse.

Geraldine Ducking was in the centre of the picture, before her a low table with a jug of water, and on her right, a journalist from the national press whom he recognized.

Not a friend. Not an enemy either exactly but one who was always ready to find the devil underneath the stone.

Next to him, sitting there with a sober face like a hanging judge was, goddamn it, Sir Ferdie. What was he doing there?

Lined up on the other side, their faces masked by one of those electronic wizardry effects, were two men.

He might not be able to see their faces but he could identify the rest of them. Those were certainly Syres's feet, he would know them anywhere, they were the longest and thinnest pair in the force. He knew the hands of the other man: he had seen Tom Gambit fold his hands, left over right, watch showing, often enough.

Gambit and Syres, just the two of them. So Luke Franks had thought better of it?

Or perhaps he was dead, Coffin thought savagely; of the three he disliked Luke Franks the most. Devious, manipulative, sly even. But he was circumspect and would watch how things went before doing anything rash.

Coffin had come in on the journalist—Mike Hooley wasn't it?—in full flood.

'In matters of this sort where the Queen's good justice is concerned, probity and honesty are of the first consequence.'

Geraldine was nodding her head. She was wearing a bright red shirt with matching trousers, a bad sign for the peace of the world. Expensive, however.

'The fact that three...' Mike Hooley hesitated, 'two high ranking police officers have agreed to appear on this programme—'

So Franks had been expected and had cried off at the last minute. Coffin extracted some satisfaction from this conclusion. That would teach Geraldine and her producer not to rely on a sod like Luke.

'Speaks for itself,' ended Hooley.

Geraldine smiled. 'In fact, they will not speak for themselves.'

Of course, they won't, thought Coffin. Silent sneaks.

'An actor will speak their words.'

Coffin heard with pleasure that the actor, it must be just the one, you could tell from the voice, had decided to give a Yorkshire accent to Syres, who was deepest Surrey, and a strong Birmingham accent to Gambit who had been educated at Radley and then Cambridge and prided himself on being classless. Which he was not.

The chief commander wondered with what evidence the actor had been provided that he produced such accents, or whether Geraldine had done so out of malice. She was capable of it and her motives were always hard to know.

What the actor was mouthing, whether truly the opinions of Syres and Gambit, hardly mattered, sniping and unpleasant as it was, but he doubted it: he could see Syres's feet twitching, and he knew that twitch. Tension.

But all the same, it was poison they were spitting out. Damn them.

Then he heard Sir Ferdie speaking in careful, measured tones, but with that croaking strange voice he had sometimes, the academic viper, he thought. He turned the sound down till Sir Ferdie's face had gone.

HE SAT THROUGH the programme. Not much in it that could be called hard fact, but a layer of nastiness was being deposited over the Second City force and over his own work like a smelly greasy sludge.

He wished Stella was here, he needed her to be there with him. Somehow her mere presence would make him feel better. But he had learnt to pass through such moments without taking to the whisky bottle. He waited for a few minutes, then dialled Docklands TV, and asked to speak to

Geraldine. She should still be there in the hospitality room offering drinks to her panel.

There was a pause, he could hear voices, and then she answered. 'I knew it was you.'

'I thought you were a friend.'

Geraldine was defensive. 'And I thought I channelled the mood nicely your way.'

'Oh, did you? And I think you shouldn't have had the programme.'

'I have a job to do, I'm a freelance lady and have to take what I am offered.'

She wasn't offered that, he thought, she went and begged for it. 'You haven't done anyone good. Not me, not the Second City, and certainly not Syres and Gambit. What happened to Superintendent Franks, by the way?'

There was a pause. 'He couldn't make it.'

'I bet he couldn't. Didn't that tell you something? He knows a loser when he sees one.'

'I can't talk here.' Geraldine's voice was showing emotion at last. Coffin felt triumphant. Not nice of him but there it was, he did. 'People are listening.'

'Why worry? It's what you want, isn't it?'

He started to put the telephone down carefully, he was angry, very angry, but he would not show it by violence.

'Wait a minute, can't we meet? I want a meeting. Come round here, or to my place, so we can talk. Or I can come to you, just as you please. I'd like to do an interview...sympathetic. Give your point of view.'

Without a word, Coffin put the telephone down.

He was asleep when Stella came home. Bob was at his feet and the cat lay across his chest, but they all seemed perfectly content.

Stella considered them. 'Haven't missed me at all, the dreary lot.'

Coffin woke up at once. 'Where have you been?'

'That's a very husbandly remark. Move over.' She sat beside him on the sofa, picking the cat from his chest.

'I told you it was important, so it is, money for the drama school, and a part for me.'

'Who's the benefactor?'

'A friend of Letty's, I believe. Anyway, he knows her, she's the introduction: he's a banker, very rich, I should think, seeing what he's splashing around.'

Coffin sat up. 'If he's a banker with money to offer, keep away from him.' How dare they use Stella.

Stella opened her mouth to speak and then closed it again. She took a breath. 'He's a lovely man, with a beautiful Armani suit. Don't be jealous, he wasn't trying to seduce me, I think he prefers the boys.'

'Seduce you, rubbish!'

Stella looked hurt. 'He did like me,' she began.

'It's a bribe. No, it's not even that, it's an attempt to get dirty money in our bank account.'

'My account,' said Stella who was still hurt.

'It's the same thing.'

Stella took a deep breath. She was a much better hand at holding on to money than her husband and they did not share a bank account.

'You touch that money and we are both in trouble.'

Stella stood up, she was not a fool. 'Right. I hear what you are saying. Alas, I was the more deceived… I'll make some coffee.'

BRENDA JAMES, the plain clothes officer, who had called on Albert Waters and been shouted at for her pains, had watched the TV programme too. She had a free evening, which did not come very often in her life because she was taking a degree at the Open University as well as helping with the difficult domestic life of an invalid sister.

So she had been determined to make the most of it: she bought herself a selection of meats and salads from Max's

Delicatessen, made a large pot of coffee, considered drinking some wine but decided she had had all she should have this week (she was a stern self disciplinarian), and settled back for a good evening of TV viewing.

She was in happy spirits because her last essay for her degree course had come back with the words: *OK. Good,* printed across it in her tutor's large firm writing. At the same time, her sister's health seemed to have taken a turn for the better so that Brenda had the feeling that this weight might soon be lifted from her. She loved her sister who was older by a good many years, but self-fulfilment beckoned.

She sat through her favourite soap, through an indifferent thriller and a news bulletin. She was half asleep when Geraldine's programme started, but she woke up at once when she realized what was going on. She watched for a few minutes, then she moved to turn the sound up louder, she was frowning.

She began to pace the room, her eyes still on the screen. After a while, she set the video so that she would have a record of at least part of the programme.

When it ended, she was still on her feet. 'I'm sure I am right... But how can I be?'

She didn't try to answer that question, but abandoned all discipline to make herself a large gin and orange. She was on the edge of the circle of detectives working on the case which had burst into fire with the body on the pyre, had dragged in the deaths of Henbit and Pittsy, and now had Albert Waters as part of it. The head in the river Thames might be part of the cycle of murders or not. She did not see all the reports as they came in, but she attended the daily briefings so she knew the general shape of the investigation. She knew that the two policemen had been drugged first with sedatives and then killed, that Henbit had probably died first with Pittsy on a later occasion; somehow they had been tricked by the killer; she knew this was guesswork and perhaps the way people wanted it to be. Because why couldn't two policemen protect themselves, be on their guard?

What was there about this killer? They had so little to go upon. But now she thought she had something to offer.

She would need her nerve to offer it, though. 'I'll do it,' she said aloud. 'I'll tell *him*. He can only laugh at me.'

Somehow she did not think John Coffin would laugh.

In the morning she played the video through again and thought better of it. Such as she could not go straight to the chief commander and ask to be heard. You had to go through the right channels. And it was only her notion.

Still, she thought it was the voice she had heard through the letterbox at Albert Waters's pretending to be him. The voice that had desired her to 'fuck off'. There was something about the timbre.

She could tell her senior officer, but he was a difficult character who might shrug it off. Also, in view of the rumours floating round, who could you trust?

She could write a letter to the chief commander, but his secretary would read it first and it might never get through to him.

Besides, it was her idea and she felt possessive of it.

She debated the problem while she ate her breakfast, she was so deeply thoughtful that she forgot what she was eating and was surprised to find herself munching dry toast with apparent satisfaction. The butter had gone from the dish so that must have been eaten somehow.

Later that day, still preoccupied with her problem, she confided in one of her friends who was in the CID with her. They had trained together and then worked as a pair. She talked about it over coffee. Not what the evidence was, she hugged that to herself, but that she had some, or thought so.

The friend was firm. 'You have to report it.'

'It's more of an idea, something I have noticed. Maybe

not hard fact.' But she thought it was. Perhaps someone else had noticed too? 'I could hang about until I saw him and then speak.'

'That would look good!'

Brenda accepted the judgement, but she was not giving up. She would find a way. What she had to say might, just might, be important. 'I don't know what to do, but I shall do something.'

'Don't get yourself killed. Let's have a chocolate biscuit.'

Brenda stood up. 'Right, we will. I'll pay.'

Her friend called after her: 'I've heard they've found a headless body in Tedder's Reach. It's not where the floaters usually end up but it got caught on a barge. What do you make of that? Must match with the head, but who is it?'

'You and I can make a guess,' said Brenda sitting down again and planting her feet with heavy weight on the floor. Suddenly she felt she weighed a ton.

Coffin and Stella did not breakfast together that morning, he was up and out before she opened her eyes.

He had been woken with the news of the body, been told of the tentative identification, and looking down at his sleeping wife had said the prayer he prayed so much lately: God keep you safe.

Then he went to start what was going to be a painful day.

He went straight to the incident room where Sergeant Eliot was already talking to Archie Young and where Sergeant Jeavons had just arrived, travel-stained and weary. Coffin looked at him. 'Get shaved and have some breakfast, you're not going to carry on like this.'

The teams investigating the several different murders had merged, it was recognized that this was a multiple murder case. Not a serial killer, possibly not a mass murderer, but one killing pair of hands wiping out person after person. Some detectives were out already, checking statements, others were following different leads, one was at work on telephone calls, and another checking records of missing women. And at least one was quietly working out the overtime report he would be putting in.

Sergeant Jeavons reappeared and was joined by Sergeant Eliot, all of them went as a group to view the body in the police mortuary. They had silently formed themselves into what was, in police jargon, a Unit Four, in other words a detective from each case being worked on. You could drop in and out of Unit Four but someone had to be there to report back to the collator and hence to all other detectives. It was part of the chief commander's hands-on policy.

They were missing something that connected all the cases, and every man here knew it, but perhaps they had it with this body.

A river police patrol had spotted the body, then got it ashore. A police surgeon had then examined it and made the first suggestion that it and the head belonged together.

He spoke without pleasure: 'Someone had to say it, it just happened to be me.'

The woman had been wearing a light cotton dress with a jacket that was still buttoned into place.

'Don't know why that wasn't torn off,' said the police surgeon, 'because she's been rolling round the Thames and thrown against God knows what, but the jacket is still in place.'

'Have you touched the clothes?' This was Coffin.

'No. Touched nothing.'

The dress which may have been pale blue, slight signs of colour remained around the collar of the jacket, was now grey and stained with mud and oil as well as other nameless liquids.

Soon the clothes would be peeled away and handed over to the forensics, and the body delivered up to the pathologist.

'I want to see the clothes when you get them off.' Coffin

was not hopeful that anything of use would be found, but he knew the value of the naked eye. Seeing was important.

'Smells, doesn't it?' said the police surgeon amiably. 'Who's going to undress the lady?' Like many police surgeons, he had developed a bawdy sense of humour. But this time, a glance from Coffin stopped him going on to his favourite joke about what you want to take to bed with you. 'Leave it to the forensic lady, eh? Is Amy there?'

Amy was there, in the background of the group. Coffin watched as her gloved hands went to work.

The jacket, the dress, the stained pants and bra were gently removed then placed on a plastic sheet. Amy ran a delicate hand over the jacket. 'Something in there.' They watched while she inserted two fingers inside an internal pocket. Then she reached for a spatula and carefully drew out a small, sodden lump. 'Believe it or not, I think we may have a letter.'

They all stared at it. 'If we can get anything up,' said Amy, 'then we may have an identification. Give me time.'

Coffin turned away. Time was not what he had to waste in his state of guerrilla war with the enemy striking their tents and moving into action. The clothes told him nothing. He did not know whether it was Phoebe lying there or not.

ARCHIE YOUNG walked close behind him. 'I want to talk.'

Coffin nodded. 'Come in the car with me.' His driver already had the door open, waiting.

'I don't want to talk in the car.'

'My office, then.'

'Some of the stuff I learned about the people you asked me about is hot stuff.'

'It's not bugged.' Perhaps it was? 'We mustn't be paranoid.'

Archie Young got into the car, settling down as if his feet hurt. 'You're right. But I promised some of the blokes

I spoke to that I would hold on to what I got. And when I say blokes, there was no blokiness... Not that sort of men.'

'Come on, Archie.' The driver was probably listening, but did it matter?

'Over the months that the investigators from the Bank of England and the City of London Fraud Squad have been digging into this money laundering business, I have got to know one or two. Not the absolute top brass, but they have knowledge, these boys. So I went to them with those questions about those people you wanted me to work on. Tactfully, mind you, with discretion. I mean, I didn't say too much about why and how I wanted to know. Made it just a kind of gossip. I'm not saying they may not have guessed, but we kept it light.'

He was pleased with himself.

'I'll talk quietly.' He bent his head towards the chief commander and began to talk.

'So they have wondered about those two as well?'

'Sure. They cast their net pretty wide. Daresay they know quite a bit about you and me. They knew about the Intelligence Unit you had set up with Henbit and Pittsy.'

'They were told by me.'

'Yes, sure.' Young did not add: But they thought you were a bit careful with the full truth. 'I got the impression they were looking into you.'

Coffin felt sure of it, but he had been investigated before, and there was nothing to dig up. Nothing that hadn't been out in the open for some time: his first marriage, his bad time, his good time, his sinking below the surface, his phoenix-like revival. It was all in the records.

'I think they might be calling on you. Just an idea.'

'In a friendly manner, I hope.'

Archie grinned. 'Not in a hostile way, of course, not as far as you are concerned, although I would say they do have their likes and dislikes. They have dug deep into Sir Ferdie and they found...well, not exactly gold, the reverse—let's say a seam of coal, and they don't love the lady either. So yes, I think there's material to work on there.'

He continued to talk as they drove back to headquarters, quietly and with circumspection. 'I made careful notes.' He handed over a file of papers.

'I'd say they have been following events in the Second City with some attention.'

'Have they any ideas?'

'Guessing.'

'Like us,' said Coffin. He added: 'If they do come, I'll see if their guess matches with mine.' And then he said; 'I'm guessing about the identity of the body.'

Young said: 'The letter, if it is a letter, will tell. But it'll take time.'

Coffin looked out of the window of the car as it drove into the headquarters yard. 'But we know who it is in the river, don't we?' And he answered himself. 'Yes, I think so.'

TWELVE

THE DAY WAS LONG for everyone in the Second City, but Coffin put other thoughts aside and got on with the routine of the day. But underneath his surface calm, dark thoughts were gathering.

The identity of the woman in the river would soon be established for sure now that the body had been recovered. The pathologists and the forensic experts working together would come up with who she was. It was so very unlikely that the body belonged to some unknown woman. This was no outsider, the dead woman was one of two people.

And he was sure he knew which.

To the rebellious couple of detectives who had appeared, even masked and silent, on television, he gave little thought. There were standard ways of dealing with such as they and the appropriate disciplinary boards would be set. He looked forward to the process. Resign indeed, that option would not be open to them: he had suspended them. The letters to tell them this had gone out; they must already know.

At some point in the day, his secretary, the new one, whose name he must remember, had brought in a cup of coffee and a sandwich which he must have eaten, because the plate was empty when she took it away. The coffee he seemed to have overlooked because the cup was still full.

'It's cold. Can I bring you another one, sir?'

'No, thank you…' he hesitated, while she waited with a very faint smile. But she didn't help him out. 'Thank you, Marina.'

Bravo, she said quietly inside herself as she closed the

door. He's got my name, I think he's getting on top of things. She had been seriously worried.

It was late evening by the time he drove home. As he walked up the winding staircase in his tower home, he heard voices. He paused to listen: that was Stella, and another voice.

He pushed open the door: Stella was sitting on the sofa with Phoebe and they were in tears.

He paused, still holding the door. 'What are you doing?'

Stella put her arm round Phoebe. 'You can see.'

He walked into the room, putting his briefcase on a chair, and stood in front of them.

'Don't loom.'

Coffin ignored this. 'I'm glad to see you are alive, Phoebe, and happy to see you with us again... But where the hell have you been?'

'You are a bully,' said his wife.

'You keep quiet.'

Phoebe stood up, tears still on her face, which had a puffy look. 'No, he has a right to ask.'

'I appointed you to a sensitive position, then asked you to undertake a special investigation. I imagine you started on it, but then you asked for a few days personal leave... I emphasize the few days because you dropped out of sight in the middle of an exceedingly complex case which was still developing. At first, I thought you were working under cover, then I thought you had ratted on me, then I thought you were dead.'

'You were almost right: I thought I was dying.' She touched her right cheek. 'I believed that the lump I had found in my jaw was cancerous and that I was going to die in a particularly nasty way. I went away because I had a specialist's appointment back in Birmingham. His first opinion was that this was likely...so I didn't get in touch. I couldn't bear to...if I talked about it, then it became real.' She paused. 'It's not so good waiting for that sort of news about yourself and having this bit of you tested and then that, while all the time the rotten thing is growing. I hid, I hid in my flat and then in hospital; I didn't read the newspapers and I didn't listen to the radio or watch television. I read Barbara Cartland and Agatha Christie, they were both great comforts. I didn't know what was going on here and frankly I didn't care.'

She had silenced him.

'And finally, the news came round that it was just an ordinary, non-malignant little tumour that they could cut out without even sawing open my cheek.' Once again she drew a breath. 'So that's it. It's out of me, I'm cured...except I'm not sure if I believe them.' She looked at Coffin. 'You don't know what to say, do you? Your wife knew, but you don't.'

'I can say I am sorry.' He looked at Stella, who shook her head.

'She didn't say anything,' said Phoebe, 'but she cried with me.'

Coffin sat down, dislodging the cat, and was silent for a long space.

'Did you hear? Hear what I am saying now?'

'I heard. But why didn't you tell me?'

'A, because I'm a coward; B, because I'm a coward; C, because I'm a coward.'

He was very nearly silenced again. But not quite. 'Now you are back, are you willing to work?'

'You brute,' said Stella.

'But a reasonable brute.' He looked at Phoebe. 'Well?'

'I'm back.'

Stella put out a protective arm: 'She's not strong enough yet, surely you can see that?'

'I'm strong enough.' Phoebe turned towards her hostess. 'Thanks, Stella, but I am.'

'Have you seen your landlady yet?'

'I went there first. Eden screamed when she saw me.'

Coffin was unsurprised; she thought you were dead and that she had seen your severed head by the river.

He knew now that it was Mary Henbit.

'You'd better start with Eden Brown,' he said. 'I think she knows more than she has said. Find out. Now she knows you aren't dead, she may talk to you.'

Stella walked towards the door. 'I'll get some drinks or coffee. A sandwich? You two will want to talk.'

Her husband turned to her. 'Nothing you can't hear.'

Stella patted his arm as she left. 'I'll be back, and perhaps some of the details I would rather not hear.'

Phoebe sat down in a chair near the table, she took a notebook from her bag. 'Nice woman, and a beauty too. You're lucky, but I think you know it. Well, tell me what I need to know.'

Rapidly he went over all that had happened since she had been away; she knew about Henbit and Pittsy, but he told her about the identification of Agnes, of Albert Waters's part and their relationship.

And then he told her that the body in the river was almost certainly that of Mary Henbit.

'The last victim.'

'I think she died not long after her husband and possibly before Agnes. Certainly before Albert Waters, who may have been the last to die. But the pathologist will have to establish that for us. There is a piece of paper in Mary's pocket, a letter, a note, if the scientists can bring anything up, then we may get something there.' He sat down and said: 'No witnesses, and the locals don't want to talk. But the investigating team are digging deep into backgrounds and movements. In the end, with forensics, we will get somewhere.' And with a bit of luck, he said to himself, you always need that bit of luck.

'But so far you have no idea of the killer...or killers?'

'Just one, I think, but one who may have had help.'

Phoebe looked at him. 'But you have someone in mind? Making a guess?'

'Of course he is,' said Stella as she came in with a tray. 'Doesn't he always?'

Coffin took a drink, while accepting with rueful amusement that both these women knew him very well. He'd better not forget it.

'It's an either or situation,' he said.

Later that night, Stella said: 'You really were a brute sending her back to work so soon.'

Coffin studied her with affection; she was brushing her hair at her dressing table with care and concentration.

'It's as well she is with Eden Brown, they can keep an eye on each other: I think they may both be in danger.'

EDEN AND PHOEBE, after the first period of caution, were glad to be together again. Eden did feel some protection from Phoebe's presence, her very survival in the world was reassuring, while Phoebe felt that Eden was a wounded sister to whom no explanations or apologies were necessary.

Shyly, Eden said that as her shop was closed, she would undertake all the housekeeping, and was there anything that Phoebe would like to eat for the evening meal? She did not eat lunch herself and she imagined that Phoebe would be at work, anyway.

'Let's go out for a meal,' said Phoebe. 'We both need a bit of uplift, don't you think? Let's go to Max's.'

Eden agreed. Good idea, she said, and then tomorrow she would cook fish, she did some tasty fish dishes.

They sat in friendly silence. It came into Eden's mind that if all this got cleared up and she stayed in this apartment then she would enjoy living with Phoebe. They might have a good, quiet, undemanding relationship. She would never marry again and she had an idea that sex was out for Phoebe for the time being. She sensed a hole there in Phoebe's life, which made something to think about, but it was none of her business.

If they both survived, there was always that thought.

NEXT DAY, Coffin received two visitors. Their arrival, in the mid morning, was heralded by a brief telephone call from the Treasury. 'Mr Fish and Sir George England will be calling on you this morning.' No time named, no polite request asking whether the visit would be convenient. It had to be convenient.

Coffin stood up as they came, Sir George was tall and thin, he was the younger of the two; Mr Fish was frankly plump. Sir George was neatly tailored in a blue striped suit, he was wearing a Garrick tie, but Mr Fish wore a light blue suit and a bright red tie. The chief commander had met them on several occasions before and had made his own inquiries into them: Sir George was reputed to have the best legal mind of his generation while Eddy Fish was the tougher brain. 'He has a lovely smile but he never lets go. Georgie keeps him under control if he can, that's why they go around in a pair.'

Sir George held out his hand: 'Good to see you again. Sorry to be so unceremonious.'

'Your secretary said you would be coming.'

'Quite, quite. Couldn't give you much notice, I'm afraid you must have a lot on your mind… The Queen's coming down, isn't she? Always makes work. She doesn't realize, of course, no idea the work she makes.'

Coffin kept his thoughts to himself; of course, HM had no idea, although she might make a guess being a shrewd woman. But you could hardly expect anyone to say: Ma'am, this is a lot of hard work. Why not stay home and walk the dogs?

Besides, a lot of people did enjoy a visit, probably he would himself when it came to it, and Stella certainly would do, making a careful inventory of the royal dress and an accurate valuation of the pearls round HM's throat and the diamonds that glittered on her lapel.

'Shut up, George,' said Fish, 'and let's get on with it.'

Not what you expected of a Treasury man, Coffin thought, but he had heard that Fish had been at Balliol.

Very quickly and tersely, in a kind of duet, but getting all the information in precisely the right place as if they had rehearsed it—they probably had—they told him that the money laundering investigation was finished and that all the people concerned were either already under arrest or would be soon.

They understood he had his own problems associated with the case, but he would be on his own in completing this investigation; their work was done.

'I know you have one or two suspects in mind,' said Sir George. 'Can't really help you, although naturally we rolled in some bits of information.'

Fish found this irritating. 'Come on, George, get on with it. Or I will. Chief Commander,' and suddenly his voice was as silky smooth as that of Sir George and the accents of Balliol emerged from hiding, 'your principal suspect was a bagman for the money launderers, carried the money from place to place, taking a rake off.'

'Thanks,' said Coffin. So this was what Henbit and Pittsy had discovered and died for; a bagman covering his tracks, and then going on killing the man Waters who had helped that bagman and the woman Agnes who had guessed. Mary Henbit had been an extra, to be wiped out just in case.

'Can we share a name, gentlemen?' he said.

MARY HENBIT got her revenge. On the next day when Coffin had his head down over his desk on which lay reports, official letters, social letters, and some rubbish which he could throw aside, he took a call from Archie Young. He sounded excited.

'I've had a first report on the letter in Mary Henbit's

pocket... It was protected to a certain extent by a handker-
chief and by the envelope. Using some magic I don't understand, they've managed to bring up a few letters in the
centre and most protected part of the letter.'

'What? Let's have it.'

'One whole word and one letter.'

'Ah.' Too much to hope for a whole sentence, but he
couldn't hold back a sting of disappointment.

'They hope to bring up some more,' said Archie Young,
somewhat hurt.

'You've got a copy? Bring it round now. I want to see
it.'

When Young arrived, Coffin cleared his desk and they
studied the sheet of paper.

'It's not a bad photograph,' Coffin admitted, albeit somewhat grudgingly.

'Comes up clearer in the photograph than in real—they
enhance it.'

'That's definitely *Bag*.' Coffin put his finger on the
word—*Bagman?* Yes, he could settle for that. He stared at
the letter, which was big and round. A capital letter.

'An A?'

Coffin was thoughtful. 'Could be.' Better than nothing.
What he would have liked would have been a big bold Sir
Alfred. You could make a start with that.

'Did Henbit do his capital As in that way?'

'I don't know,' admitted Young, who felt he wasn't getting the thanks he had expected.

'Get hold of one of his files and see what you can do in
the way of a match.'

He worked on for the rest of the day, then towards evening, as he was packing up to go home, Archie Young
walked in. He just about knocked first, but he was in the
room before Coffin had done more than open his mouth.

'I've got some specimens of Henbit's writing you ought
to see.' He planted a photocopied sheet of paper in front

of Coffin, then followed it with a second. 'He did not write his As in that way.'

The chief commander examined both documents carefully. Felix Henbit had been writing a report on an armed robbery.

'No.' He sounded satisfied. 'But I never thought he did. I don't believe you did either.' He raised his head. 'Let's call Sir Alfred in.' Or Sir Ferdie as he liked to be called, for no reason that Coffin understood.

Archie Young raised an eyebrow. He had a thin, narrow face and the eyebrow made him look thinner and more sceptical than ever.

'Yes, really.' Coffin was triumphant. Here I come, killer. You lying, sneaking, greedy, violent killer. I guess you enjoy killing. Well, enjoy this: I'm on to you. It's over.

BRENDA JAMES thought about the television programme in which the two policemen had appeared. The programme had worried her. She listened and pondered. Should she say something to the chief commander? Cheek on her part? Would she be brave enough? She doubted it, but after all, murder was murder—one had a duty.

She thought a lot about duty and her own duty in particular.

She mulled over her problem all the next day and might have gone on indefinitely but something, she never knew what, perhaps a second restless night, propelled her into action.

She made her way to the chief commander's office, watched Archie Young leave, then muscled her way in. At the end of the day, there seemed less than the usual resistance, and anyway, she got in.

'Sir,' she said breathlessly, 'I think I recognized a voice.'

COFFIN THOUGHT about life and his place in the scheme of things; finally, he knew what he would do. He picked up the telephone and placed a call.

'Geraldine? Ah good, it's you.'

'It's always me at the end of this line.' The voice was sour. 'Are you going to give me that interview?' When I think of all I've done for you, the tone said.

'I can't give you an interview, Geraldine. But would you like to take part in a happening?'

'Do they still have them?'

'I'm having this one. Meet me at Albert Waters's house in two hours' time. And you can bring a photographer.'

'Who else will be there?' Geraldine said suspiciously.

'No other journalist. This is just for you.'

Geraldine expressed satisfaction, it was about time she got what was hers, her voice conveyed.

THIRTEEN

COFFIN KNEW that he ought to get in touch with Stella, to tell her that he would be late home and not to worry, he would try to join her when he could. He knew that they had some evening engagement together but he could not recall exactly what it was or if it was important. He had an idea it was to do with raising more money for St Luke's Theatre. Just lately it usually was. Stella would not mind whether he was there or not, she said that on these occasions he was more of a hindrance than a help, as the look of bleak policeman-like honesty was not the way to get the money rolling in.

Just for a moment, he wondered uneasily if any laundered money had flowed into the St Luke's foundation from any benefactor. He was not himself a trustee of the foundation, although his half sister Letty Bingham was, but he was on the guiding committee and if any dirty money had flowed that way then the present trouble he was in would be minuscule compared with what would be coming.

One could but pray.

He had a little time before he need take action, so he telephoned Stella and for once she answered straight away.

'Been thinking about you. Is everything all right?'

She could pick up moods. 'Not too bad,' he said cautiously. 'Things are moving.'

'You mean you are pushing them,' she said astutely.

'Sometimes you have to.'

'But you are not sure of yourself? Is that why you rang me?'

'I always feel better when I have spoken to you.'

Stella was quiet for a moment. 'That's one of the nicest things you have ever said to me. Do you mean it?'

'More than you realize.'

'Right. Then let me say this: I have seen you before in this state, and it always comes right. Have faith in your own judgement.'

'Bless you, Stella.'

'Something is going to happen, that you will have caused to happen and it is going to be soon?'

'Yes.'

'I will be thinking about you.'

He put the telephone down after a few more words, feeling better. It was like a blood transfusion, talking to Stella when he felt like this. Who could have predicted that marriage would bring this with it?

There was still time before he had to set out. He forced himself to settle to work, only to be surprised by a knock on the door and a sudden entrance.

'Joey!' He stood up, and said more slowly, 'Is it Joey?'

'Of course it is. You saw my name? You knew I was coming?'

'Yes.' Coffin looked down at the list of engagements on his desk: Inspector Lessiter. How could he have passed it over? 'Yes, of course. Sorry, my apologies.' He stood up and held out his hand. 'I've had a lot on my mind. And you've changed.'

'A lot of years have passed.' Joe Lessiter did not say how many, but he smiled. He was a tall, well-built young man, with a bright-eyed, long-nosed face and a great air of self-confidence. 'You haven't changed, sir. Or not much.' A few grey hairs, some lines around the eyes.

'You were the best cadet I ever had, I was sorry when you moved on.' Years ago the two, one very junior, had worked together in south London. 'I heard you had gone into security.'

'I was seconded. But I've had no regrets.'

'No, I should think not.' Responsibility became him. Lessiter looked like a man in control of himself and of others. I could do with him here, Coffin thought.

'This is my first time in your territory.' He grinned, reminding Coffin of the old Joe. 'In fact, this is my first big job; HM herself, and I want it to go right.'

Coffin nodded. 'Let's get down to it.'

They bent over maps and timetables, everything had been checked once but Lessiter must check it again.

Before everything was folded away, Lessiter spread out a half circle of photographs on the desk in front of Coffin. 'If you see any of these faces around, they are trouble.'

'I have my own copies, and they have been circulated. No sightings so far.'

'No.' Joe shuffled all his papers away. 'I don't think they will be there. It would be easy if one knew what face to look for, but it's always the outsider who gets through, damn him.' For the first time, he let the tension show. 'It's always the worst time when you've planned and prepared and just have to sit and wait.'

'Don't I know it.' He met Lessiter's interested gaze. 'I'm into a brute of a case now.'

'I had heard talk.'

'I bet. I think I know who and I think I know why, but no real proof. I've got to bounce the killer into confessing.'

'And he's tough?'

Coffin thought before speaking. 'This killer is very tough, but doesn't like the idea of publicity.'

'What killer does?'

'This one in particular loathes it.'

'Got a public position to keep up?'

'You could say that.' Coffin could see Joe running names through his head, no doubt he had some ideas of his own, he would have looked into what was going on in the Second City. 'I have someone who will swear to a voice, and I have a letter written by a dead man, but it's guessing and it wouldn't stand up in court unless the killer screams. I want that scream.'

As Joe Lessiter stood up to go, he said: 'You have a lot of support among my bosses.'

Coffin's eyebrows shot up in question.

'No, not HM. Next along the line. Thinks you are doing a great job.'

As he moved towards the door, he said: 'Back to the grind. Mustn't fiddle while Rome burns. Good luck. Or break a leg, as they say in theatre.'

Now what did he mean by that crack about Rome? Coffin asked himself. It was time to leave and as he tidied himself up in his cloakroom before departing, he took a look at himself in the glass over a handbasin. Was he sprouting Prince of Wales feathers above his head?

Two blood transfusions within the hour; first Stella, and now this. He felt good.

HE WASN'T SURE what he was going to do, but he knew he would move through the 'happening' as if he did. It would come.

The great heat had departed from the day but it was still humid.

'Hello there, Geraldine; you got here?'

She was grouchy. 'Not with pleasure.'

You can't have everything, he thought.

'What's Sir Alfred doing there, sitting in his car?'

'You'll find out.'

'I hope *he* will.'

Coffin felt good now, he could sense things falling into place. 'He will in time.'

THERE WAS A CRACKLE of thunder in the air. He hadn't seen any lightning flash, but sometimes in London with all the other lights in the sky you did not.

'This way, Geraldine.'

He had a key to Albert Waters's house, yet he did not go in through the front door, but led her and the photographer from her paper round the back. The house was stuffy with smells of living and dying.

'God, what a stink!'

'You've smelt worse, Geraldine.'

'What's that old goat doing outside? You never answered.'

'Sir Alfred will be helping us.'

The photographer stumbled behind her and nearly fell.

'Watch it, Gus,' she said. 'Don't be a casualty.'

Gus had his own irritation to express. 'It's not a good light in here.'

'You've brought a flash, I suppose,' said Coffin. He did not make it a question, and Gus, feeling no obligation, did not answer.

'Let's go into the living room first.'

Geraldine blinked. 'The light's on.' She sounded surprised.

'Yes.' His team had already been in the house earlier that evening. 'Happenings' may look spontaneous but they have to be planned for with the care of all productions. He had learnt a lot from Stella about drama. 'We need a bit of light. Sit down. Gus, you too.'

Geraldine chose the only comfortable chair with unerring precision. Gus took an upright chair and Coffin stood. He was running a risk and he knew it but it seemed to him the only way to play it: to push ahead of proof and evidence and go for a straight confession. His mind shifted back to Sir Alfred sitting in his car outside. Well, he wasn't on his own, Coffin had laid on a complement of police officers, some visible, others tucked away on that rough patch of ground where Albert Waters had constructed his funeral pyre. If the worst happened, then he hoped they would get the fire brigade in. Joke, he said to himself.

Geraldine's mood was not improving. 'Did you get a shot of Sir Alfred in his car?' she snapped at Gus.

'I did as it happened. Full face. He wasn't pleased.'

She turned to Coffin. 'Come on, let's get on with this. If I'm to do an article, I need some action.'

'It's about to happen.' He switched off the kitchen light, but enough daylight came through the drawn curtains for them to see each other. 'All set?' He motioned with his hand. 'Now we go into the hall, stand behind the front door and you do your bit, Miss Ducking.'

He walked ahead of them into the narrow hall which managed to smell damp even in a heat wave. It was darkish, though. He reached out a hand for the light switch and paused. It would be a kind of signal to those outside that the happening was begun. And then he decided against it. 'Switch the light on, please, Geraldine.'

'I don't know where the switch is,' she began, but her hand had already gone out to it, and Coffin rested his gently upon it.

'Yes, you do.' He pushed her forward.

'Now you, Geraldine, stand behind the front door. Gus, camera ready to snap what happens. Do you have a tape as well?'

'No.'

'But *you* do, Geraldine?'

'I do, as it happens.'

'Switch it on, I want sound effects too.'

'It's on already... I don't get this.'

'Stand right behind the door and wait.'

'What do I do?'

'I'll tell you: when there is a knock on the door, I want you to kneel down or crouch as suits you best and shout out "fuck off" in your best growl.'

Geraldine jerked as if an electric current had passed through her.

'You know how to do it,' said Coffin with sudden ferocity. 'You've done it before.'

There was a knock on the door. *Bang. Bang. Bang.*

Geraldine turned towards Coffin, the electricity which was pulsing through her body had reached her face, twisting it into strange shapes. 'You bugger.' It came out more as a whistle than a growl.

'That's not the voice I wanted, try again.'

There was another triple knock on the door. *Bang. Bang. Bang.*

'Outside is one of my officers: it was she who tried to raise Albert Waters. She knocked on the door and got a dusty answer. But he was already dead. So who spoke? She thinks she recognized your voice.'

'What rubbish.'

'And then there was that letter that Felix wrote to his wife and we found in her pocket. You missed that, Geraldine. It was a D, that letter, I know it and the whole world will know it soon.'

The knocking came again.

'Come on, Geraldine, do your stuff for me and Gus.'

Geraldine hit at him, spitting and swearing.

'But you don't need to say anything, I will do all the talking later; what you have to say is written in your face, and Gus has got it all on film.'

Geraldine began: 'I didn't...'

'Oh, not on your own, you had help. With Henbit and Pittsy, oh yes, and you had helpers. And with Agnes, you were there. My guess is that you killed Agnes, who trusted you but was getting nervous, in her own house and with your own hands. Were you ordered to do it, or be dumped yourself? We will get proof, Geraldine, forensic evidence is very useful.' He put up his hand. 'Don't try and hit me, Geraldine. It just makes me remember your victims. Like poor old Albert, no angel, true, but you used him. I think it was your idea to use Albert Waters. And you killed him as you killed Agnes with your own hands, because those who were behind it all would want to make sure you were involved. Guilty, Geraldine, guilty.'

She opened her mouth. 'I'm not saying anything. I want a lawyer.'

'You shall have your lawyer. But you will talk, and you will tell me who instructed you to kill and helped you to do it.'

'I'm not talking.'

'I should if I were you. Don't protect them, because they will sacrifice you.'

He saw that arrow go home as a streak of white stretched across her face. Good, he thought. Good.

'I hate you,' she said.

'Good, and if it's any comfort, I hate you.'

OUTSIDE, STILL SITTING in his car, Sir Alfred was getting restive. 'What I am doing here?'

Coffin said cheerfully. 'You were just stage dressing—you've done your part. We'll have a talk later. I have some things to say to you.' Sir Alfred showed signs of anger. 'No, don't huff and puff. Not now. I'm off to see my wife.'

As he drove home to Stella, aware that behind him, the police team headed by Archie Young were in charge, he rehearsed what he had to say to Geraldine Ducking.

'You are the bagman we were looking for, carrying money on your travels and then salting it away as ordered by your masters. All right, I don't think you did all the killings on your own. You had help and we shall be questioning you about that. Archie Young will be doing the questioning. And there is Phoebe Astley. You know her? For personal reasons, I think she will want to get into the act.'

He thought for a bit as a red traffic light halted him. 'How had it gone? Start with Felix Henbit. He had been suspicious of Geraldine. Why or how might never now be

known but it had probably been some words from Agnes
Page. Henbit had written a note to his wife, perhaps warning her off shopping in any of the boutiques. He had been
working with Pittsy who shared the information with him.
Henbit had gone first, drugged and killed, then Pittsy and
then Mary Henbit. Sometime earlier, you, Geraldine, and
whoever else killed Agnes Page and got her father, if he
was her father, to help burn her body. You had help there,
we must get you to tell us about that killing. Was she your
cousin? And Albert Waters? Uncle Albert, was he? There
was a family connection and that was why he helped you…
He probably helped with Henbit and Pittsy.'

The traffic lights changed and he moved on. His thoughts
changed channel too. 'Sir Alfred, I made use of you this
evening, and I don't mind admitting that I suspected you
of being the bagman. You do flash the money around, you
know. That car you were sitting in now, your own, I believe, and not the university's? I'd like to know where the
cash comes from and one day I will find out. For a boy
from a poorish family you don't act impoverished. Perhaps
I shouldn't be curious, but I know you have some expensive
private hobbies into which I will not go now but which put
you under suspicion. I don't know whether I like you or
not, Ferdie. You asked me to call you that, didn't you? But
I'm not sure if I shall, not until I make up my mind about
you.'

He drove on. He put up his hand to his cheek, drawing
it down, then looking at it. Blood.

Geraldine had clawed down his face. Do you know what
put me on to you, Geraldine? Well, a feather in the wind.
It was when one of my bright young men discovered that
Albert Waters's grandfather was called Tom Ducking. That
made me think, Geraldine. They're all related. One bloody
clan.

A block in the traffic, and once again a change in his
thoughts. He'd better clear up things in his relationship with

Phoebe Astley. A bit of a residue there. He shifted in his seat.

'Let's think about something else,' he said to himself. 'It'll sort out.'

The traffic moved on and he moved with it.

He saw St Luke's Mansions ahead of him and there was a light in the tower which made him think Stella was at home.

I am coming home, Stella, after putting on a drama which has forced a killer to confess. Because Geraldine was now making her confession to Archie Young. I may still be in trouble, although I think I have beaten the guts out of my rebels, and I may be able to present myself to you as Sir John.

It's a raffle, I may win a prize or it may be the booby one. But I am going to go in and say: May I kiss you, Stella?

If she says, yes, then I shall know life is on my side.

STELLA WAS IN their living room in the soft lamplight, with Tiddles on her lap and Bob at her feet; she was listening to the *Marriage of Figaro* on tape.

She stood up at once, and went towards him. 'You are hurt and tired.' She put her arms round him.

'Can I kiss you, Stella?'

She put her hand gently on his bloodstained cheek. 'What, unwashed and unshriven?' She drew him down on the sofa. 'Yes, and welcome.'

This is more than life just being on my side, he thought: it's fighting for me. He told her what had happened.

Stella was thoughtful. 'I never really liked or trusted that woman. I didn't like her eyes.'

'You were right.'

Stella continued thoughtfully, 'Did you really have a case if you hadn't bounced her into a confession?'

'She hasn't actually confessed yet,' Coffin admitted. 'But

she's talking and Archie will get it all out. And yes, we do have a case. The Treasury blokes have all the financial stuff, and we can now go through her flat. The forensics will do their best.'

'What about the letter in Mary Henbit's pocket? Will you get more from that?

'I doubt it; I don't believe the cleverest lab work can get more out of it. But she didn't know that.'

In other words, as so often, he had chanced his arm and got away with it. Stella shook her head and smiled. He didn't change. She did admire him, but no one would call him an easy man.

'What exactly did Geraldine do?'

'She was what they call the bagman; she collected the dirty money on her trips abroad and brought it back to the Second City, she skimmed some off, too, I daresay. Anyway, she was well in, our own special carrier of money to launder. There would be others, of course, for different cities.'

'Why did she do it? She was clever, she had a career.'

'Looked like easy money at first, I expect, and she liked luxury. Then it got nasty. I don't suppose the killing was her own idea, it was required of her. She had help, but they saw she was deep in. And she certainly killed Albert.'

Stella was thinking. 'Agnes may not have been his daughter, but a niece or a cousin. They are clannish, these Dockland families.'

'We will find out.' He felt very weary now.

'What about the ones you call the helpers? Will they be caught?'

'Oh yes, in the end. Not the really big men, they will still be sitting in their offices in Rome and Istanbul and Hong Kong.' Only the little men like Teddy Timpson.

Stella thought about it. 'Are you in any personal danger?'

'No, I might have been, and they certainly used the dirty tricks brigade, but I seem to have seen them off.'

Stella looked away, not quite content.

He caught her mood. 'I'm not as cocky as I sound.'

'Never thought so for a minute.'

'I may go down the drain, Stella. It's evens.'

'You've said that before and survived.'

He drew away. 'Something terrible happened just before I left. I had a bit of news: Teddy Timpson hanged himself.'

She was shocked. 'Oh, my dear, how, where? At home?'

'From a tree.' He saw her horrified look. 'No, not the Coffin Tree, although there would have been a touch of the cathartic in that. He knew he was being investigated for taking bribes, and he knew the dirt we would dig up once we started. No, he chose a tree in Greenwich Park. He went in at dusk and managed to hide himself. So he wasn't found at once.'

Stella put warm comforting arms around him. 'Let's go to bed, that's the best cure for you.'

WITH HER HEAD on the pillow, she said: 'You bring me luck.'

He raised himself on one elbow to look down on her.

'What does that mean?'

'I'll tell you one day.'

I'd like to believe it, Coffin thought, but I didn't bring luck to Felix Henbit and Mark Pittsy, or Mary or Agnes Page. Or even old Albert.

Later, he said: 'I wonder what really brought Phoebe back…she said this and she said that, but I never felt quite sure what was the true reason…'

'Oh, I know,' said Stella. 'She thought she had a mortal illness, would soon die and she didn't want to die in Birmingham.'

'As simple as that?'

'Life often is simple.'

He drew her to him. Darling Stella, it wasn't true and he

doubted if she even believed it, but he never doubted her courage and optimism.

'I wonder why she wanted to die in London,' he said, reverting to Phoebe.

Stella smiled but said nothing except to herself: You will never understand women: it was because you are here.

IN THE NIGHT, the Coffin Tree in the rough ground opposite Albert Waters's old house in Fashion Street, caught fire and burnt to the ground. No one knew how it happened. Some people, like Albert's old neighbour, said Albert set fire to it with ghostly hands.

But others, more cynical, said that the chief commander had contrived the fire somehow. After all, it had his name on it.

Death and Faxes

First Time in Paperback

A MOLLY MASTERS MYSTERY

Cartoonist Molly Masters has returned to her hometown with her two children…and steps smack into trouble she thought she'd left behind. Her scandalous high school past—a scathing poem about a teacher had made front page of the school paper—comes back to haunt her. Now there's a letter from the teacher with a cryptic message, but poor Mrs. Kravett is dead before Molly can respond.

Then come the death threats—by fax.

Leslie O'Kane

"O'Kane's engaging mystery takes a slanted entertaining glance at high school figures we all loved to hate." —*Publishers Weekly*

Available in September 1997 at your favorite retail outlet.

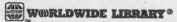

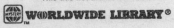

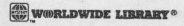

If you enjoyed the mystery and suspense
of this novel by

GWENDOLINE
BUTLER

Don't miss the opportunity to catch her
previous John Coffin mysteries also from
Worldwide Mystery™:

#26110	COFFIN UNDERGROUND	$3.99 U.S. ☐
#26121	COFFIN IN THE MUSEUM OF CRIME	$3.99 U.S. ☐
#26157	DEATH LIVES NEXT DOOR	$3.99 U.S. ☐
#26171	CRACKING OPEN A COFFIN	$3.99 U.S. ☐
#26200	A COFFIN FOR CHARLEY	$5.50 U.S. ☐

(limited quantities available)

TOTAL AMOUNT	$	
POSTAGE & HANDLING	$	
($1.00 for one book, 50¢ for each additional)		
APPLICABLE TAXES*	$ _____	
TOTAL PAYABLE	$ _____	
(check or money order—please do not send cash)		

To order, complete this form and send it, along with a check or money order for
the total above, payable to Worldwide Mystery, to: **In the U.S.:** 3010 Walden
Avenue, P.O. Box 9077, Buffalo, NY 14269-9077. **NOT FOR SALE IN CANADA.**

Name: _____

Address: _____ City: _____

State: _____ Zip Code: _____

*New York residents remit applicable sales taxes.

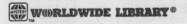
MYSTERY **WORLDWIDE LIBRARY** ®

WGBBL1